CW00555427

THE FOLDER

By

Conny Ge

Copyright © Conny Ge 2019
This book is sold subject to the condition that it shall not, by
way of trade or otherwise, be lent, resold, hired out, or otherwise
circulated without the publisher's prior consent in any form of
binding or cover other than that in which it is published and
without a similar condition including this condition being
imposed on the subsequent publisher.
The moral right of Conny Ge has been asserted.
ISBN-13: 978-1795039963

This is a work of fiction. Names, characters, businesses, organizations, places, events and incidents either are the product of the author's imagination or are used fictitiously. Any resemblance to actual persons, living or dead, events, or locales is entirely coincidental.

CONTENTS

PART 1. THEN..1

   CHAPTER 1..1
   CHAPTER 2..7
   CHAPTER 3..14
   CHAPTER 4..26
   CHAPTER 5..33
   CHAPTER 6..39
   CHAPTER 7..43
   CHAPTER 8..48
   CHAPTER 9..51
   CHAPTER 10..55
   CHAPTER 11..61
   CHAPTER 12..66
   CHAPTER 13..71
   CHAPTER 14..75
   CHAPTER 15..78
   CHAPTER 16..82
   CHAPTER 17..85
   CHAPTER 18..91
   CHAPTER 19..95
   CHAPTER 20..102

PART 2. NOW...107

   CHAPTER 21..107
   CHAPTER 22..113
   CHAPTER 23..117
   CHAPTER 24..122
   CHAPTER 25..125

CHAPTER 26...129
CHAPTER 27...133
CHAPTER 28...137
CHAPTER 29...143
CHAPTER 30...146
CHAPTER 31...153
CHAPTER 32...160
CHAPTER 33...164
CHAPTER 34...169
CHAPTER 35...174
CHAPTER 36...179
CHAPTER 37...182
CHAPTER 38...186
CHAPTER 39...189
CHAPTER 40...192
CHAPTER 41...196
CHAPTER 42...199
CHAPTER 43...206
CHAPTER 44...213
CHAPTER 45...217
CHAPTER 46...220
CHAPTER 47...225
CHAPTER 48...229
CHAPTER 49...232
CHAPTER 50...237
CHAPTER 51...242
CHAPTER 52...247
CHAPTER 53...250
CHAPTER 54...255
CHAPTER 55...262
CHAPTER 56...267

PART 3. THEN...272

    CHAPTER 57...272

    CHAPTER 58...278

    CHAPTER 59...282

    CHAPTER 60...286

    CHAPTER 61...290

    CHAPTER 62...293

    CHAPTER 63...297

    CHAPTER 64...301

    CHAPTER 65...306

    CHAPTER 66...311

    CHAPTER 67...317

    CHAPTER 68...321

    CHAPTER 69...324

    CHAPTER 70...328

    CHAPTER 71...332

    CHAPTER 72...335

    CHAPTER 73...339

    CHAPTER 74...343

    CHAPTER 75...347

    CHAPTER 76...351

    CHAPTER 77...355

    CHAPTER 78...359

    CHAPTER 79...362

    CHAPTER 80...366

FINAL PART. NOW 373

    CHAPTER 81 373

    CHAPTER 82...377

ABOUT THE AUTHOR 381

ACKNOWLEDGMENTS

Thanks to my family and friends for their patience and for emotionally supporting me while fulfilling my dream of writing my own fiction novel.

PART 1

THEN

CHAPTER 1

28th Of June 1983

"It's your fault!" David Hunt blustered. His voice was trembling with rage.

It had just gone past nine on a warm summer evening. He was in his flat. It felt empty without Lucy. Pacing up and down in his bedroom, the phone pressed to his ear and only dressed in boxer shorts, he felt the whole world was crashing down on him. The air in the flat was thick and David felt near to suffocation. It had been muggy all day and he wasn't sure if this was the reason or if it was caused by his emotion. Light was still shining through the half-closed shutters creating funny shapes on the satin silk cover crumpled on the bed.

The liquid whiskey slewed in the tumbler whilst pressed in David's other hand. He took a big sip and gulped it down. His torso was shaking badly. David slumped onto the edge of the king-size bed, dragging the wire connected to the phone along the carpet. The last few months had taken its toll. Feeling like a wretch, he was at a loss. Squeezing the tumbler between his thighs, he wiped off the sweat from his forehead. His dishevelled hair jutted out in all different directions.

"You took everything from me!" David scolded into the phone. He paused and listened. He shook his head, unaware that the person on the other end was unable to see him.

His gaze averted to the shotgun, his only pride left. It lay next to him half covering the pillow. It was an inheritance from his granddad. His granddad used to go hunting with him when David was a kid. He taught him all the necessary bits a man needed to know. David's voice altered to a high-pitch tone. He began to laugh hysterically. "It will be all your fault and the world will know about it." His free hand forming a fist, David paused for a second. His vocal changed to a profound menacing tone as he went on to make the warning clear. "I made sure of that!" David slurred, slammed down the phone and threw it into the corner.

He had finally had enough. Not even one second longer would he listen to the voice he hated so much! David poured the rest of the content down his throat. The glass slid through his fingers to the ground. It landed with a thud on the rug squirting leftovers from the liquid around the carpet. Afflicted by hiccups, David gaped at the letter which stared back at him from the floor. It had remained unscathed from the splash. It was the last letter to his big love Lucy. He hoped she would understand. Lucy! David shook his head in sadness. His longing for her was excruciating.

Glancing around in his bedroom, the decoration had been chosen by Lucy, everything reminded of her. The black and red furniture, the grey curtains, the white rugs and even the goddamn wallpaper with the flower pattern! A big moan came out of his mouth. He flinched as he spotted his reflection in the built-in mirror of the wardrobe. Lucy had already taken most of her belongings. The wardrobe was nearly empty, only a third was now filled with his clothes. Still a few items of his beloved Lucy were scattered around, and all the memories with them.

David pressed his palms against his forehead. The whiskey had certainly reached his head. He wasn't a big drinker. Never had been! He usually detested drunks. Never understood how it could calm someone. Your problems didn't go away with getting hammered. Yet tonight was a different story. It encouraged David. It soothed him. It gave him strengths and made him forget. And he certainly didn't need much to make his head spin. The last refrain from The Beatles playing the song 'Yesterday' from the record player in the lounge next door was interrupted by another attack of David's hiccups.

Precipitately David clutched for the shotgun, planted it on his lap and leaned back. The back of his head found comfort in his open palms. David shut his eyes, his lips pressed together into a thin line. His mind raced off to the past. If he was only able to turn back the time, so many things he would have done differently. Twisting and turning his thoughts on what could have been done to save the situation, he lost track of the time. A knock at the door interrupted his thoughts. David's eyes flew open in surprise. He wasn't expecting anybody. He battled with himself over whether he should ignore it.

For a split second he thought it was Lucy, who had changed her mind and decided to come back to him. But didn't she still possess a key? Surely she did. He paused for a moment, before curiosity took over. He arose from his bed, pushing off the shotgun. With wobbly knees, David reached for a T-shirt scattered on the carpet and covered with the fabric his nudeness. He trudged to the hallway and slowly pulled open the front door. To nobody! Gazing into the twilight, his eyes darted rapidly from left to right. It was a quiet neighbourhood, mainly consisting of elderly residents, who were long since in their night gowns.

To gain a better view, David stepped outside. Not even a single soul was loitering around. Probably the kids, from further up the road, were playing a prank. David retreated inside. With his left foot he kicked the door shut and aimed straight for his bedroom. His shirt slipped from his chest. With slumped shoulders he once again collapsed on his bed. His shotgun still resting on the bed peeped at David. He yearningly grasped for it. He laid it on his bare chest and began to caress the barrel like a baby. The coldness provided his skin with a calming, prickling sensation.

With closed eyes David's mind once more made a trip down Memory Lane. This time it was to his children. Their happy, young, innocent faces appeared in front of his eyes and a sad smile escaped his mouth. The notion of never seeing them again was still inconceivable. Suddenly their faces, covered in tears and blood, glared at him. David realised it was his blood. His eyes popped open in terror. In an attempt to shake off the picture he rubbed his eyes and rolled to the side. The shotgun slid off his chest. What was that? Still appalled, David knew the answer.

Although persuading himself again and yet again that his children were better off without him, would they not be somehow damaged? He shook his head abrasively in an attempt to discard the thought. He had no other choice. Too many things had happened and there was only one way out of it. It was time to end it all. The aura of grey was widening with no future for him in this world. Only one shot and all the pain would go away. He abruptly sat up and reached for the letter from the floor. With a big swallow, David pulled himself together and composed one last sentence to his beloved Lucy.

*

The elderly man from two houses further down the road almost struggled to keep up with Alfie. Alfie was his dog, a white-coloured poodle with black streaks. Alfie's long ears flapped against his fur as he pulled away from his master. The elderly man had to use all his strengths to keep hold of the leash. He cursed under his breath. It was getting late, drawing close to eleven and he was supposed to be sitting in front of his TV right now. Yet Alfie had better thoughts. He had kept scratching at the front door for so long, the man finally gave up and took him out for another night stroll. Considering he had taken Alfie out for a walk just an hour ago.

The full moon glowing in the sky alongside the streetlights gave the man enough brightness to find his way around. A light breeze refreshed his face. The man sauntered past the cream-coloured two-storey house, the last house in the road. He knew the owner of it, a single mum with her young child who rented out the ground-floor flat to a young couple. To scratch a living, so the people here said. He was approximately twenty metres from the cream-coloured house, when the sound of a faint shot filled the air. The man cringed and turned around. His eyes anxiously whizzed from left to right. What was that? A gunshot? Confusion effused from his face. Didn't it come from the cream-coloured house?

He pulled on the leash, to keep Alfie close. The dog began to whimper, but reluctantly obeyed. The man craned his neck, as if it would help to gain a view of the entrance. The entrance was out of his sight on the other side of the building. He considered turning around to check if it had indeed erupted from the cream-coloured house. Yet the whole interior was in darkness. Either the occupants were asleep or nobody was at home. For a few seconds the elderly man stayed put and listened. When he was greeted by utter silence, he scratched his ear, putting it down to his bad hearing. Too many western movies in his head, he thought, and navigated Alfie back to his own house.

CHAPTER 2

29th Of June 1983

The sun was dazzling right into Emily's eyes. It was nearly midday and Emily peeled the last spuds in the sink for their lunch today. The heat pouring through the kitchen window gave an indication of what to expect today. Perhaps it would be a nice day to go to the outdoor swimming pool? The children would love it. Every now and then, Emily peered through the window to keep an eye on her children playing in the garden. She had to stand on tiptoe to glance outside; the sink between her and the window didn't help. Emily usually wore stilettos. Belonging to the group of petite women, stilettos endowed her with confidence and security. Without them she felt like a child.

At home was a different matter. She chose comfort over appearance. Her pretty face surrounded with blonde angel locks and huge brown eyes drew the attention of men. Still, a deep sadness was reflected in Emily's young face. It had been there for a long time. A smile crossed her lips as she watched Thomas, her older one, stood behind Zoe, teaching her how to twist a ball on a finger. Surprisingly today the children were not at loggerheads. Every day was different and it was impossible to predict how it would go. Emily wasn't sure if it was caused only by the separation, or if a small evil was hiding inside Thomas.

Since the day her husband had moved out, Thomas, who was turning seven in a few weeks' time, was suffering with temper tantrums more than ever before. And Zoe, his three-year-old sister, was far too young to understand her brother's moods. It was also her son's jealousy Emily struggled to cope with. Before Zoe came along, Thomas had her full attention. As in any family, that changed when Zoe was born and Thomas didn't like the fact that he wasn't the only number one anymore. And now she had to cope with it alone. A big sigh escaped Emily's lips.

Switching on the hob to boil the potatoes, Emily contemplated whether she should start with the chores right now or leave it for later. The day never ended with two small children and a house this size. The house wasn't that big at all, just the usual three-bedroom family home. The kitchen was even small, just big enough to fulfil its duties of cooking and cleaning. However, the garden spoke for itself. It was a massive green area with planted vegetables and flowers. It wasn't that she didn't like it. Indeed she loved to plant, especially flowers. To observe them flourish every spring made Emily's days. But often she felt too overwhelmed with all the tasks that came along with raising two young children and maintaining a home.

Placing her palms on her hips Emily straightened her body. She was only in her mid-twenties, shouldn't she be out there and actually enjoying life? When was the last time she went out for a dance? She couldn't even remember. But then her mother would tell her, 'You chose this life, now get along with it.' However, she hadn't visualised her life to be like this. Her children weren't even attending school yet – Thomas was enrolled for school in September – and she was already a single mum. Emily had always dreamed of a big happy family. Sadly it wasn't the case here. The break-up from her husband still hurt. A single tear rolled down her cheek.

The sudden jingle of her doorbell caused Emily to cringe. She wasn't expecting anybody. Emily glanced at the clock above the kitchen cupboard, puzzling who it was. Perhaps it was her neighbour, wanting to borrow something. It was often the case lately. She wiped off her palms on her apron and ran her hand through her hair in an attempt to adjust it. Within seconds Thomas head popped through the kitchen door followed by Zoe. He must have heard the doorbell. He was a very curious boy. It was impossible to keep something from him. "Who is it, Mum?" he asked with big eyes staring at her.

"Well, how would I know?" Emily shrugged. "I am not expecting anybody. Get the door, Thomas!"

You didn't have to say this twice. Thomas rushed to the front door, Zoe in tow like a duckling behind her mum. Emily took her apron off and proceeded to the door, too. Along her way, she quickly grabbed a pair of stilettos from the shoe rack and slipped swiftly into them, before joining her children at the door.

The front door was swung open and Thomas shouted over his tiny shoulders, "Mum, some strangers. Come quick!" He gestured wildly with his hand. As Emily approached, her face dropped. Her mouth twisted into an angry grimace. On her doorstep stood two men she had never seen before.

One was tall and slim in his early thirties; the other one was small and chubby in his late forties. Both dressed in dark suits. Emily frowned. The one thing she detested most was hucksters. "I am sorry but I am not buying anything," she said, angry, and was about to shut the door in their faces. The taller one stepped with one foot inside preventing the door from being slammed in their faces. "How dare are you?" Emily yelled.

"Listen, we are not here to sell anything. We are detectives from the crime investigation department," the taller one growled. They both produced their badges.

Emily's disgruntled expression suddenly changed. Her face went ash pale and she nervously rubbed her temples. The sudden unease surging through Emily's bones threw her off balance. She was set back on her heels. "What has he done now?" she managed to say, referring to her husband. She sensed straight away it had something to do with David. Not that he'd ever been in trouble with the police, yet instantly she knew it was about him.

"Who has done what?" This time it was the smaller one who talked. He strode forward, almost colliding with his partner's back.

"My husband, David, it's about him, isn't it?"

The taller one rolled his eyes in exasperation. "Please, can we come in? We don't want to discuss this out here." Unable to think straight, Emily stepped to the side and gestured for them to come in. They followed her into the living room, Zoe and Thomas in front of their mum. Zoe looked frightened. She didn't leave her mum's side. She was afraid of any man who wasn't close family. The taller one certainly gave her the creeps. With his bushy moustache he resembled a bad person she had once seen on TV, who shot a deer. Since that day Zoe didn't like men with beards.

Thomas on the other hand felt a rush of excitement. It was the first time he was facing two police officers. Yet he had always imagined them differently, probably because they weren't wearing any uniform. Thomas desperately searched for their guns by eyeing them up and down.

"So what's this all about?" Emily queried, offering them with her hands to sit down on the sofa. The atmosphere in the room was tense. Emily lowered herself onto the armchair opposite her visitors with only the table made out of oak between them. She began twitchily fondling through her daughter's blonde hair, who was leaning against her mum's thighs.

"Not in front of the children. Can you send them away?" the smaller one demanded. He sounded quite abrupt.

Emily felt instant animosity towards them. She didn't like the way they ordered her around in her own house. Still, she obliged. "Thomas, take Zoe and go to Sarah!" Sarah, who was their next-door neighbour, was also a good friend of Emily.

Thomas grimaced as he remained in the centre of the room. With a sullen face, his chest out and arms crossed, he acted like an adult. He didn't want to leave. He wanted to know what they had to say. If it was about his dad, he had a right to know. Thomas didn't stir from the spot, his pants sagging off his waist.

"Thomas, go now!" Emily raised her voice as she frowned at her son. She gave her daughter a push and Thomas, who had no other choice, took Zoe's hand. They both vanished from the room. The set of vintage dinnerware in the glass cabinet, that was adjacent to the sofa, began to clatter when Thomas banged the front door shut.

Out of the house, Thomas quickly descended the outdoor steps dragging his sister with him. But instead of heading to the neighbour, Thomas poked along the building making his way to the rear garden. He motioned to his sister to follow and placed his index finger to his mouth. "Sshh!" he ordered and continued waving his hand as he sidled along the wall.

Zoe obeyed and stooped down as they made their way to the rear garden. Keeping their heads low, they climbed up the embankment towards the patio door and knelt on the grass. Thomas once again placed his fingers to his lips indicating to his sister to keep quiet. The patio door was left ajar. The voices of Emily and the two policemen were vaguely audible. Zoe grabbed at her brother's shirt annoyingly. As usual he left her out. He had the better position right next to the glass door. She had the crappy one. No chance would she able to hear clearly from this angle. Thomas loured at his sister and pressed his palm over her mouth.

Tears rolled down Zoe's cheeks, landing on Thomas' fingers. The sudden urge to be with her mum instead of her annoying brother, was overwhelming. Why was he always so mean to her, treating her like a baby? A deep, drawn sigh escaped from Thomas' mouth. His sister was getting on his nerves. He nervously glanced inside terrified that he may have been caught. He didn't want to be arrested for not following orders from a police officer. Fortunately they hadn't noticed.

And then Thomas heard it. The words were clear as crystal out of the taller one's mouth. "Your husband shot himself in his head. He is dead." Thomas' face went as pale as clay.

CHAPTER 3

Zoe

Everyone called him Big Mark. He was the same age as me, nine years old. We went to the same class. With his massive body, Big Mark could easily get away with eleven. Most of us feared him. He found joy in belittling the smaller ones, particularly me. With my slight build, I was the perfect target for him. It was one of the reasons I abhorred school. As I stood helplessly in the immense school yard with Big Mark hovering over me like a lion, I wished my mum was here. The yard wasn't that big, still for me it seemed huge. I glanced wistfully to the school entrance. Home was only five minutes away.

Right now I was tempted to dash down the stairs, over the field to be reunited with my mum. It would take me only a matter of minutes. But wait, hold on, Mum was at work, wasn't she? I could feel tears rolling down my cheeks. Big Mark continued his verbal attack on me. I felt overwhelmed by sudden trepidation. My eyes wandered off to the grey school building. I was hoping to catch the sight of a teacher. My efforts turned out to be futile. Wherever I turned, only pupils were visible. A sudden coldness crept over me. I felt goose bumps popping up on my forearms. I grabbed the front of my coat and tightened it around my small body.

The fallen leaves, covering the ground, crunched beneath my feet. It was a sign that autumn had arrived. It meant my birthday was around the corner. Any other time I would have been thrilled. Right now it didn't mean anything to me. I only wished big Mark would go away. He even drew the attention of the others now. Classmates converged to watch the show.

"Look at you. You are a loser. You don't have even a father, ha ha…!" That was his favourite phrase. He was going on and on with that. It hurt! Why did he have to say such ugly things? Like it was my fault that I had no dad? I could feel my shoulders sagging from my upper body. With my head down, peering to the ground, I attempted to sidestep Big Mark.

All at once Big Mark went silent. I glanced up. First I wasn't sure what was happening. When I followed Big Mark's gaze, who tremulously looked over my shoulder, I met my brother's eyes. My brother Thomas was swiftly approaching us. His green eyes looked even greener, disgorging aggressiveness into the air. My heart began to pound; on one hand with relief and excitement, on the other hand with awe. Thomas, getting closer, scowled at Big Mark with a wheeze. Big Mark lifted up his hands in defence. For once he was quiet as a mouse. He was frozen to the spot and his eyes moved rapidly from left to right.

Although Big Mark had the size of an eleven-year-old, he was scared of my brother. I managed to suppress a sneer. My brother was three years older and was known to be of belligerent nature. I had first-hand experience of it. I dodged and Thomas instantly leapt forward, grabbed Big Mark by his shoulders and threw a punch to his face. "If you ever pick on my sister again, I'll kill you," my brother ranted.

Big Mark, aware of the others, felt suddenly embarrassed. His affected cheek began swelling up. He rubbed it to ease the pain. I knew what was coming. If Big Mark gave in now, he would look like a loser.

He pulled himself together. With his chin up and his front out, he stepped forward and lunged at my brother. I squinted my eyes in apprehension and quickly covered them with my palms. A thud caused me to let go and pop open my eyelids. I saw both of them wrestling on the floor. The audience had expanded, gathering behind and right beside me with curious faces. Some cheered for my brother, others for Big Mark. The fight didn't last long. Thomas was indeed the stronger one. Big Mark gave up almost immediately. He leaped to his feet and managed to run off before the second punch could land.

More tears were splashing down the collar of my coat. Thomas, who was still crouched down to the concrete, quickly arose and led me away. He placed his arm around my shoulder and gently thrust me towards the building. The others glanced at us, some with a pitiful expression on their faces. Most of them knew we had no father. Sometimes I wondered why me? All of my classmates had both parents, not even one of them was missing out. Only me! I dipped in my jeans pocket and fished a tissue out to give my nose a blow.

Thomas did his best to console me. He lightly rubbed my upper back and gabbled smooth words to mollify me. I rarely saw this side of him. All the more I enjoyed it and wished it wouldn't end in front of my classroom. My brother promised to accompany me home after school and I vanished through the door. Two hours later I waited outside the building. Back in the classroom, Big Mark had kept his head down. I was confident I wouldn't have to worry about him anymore. His demeanour showed me that he was too frightened of my brother.

Not long and Thomas showed up alongside me. He took my hand in his palm and together we strolled home. The street we lived in was a set of housing blocks provided for families of the armed forces. They all resembled each other, only discerning in colour. When we reached our block, I lifted my head and peered to the bedroom of my mother. The building contained of six flats. We resided on the top floor. After the death of my dad we moved to Mitzen. The town had a big barrack and mum was promised a new flat and work here.

I gaped at my mum's closed shutters. I sensed Thomas' gaze following mine. I promptly averted my eyes in the hope Thomas hadn't seen them. The day had started awful. The sight of closed shutters made matters worse. It put me in a bleak mood. Disheartened, I looked up at the sky. Dark clouds auguring that rain was on its way completed the picture. We climbed up the stairs and when Thomas unlocked the door, I scurried past him along the corridor before finding myself in front of my mum's bedroom door.

Our flat consisted of two bedrooms, a living room combined with a dining room, a kitchen and a bathroom with a separate toilet. I shared the bedroom with my mum. Mum wanted my brother to have his own bedroom since he'd turned twelve. It was time for him, she used to say. I understood and it usually didn't bother me. Only when my mum was not herself, I rather wished to have my own room. I puzzled what I would discover behind the door and began to pray. Mum was supposed to be at work. Yet the closed shutters could only imply two things. Either Mum had forgotten to open them this morning or she was still in bed.

I knew it was the latter. Under other circumstances I would have been pleased to see Mum at home. I was usually too scared to be alone with Thomas. He was often very volatile and truculent towards me. However, today I would have rather preferred my mum to be at work. Because if my mum was still in bed at this time of the day, it signified she was ill again. And it made me very sad to see my mum like this. I quietly pushed open the bedroom door and tiptoed inside where I was confronted with darkness.

"Mummy?" I whispered. When I didn't get any reply, I turned on the lights. As the room brightened up, the first thing I spotted was the bulged blanket. I recognised my mum's tousled hair protruding from underneath the duvet. My mum's composure indicated that she was rolled up in a foetal position. I intercepted mumbling under her breath. One quick glance at the bedside table and I understood. The empty bottle of vodka and a glass filled with a quarter of liquid spoke volumes. I turned the room back into darkness and pulled the door behind me.

It struck me that Mum wasn't even bothered to hide the bottle anymore. She usually did. It didn't make much sense to me, when Mum hid her glass of beer, wine or her glass of vodka. What was the purpose in it? We knew of her drinking habit anyway. Perhaps she was hiding it from herself? Although I was still a child I knew exactly what it meant when Mum was drunk. It wasn't that Mum wasn't capable of looking after us. We were old enough to make our own sandwich. It was more the arguments and often violence that followed. Thomas was a fractious child. And when he saw Mum drank, he usually got choked up about it.

Thomas was only twelve, but already a strong boy. It didn't help that Mum was a tiny person. As I revolved, my brother was right in my face. "Mum is sick again," I stuttered and perceived melancholy in my own voice. But then my heart began to race and immediately I regretted my words. I placed my fingers on my lips to keep my mouth shut. But it was too late. I could see it in my brother's face. It was turning red and his lips were quivering. I glanced at him beseeching. "Please don't hurt Mum," I begged. I feared he would beat Mum. It wouldn't be the first time and probably not the last.

Sometimes it was so bad that either the neighbours called the police or Mum did. We were regular customers by now. I began to pray, conjuring God that today was not one of them. I was convinced my mum would be OK tomorrow. She was just in need of sleep. "OK, best I don't go even in there," Thomas said contemptuously and headed for the kitchen.

I heaved a sigh of relief and jogged behind my brother. I came to a halt in the doorway and observed Thomas preparing himself a sandwich. A loud rumble unfurling from my own stomach reminded me how hungry I was. "Can I have one too?" I asked.

"Can't you do it yourself?" Thomas snarled and rolled his eyes.

I swallowed and turned away. My vision was once more blurred with upcoming tears.

"OK, OK, do you want the same?" Surprised by the sudden change, I pulled at the sleeve of my jumper and wiped off my eyes as I revolved to nod. Five minutes later we sat in the lounge side by side, watching TV with a mouthful of ham sandwiches between our teeth. Thomas, as always in control of the remote control, switched the channels constantly. I was not allowed to choose. But at least today, considering that Mum was ill again, Thomas was in good mood. No way did I want to spoil this moment.

The image of my dad sneaked into my mind. Unlike Thomas I could not remember him. I was only three when Dad passed away. Mum told me he died in an accident. As if my brother could read my mind, he suddenly turned towards me. His hands connected with my shoulders and he rotated me to face him.

His green eyes bore into mine and he rubbed his chin thoughtfully. "Zoe, Father didn't die in an accident!"

I almost choked at his words, whilst still chewing on the last bit of my sandwich. I managed to gulp it down and tilted my head. "What are you talking about?" I slid my hands on each side underneath my bum, shifting on the sofa.

Thomas had my full attention now. I actually never fully understood the meaning of my father's death. I only knew he wasn't coming home. It was like I never had a dad. Not even one single moment with him could I recollect! I only knew my mum's tales. My mum occasionally reassured me that Dad had loved me very much, that I had been his little princess. Unfortunately it didn't mean anything to me. Even at school when classmates talked about their parents, their dads, it didn't make much sense to me. I was the girl who had no dad, who never had a dad. I felt a lump in my throat as I waited for Thomas to continue.

"Father blew his brains out. He killed himself, couldn't handle all the pressure in the army and at home!" He said it as a matter of fact. I could feel my pupils widen.

"What are you talking about?" I froze, feeling abruptly unable to move. What on earth was he hinting at? I felt Thomas' exasperated look. He now shook his head, but I just shrugged my shoulders.

"Dad had massive problems in the army, something to do with his flying. It's all in the folder." Thomas' head veered towards the large cabinet behind me. He pointed to it with his chin. I turned around. I knew my dad had been a pilot in the army. Not much else did I know.

"Where is it?" I queried.

"Wait!" Thomas dragged himself to his feet and vanished from the room without a sound. I began chewing on my nails. A bad habit when I was nervous. What was he up to now? I leaped to my feet to go after him, when Thomas returned hauling a chair behind him.

He positioned the chair in front of the cabinet and ascended it. I plummeted back onto the sofa and watched my brother reaching for the top. Within seconds, Thomas presented a grey folder and excitedly waved it in the air. "It's all in here, in this folder!"

I looked at him, muddled. "What's in there?" I found it hard to believe that whatever Thomas was talking about could be in a folder.

Thomas rolled his eyes, totally bugged. He tapped the front cover with his index finger. "About dad, the truth is in here!" I grimaced in confusion. I had no clue what Thomas was talking about. Still I sensed something important was in this folder.

*

Now in my late twenties, I was ready for the truth. After travelling around the world and working in different places I had changed. As a child I was always hiding the fact that my mum was an alcoholic, my dad had killed himself and my brother being not an older sibling to me but a very difficult child who I was afraid of. Now as an adult I realised that the past wouldn't just go away. It haunted me, especially when I went to see my mum. She was better now, yet she still drank to a certain degree. It saddened me to see her when she was down.

As a child I often blamed my dad for everything.

Why did he have to leave us? Why did he have to shoot himself? If he had not killed himself, beyond doubt we would have grown up differently. Many times I questioned myself, why us, why me? I prayed to God, not only praying, I actually begged to make my mum better. But nothing changed. My maternal grandparents blamed my dad for my mum's drinking problem; first it was his infidelity and then because of his suicide. My paternal grandparents blamed my mum for father's death.

It was the days when, after a visit to the paternal grandparents, Thomas returned home. When he found alcohol in the flat! When he saw my mum drunk or even when she wasn't drunk. It was then when he shouted, 'Peg out, you killed him. They told me, it's your fault, you put him to his early grave because of your drinking.' It was Thomas' way to cope with it, by attacking Mum and blaming her for the death of my father. He often couldn't control himself. He once told me he didn't mean to hurt Mum, but it drove him nuts to see her drunk.

Still I believed that Thomas' behaviour caused my mum to drink even more. It was bad growing up without a dad. And maybe because he was a boy, he possibly lacked a father more than me. It might also have been the fact that he remembered more. Although Thomas had been only six, nearly seven when Dad passed away, he mentioned from time to time that he recalled the arguments between our parents. Thomas was even the one who told me that my father had been a womaniser. I was growing up very quickly. I took care of the household and stood at my mum's side.

When not intoxicated, Mum was a great person. Indeed she was very talented in many ways. She was also full of life. But when the alcohol sneaked in, the wonderful person disappeared. Once my mum was that drunk, the police had to call the ambulance to take my mum away. They feared she had alcohol poisoning. When social services got involved, indicating that the children would be better off somewhere else, my mum called her parents and threatened suicide. Thanks to my dad's cause of death it was taken very seriously. And my grandparents stopped it from happening.

Over the years my mum tried to beat the devil with rehabilitation centres and AA meetings. Sadly she wasn't strong enough. The pain she had endured in her life was too strong. The alcohol was a necessary devil to keep the agony away. It was like a circle, my mum couldn't break free. She got better at times, but then depression slunk back into her life and as always she found solace in alcohol. So one day shortly after I came back from backpacking my mum was once again off her head. I got furious and blamed God afresh.

And then on the spur of the moment I remembered the folder. The one my brother had told me about all those years ago. It was still on top of the cabinet. My mum had kept it always in the same place. After my father's death we had moved several times. So the folder did. Inevitably and each time it found its position back in the same spot. That day and without my mum's knowledge I took hold of the folder.

Why now? No idea! It was most likely triggered by the fact that my mum suffered again. And perhaps searching for answers would help me to understand.

The front cover was labelled with black ink, 'The helicopter incident 1983'. My dad had been a sergeant and helicopter pilot in the armed forces. From tales I knew he had been involved in an incident. He had suffered with the aftermath and had taken it to heart. Unable to ask my mum about my father's death, it was too painful for her to talk about him, I decided to take it into my own hands.

And that was the first time I looked at it. As a child and teenager, my father was not a subject you would talk about. I thought it was mainly because of the way he died. But then after reading the folder, I wondered if there was more to it. Was it to keep the past buried? Or was it something else? Convinced that there was more to his death, I promised myself not to stop until I knew the truth. I was positive the folder was the key to it.

CHAPTER 4

Then – 20th February 1983

"Roll on the weekend!" Mike the mechanic rubbed his hands in delight. He sat next to David Hunt who operated the helicopter. "Can't wait for this day to come to an end!" he continued.

"Same here." David grinned. As a helicopter pilot and a sergeant within the German Air Force a weekend off was rare, all the more to enjoy. Glancing at his instrument panel, David noticed that the altitude showed 300 feet. Not long and they would reach their base in Bueckenau, one of the bases for the army aviation squadrons in the North of Germany.

In company with two other pilots, they flew in tandem through the Buchesener Valley. David with the most flight experience was leading the way. Alex Feld in a second chopper was right behind him. He was like David, a sergeant in his late twenties and aiming for a military career. The third machine was steered by Andrew Mann. He was in his mid-twenties and the same rank as his colleagues. In contrast to his comrades he behaved occasionally heedlessly.

It was a very cold winter day in February with the sunset in tow. The land was covered in a blanket of snow with icicles dangling from the trees. The bright blue sky provided optimal vision for the air traffic. The task today, conveying a colonel and a major from one place to the other, was completed. The pilots were in a fantastic mood with the end of the day drawing closer. Once the air was clear with no superiors in immediate vicinity, they enjoyed themselves behaving like free birds in the sky. They began pulling a few stunts in the air and waved at each other.

The flight mission they had been given, was an altitude of minimum 400 feet and only 150 feet by weather deterioration. The weather was good, still all three pilots flew below 400 feet. It was much more fun floating lower. Flying gave David a feeling of freedom and independence. David's childhood wish to become a pilot came true at the age of twenty-three. One day, he hoped, he would be flying one of the big charter planes and go around the world. He was a very ambitious person.

When he set his mind on something, he didn't give up until he reached his goal. He proved it when he fulfilled his dream as a helicopter pilot. Despite the fact that he was already married, had one young child and another one on its way he passed the training with flying colours. David himself grew up in a big family. He came from a worker family and, as the oldest of five children, he learned from a young age to look out for himself. The opportunity to commence the flight training arose, after he had completed his national service that is compulsory for all young men in Germany.

As a quiet man, people who didn't know him thought of him as a reserved person, one who was not capable of passing the training. However, they got it wrong and often misinterpreted him. David indeed had a very strong personality. Only the ones who knew him such as family and close friends were aware of his determination. David swerved his head left to glance at the glittering snow. He recalled the previous night and the amazing sex he had. His face lit up whenever he thought of Lucy, his new partner. They had moved in together a few months ago. It was getting serious and his life was changing for the better.

Then David's biggest problem was the female gender. David had charm and a handsome face. Women were falling for it. Once he got into serious trouble. He had laid his hands on the wrong woman, the wife of one of his former superiors. He was forced to move to a different base, followed by disciplinary actions. It happened a few years ago, when he was still with his wife. David wasn't proud of that and pushed the bad memories away.

"Mayday, mayday!" All of a sudden Andrew Mann's panicked voice filled the airwaves.

David was startled. "Bloody hell. What's going on?" he said more to himself.

Mike grunted next to him. "Oh dear, it's Andrew, I think he caught something."

David glanced at Mike. "What do you mean he caught something? Don't tell me he kissed something in the air again?" Just recently Andrew was involved in an incident where he flew into a telephone line. The radio blinked again, followed by a gasp.

"Shit, shit, shit! I collided with a power supply line." A clarion desperate breath was transmitted via airwave.

David rolled his eyes in exasperation. His mouth opened to retort, but Alex Feld was quicker, his voice roaring through the airwaves. "Not again, Andrew. Buy some spectacles for God's sake!" David silently agreed with Alex. He slammed his wrist against the cyclic stick and threw an irritated glance to Mike, who was on the lookout for Andrew.

"It's not funny." Andrew's voice echoed back. He clearly sounded upset.

No surprise. It didn't look good for him. Colliding with something in the air twice within a period of six months was not what you would expect from a pilot. "I've still got it under control, but I have to descend," Andrew panted.

David did a sharp turn by manoeuvring the machine to the left to join Andrew on the ground. "On our way," he groaned into his radio.

"Me too!" Alex shouted caustically. No chance they would be able to finish on time now. It was Friday afternoon and they all had plans.

David was supposed to have his children for the night. He was looking forward to it. "Not good," he said to Mike.

"Yeah, so annoying, I was supposed to see my bird tonight. Haven't seen her for two weeks! Damn you, Andrew. I think I am going to buy him some glasses,"

Mike replied with a slight smirk on his face.

"That might be a good idea. I hope the damage is not too bad. Let's find out, shall we? Luckily we have you on board." This time it was David who smiled.

Several minutes later both David and Alex touched ground beside Andrew. The snow was more than 20cm deep. Not ideal for a helicopter to land. David emerged from the helicopter with the engine running. His boots vanished in the snow. He rubbed his hands together with chattering teeth. David reckoned it was more than minus ten degrees. Andrew, who stood next to his machine, eyeballed the damage. A trail of relief crossed his face. "I don't think it's that bad. I might be still able to fly it!" he shouted loudly towards David and Alex as they both advanced. Mike trudged behind them with his tool box in his hand.

Mike got straight down to work. He began to examine the machine. Like the other two choppers, it was an Alouette II, a light helicopter made in France. He scrutinised underneath the cockpit, where the impact took place, and twitched his moustache. "Well there is only a bit of damage to the paintwork, nothing serious. Obviously it needs to be checked out properly, but there is no major defect I can see," he concluded.

"So am I able to fly it back to the base?" Andrew's eyes glimmered with hope.

"Yes, this shouldn't be an issue. But are you not supposed to report it first?" Mike glanced from one pilot to the other. Alex shrugged his shoulders, whilst David kept his head down. His toes inside his boots wiggled with coldness. "I thought you guys have to wait for the assessor, before you are allowed to take off again." Although Mike was not a pilot, he was long enough a mechanic in the air force to know the rules. Andrew averted from Mike's glance and stared at his feet.

Suddenly he looked like a young boy who had been told off by his teacher. He muttered nervously, "Shit, I've just flew into something the other day. This time I will be in serious trouble. I don't want to lose my licence." Due to the running rotors of all three helicopters, he was barely audible.

David pursed his lips. He silently cursed Andrew. He stepped sideward. David's gaze wandered off to the sky, following the wire of the power line that was shrouded by trees. "What's the damage up there?" He shielded his eyes against the reflection of the sun. "Did it cut through?"

Andrew waved aside. "Don't think so. I only struck it lightly."

Alex, who stood next to Andrew, sighed. "The problem is, we have to get somebody out here to guard the machine until Monday. They won't send an assessor out today. We know that." David nodded in agreement. He stuck his hands in his pocket, to fight against the numbness in his fingers. He was yearning for a hot bath.

Andrew clasped his palms against his temple and whinged, "It might be ourselves who have to babysit the machine. Kind of a punishment I could imagine. Shit, the captain is going to kill me."

Abruptly one after the other turned their head to David as if it was up to him to decide. Although David was the most experienced one when it came to flying, he certainly wasn't in charge here. With an 'I don't know' gesture, David began to reason. "Well guys, you know how it works. You can't take off just like this. It has to be reported immediately. Otherwise we might find ourselves in trouble."

Andrew's face went pale. "Look guys, there is almost no scratch. The captain will be fuming if somebody has to come out to guard the machine over the weekend, especially in these weather conditions. I would suggest we all fly back and I will report it on Monday."

Alex, David and Mike looked at each other. On one hand it made sense what Andrew was suggesting. On the other they could face serious consequences. "Well I am not sure if that's a good idea," David pondered.

"Guys, please, come on. It's not just this, you know that. We were supposed to fly a minimum of 400 feet and we didn't. It will come out. And most likely we will be punished for it. I will speak to the captain on Monday," Andrew coaxed.

Alex nodded. "Well, Andrew is right. We flew against the flight mission. And yes, it will be difficult to send somebody out here in this thick snow. And worst of all it won't change a damn thing. The damage is done." They discussed it for another five minutes and came to the conclusion to follow Andrew's advice. At this very moment, none of them could predict that they were about to commit a disastrous mistake, which would change their lives forever. And not far from where they stood, a whole village was left without electricity.

CHAPTER 5

David parked his car in his usual spot. It was half past seven Monday morning. Life in the barracks was already wrapped up in daily activities. Soldiers visible in their battledress were lined up in order to get ready for their morning parade. The buildings were of the late 1940s, built after the Second World War. They were of a standard grey colour emanating a dull ambience. Going through the gates David walked past the buildings set in a row containing the dormitories for the soldiers.

Being one of the soldiers, who used to live on and off at the barracks, David was glad these times had gone. When his marriage fell apart and before moving in with Lucy, he spent most of his time here. He glanced at the two massive halls behind the dormitories which towered over the whole compound. They housed the helicopters, twelve in total with a workshop on-site. Before David became a pilot, he was a helicopter mechanic at the barracks. His knowledge about the mechanism of a chopper was excellent. Thus, he was confident the damage Andrew had caused was pretty minor. Yet the whole weekend, he had been afflicted by uneasiness about their actions on Friday.

David entered the building opposite the hall. It accommodated the changing rooms for the soldiers, the offices and the canteen with a kitchenette. Five minutes later he was fully dressed in his uniform ready to meet his superiors. He flattened his shirt and brushed through his hair while he loped along the dreary corridor. He lightly knocked at his captain's door. The familiar voice of his captain ordering him to step in echoed in his ears. David did as he was told and pushed the door open.

His colleagues Alex Feld and Andrew Mann were seated opposite Captain Max Boll, who was plunged into his swivel chair behind his small desk. The captain was of a short built and slightly overweight. He was only in his early thirties but his receding forehead indicated that he was not far off from becoming bald. Behind Boll, propped up against the window sill, stood Benjamin Kraft the major. He was in charge of the unit and fairly new to the team. David was yet unsure about him. Rumours said that he was an old friend of the captain.

The room itself was not very big. The captain's desk situated near the window, some filing cabinets alongside the wall and a few chairs, now occupied, took away most space in the room. It was certainly not for people who suffered with claustrophobia. The desk was as ever messy, with files and paper scattered around the surface. It didn't surprise David. The captain was known to be disorganised with his

34

paperwork. A framed picture displaying the captain's wife and daughter embellished the desk.

He had met Boll's wife when he installed his captain's sauna. She was an attractive woman. David couldn't comprehend what a woman like her was doing with a man like Boll. She was tall with long blonde hair and possessed a curvy body, a man would die for. The thought of her made David's mouth water. The captain in contrast wasn't nice. And not just his looks let him down, also his personality stank. Andrew Mann who sat to the left, his back towards David, looked like a drowned rat.

"Sit down!" Boll commanded, pointing to the empty chair in the left corner. "We already have discussed the situation. And like I said to these two…" Boll pointed to Andrew and Alex. "What on God's earth was going through your brains, when you made the decision to leave the scene? You all know what the procedure is!"

David didn't like the way this was said to him. Discomfort was crawling through his body. He glanced at Benjamin Kraft, the major, for consolation. But his gaze was focused on an unidentifiable object outside the building.

"Especially you, Sergeant Hunt, the most experienced of you all. You should have known better what to do. I am deeply disappointed by your actions!" Boll banged his fist on the desk, causing the framed photograph of his family to rise up into the air. It was his way of demonstrating authority. A lump was building up inside David's throat. He had not imagined the meeting to be like this. The feeling, that he was solely blamed for their actions after the incident, sank in. David, still on his feet lowered himself onto the chair.

He clenched his fingers into the rim of the seat, pressing the chair against his bum and moved forward to be side by side with his comrades. He turned slightly to his right and glanced at Alex and Andrew for support. At the end of the day they were all in this together. Sadly he was confronted with silence.

Unsure about their quietness, David stirred edgily in his seat. "I am sorry, Sir, but I am sure you were aware of the weather conditions. And the circumstances given, we thought it was better to fly back to the base as there was almost no damage to the chopper," Dave apologetically replied.

"Yeah, yeah, save me all this soap, I've heard it a few times now," Boll groaned loudly.

Kraft, who had been quiet until up to now, slowly turned around. He was a tall man, almost 190cm and had a muscular body. His dark blond hair was combed backwards, protruding his bushy eyebrows. His deep blue eyes bored into David's. "Obviously you all were flying to low, no doubt about that. I was told the flight mission given on that day, was a minimum of 400 feet, and 150 feet by weather deterioration. However, as far as I can recall, let's forget about the coldness, the weather conditions were excellent. Isn't that correct, Captain Boll?"

Kraft had a firm voice which tolerated no dissent. His head was touching his chin when his gaze sank to Boll.

"Yes, that's correct." Boll slightly lifted his eyes to the major, nodded, and returned his stare to David.

The interrogative look of both of his superiors made David wonder if they had spoken to Alex and Andrew in the same way. David leaned back in his seat and took a deep breath. He began moistening his lips with his tongue, searching for words.

"Well, Sir. I know we had instructions to fly a minimum of 400 feet and we failed to obey. Therefore, it is our entire fault. But you know how it is. On our way back, after we had dropped off the last passengers, we began a bit fooling around. That's all. The order wasn't even written down anywhere, so we got carried away. I am conscious this is not an excuse. However, we can't change it anymore. What's done is done. Apologies again, Sir!" David reasoned.

"And that's the point!" Boll interrupted and again banged his fist against the surface of his desk. This time it was with a rush of excitement. "It's not somewhere on paper. If we all stick to it and say the mission was to fly a minimum of 150 feet, we can assist Sergeant Mann by sharing the burden." He nodded towards Kraft and continued. "But if we tell the truth, then…" He shook his head in a steady motion with a frown.

"We all find ourselves in serious trouble, especially Sergeant Mann. His licence will be gone forever and most likely he has to pay for the whole damage. As I have told the others already. Your careless behaviour didn't just cause damage to the machine. A whole village was left without electricity after the impact."

David furrowed his brows. That was new to him. Still, he wasn't keen on lying. However, the fact that a whole village was left without electricity changed the circumstances.

His comrade could find himself in serious trouble, especially after he had flown into a telephone line only a few months ago. And David certainly didn't wish this on anybody. After all, it was about camaraderie. And perhaps if they had followed orders, this would never have happened. Who knew? It made sense what the captain suggested. They had to stick together. Still, David had a vague apprehension about the whole thing.

Nevertheless, he agreed to the captain's plan and lied. They all lied. Instead of admitting that 400 feet had been the stipulated altitude, it was altered to 150 feet. The altitude they were supposed to fly only by weather deterioration. And this time it was put on paper. Andrew would hopefully be spared without facing enormous consequences. At this point David didn't realise that the captain had his own plans and that this was a set-up.

CHAPTER 6

Lucy was trying her best not to cry into the phone. A streak of curly brown hair slid onto her cheek and tickled her skin. She swiftly tucked it behind her ear. Sitting at the kitchen table in her flat in Bueckenau, where she resided with her partner David, her pretty young face was buried in one of her hands. The other one was holding the receiver. They had moved in together about six months ago, yet the relationship was falling apart.

She had met David the previous year in Lucy's home town in Hanwau. Lucy had been employed as a switchboard operator at the local barracks when David attended a four-week course. They instantly fell in love. From the start they were crazy for each other. Lucy transferred to the barracks to Bueckenau, to be closer to David. Not long after that they shared a flat together. She smiled lugubriously at the thought.

The questioning of her mum flustered her even more. Lucy barely managed to hide it. "Yeah Mum, David is still not flying. I have no idea how long this will go on for." She was tempted to tell her mum about David's sudden mood change. Since he was grounded, he wasn't the same person. Worst of all she suspected he was cheating. Lucy was cognisant that David had been unfaithful to his wife Emily. When Lucy had met him, he still lived with Emily. He had insisted that their marriage was over.

Yet it had gnawed on her conscience, especially as there were two young children in the game. She was not the type of person to destroy a family. She confronted David to give him the choice and David decided for Lucy. She had never met Emily. She had only spoken to her once on the phone during which Emily sputtered some comments about David's adultery during their marriage. That time she didn't think much of it.

Right now she thought differently. She didn't have any proof of his infidelity, however she could tell. Their sex life used to be great. She recollected times when he couldn't get enough of her. And now they behaved like an old couple. David frequently came home late and the other night he didn't come home at all. Perhaps it was a mistake to share a flat after knowing each other for only six months. Lucy had known from the start that it would be no bed of roses.

She accepted the fact that David had commitments. He still had to look out for his family, not just financially. His children needed him as a father and David in turn needed them. Lucy didn't mind. She liked the kids to come over. They always had so much fun together. Yet suddenly precarious about their joint future, she wondered if her mum had been right. She had warned Lucy on numerous occasions about David.

Not that her mum didn't like him. However, she had not approved that David was still married with two children. Eventually Lucy had managed to convince her mum that the marriage had been long over before they even met. And her mum finally began to accept them as a couple. "I know, I know. He hasn't done anything wrong. That's just how it works in the forces. It takes time until the investigation is complete," Lucy said whiningly to answer her mum's question as to why it was taking so long to come to a decision.

Almost two months had passed since the incident and David was patently suffering. When her mum began to challenge her, picking up on Lucy's dolorous undertone and suspected that David had somehow hurt her daughter, Lucy gasped. She uncrossed her legs and stretched them. Although Lucy was tempted to confide in her mum, she feared her mum would come straight over to take her back home. She would most likely demand to end this relationship.

Lucy tried to push David from her mind, yet she wasn't succeeding. Tears welled up again and she quickly muttered into the phone, "Mum, I have to finish. Somebody is knocking at the door. I will call you soon." She managed to put the phone down before bursting into tears. She slumped forward, her wet eyes landing in her open palms. Of course there was nobody at the door.

Lucy just didn't want her mum to know that she was crying. She struggled to come to terms with David's potential unfaithfulness. They were seeing each other for only one year and he already cheating? Wasn't the first two years supposed to be the time where you were most in love? The only conclusion Lucy could draw was that he would eventually leave her too. Sobbing like a baby, Lucy realised she had to draw an end to it.

She didn't want to end up like his wife, always wondering in which bed David slept next. Still she wasn't ready, not yet. She wanted to give David one more chance. She forged out a plan in her head to spy on him next time he went out. She needed to be sure what he was up to. If he was telling her the truth and he indeed stayed the other night at a friend's house, as he had insisted, then there was nothing to be worried of.

CHAPTER 7

Two months later David, deluged with discontent, was once again on his way to the captain's office. He was still prohibited from flying. Not that he had expected it to be any different. After his captain had changed the altitude, all three pilots were recorded on tape. When it was David's turn, it felt more like an interrogation than an interview. David tried to explain that he hadn't been in charge that day. If he had, under no circumstances would he have left the scene without reporting it there and then. But whatever he said, the captain turned his words against him. He pinned the blame on David, justifying it by alleging that he, as the most experienced pilot, should have known better. On paper David was announced as the commander and that was the end of it.

As a result David's pilot licence was temporarily revoked. He was placed on restricted duty and a disciplinary enquiry was under way. The payroll office eliminated his flight allowance, causing him to increase his debts. It was a big financial loss. He struggled to support his wife and two children. The fact that he had always lived a bit over his budget didn't make it easier. It had long crossed David's mind that he had been set up. By lying about the altitude, his captain had him in the palm of his hand. If David had known all this beforehand, he would have never agreed to it. David contemplated raising his suspicions higher up and admitting his part in the lying. But then David didn't want to make it worse. It was unwise to upset your superiors. They could easily destroy your career. He decided to hold back and to await the outcome of the disciplinary enquiry. Today, his captain was going to tell him how long he was grounded for. After a brief knock David sauntered into his captain's office.

Boll was expecting him. He sat as usual behind his desk, his palms on top of each other on a bunch of loose papers. As ever the desk was in a dishevelled state. How on earth did his captain manage to gain control of it? David zestfully grabbed a chair and placed it opposite his captain. David, confident he would be back in the air in no time, placed his hands on top of the chair and expectantly looked at his captain. He was already suffering with withdrawal symptoms. Two months without flying was a very long time for somebody who was passionate about it. Boll's face remained neutral. It slightly unsettled David. Would his captain not have a smile on his face to deliver some good news to one of his soldiers? The feeling of discomfort returned. Boll gestured to sit down. David struggled to suppress his dislike towards his captain.

Boll was a hypocrite and David had lost trust in him

since the incident. He plopped onto the chair, his fingers intertwined in his lap. They had not been on good terms at all since that day. It didn't help that every time David tried to speak to his captain, he was ignored. Incredible to think that just one year ago, David had installed Boll's sauna. He inconspicuously wagged his head. Still David hoped for the best. His face brightened up, full of aspiration. He even endowed a smile to his captain. Boll had his head focused on a pile of documents in front of him. He moved his chubby index finger to the top and began to thump on it. His neutral gaze had changed to a grumpy expression. He shook his head and finally glanced up. Not a good sign, David thought. The atmosphere in the room became all of a sudden tense.

David disengaged his fingers and ran them through his hair. "Is it that bad?" he asked.

Boll stood up and turned towards the window. With his back to David, he sighed. "I am very sorry, but I have bad news for you."

"What do you mean 'bad news'? I am not expecting to be back in the air tomorrow. I know it takes times and I will be punished for a while. But it can't be that long, can it?" David countered with a half-smile and leaned forward. In an attempt to read the document, he jiggled to the front edge of his seat. The legs of the chair suddenly began to bounce on the floor. David quickly grasped hold of the desk to prevent his fall. The noise didn't escape Boll. He turned around and threw a dispraising glance at David. David in turn returned his look inculpably. "Could you just tell me, Captain? Don't tantalise me."

Boll nodded. "I will. But first of all I want you to

know…" His gaze fell to the floor. "I tried my best. For all of you! But sometimes it's not good enough."

David ran out of patience. His face turned red, which was not a good sign. He angrily stared at his captain, who once more showed his back to David. The camouflage pants were wrapped tightly around the captain's legs, indicating that he had put on some piles afresh. David was tempted to snap the sheet from his captain's desk, but managed to control himself. Boll finally revolved. David blinked. Did he not just see a smirk on his captain's face?

"Before I show it to you, I want you to know it's not just you." Boll continued. "Alex Feld got off lightly. He has been grounded for only six months. But Andrew Mann…" Boll shook his head. "Well, he has been punished for sixteen months. I don't have to tell you what that means!"

No, he didn't. David knew exactly what it meant. His comrade would probably never fly again. After twelve months' prohibition, a pilot's licence expired automatically. If you wished to fly again, you had to repeat the whole training. And David didn't think Andrew would get another chance. Not as it happened the second time. But that wasn't David's problem. "I am very sorry to hear that. But what about me? How long for me?" Surely it couldn't be any longer than Alex's?

Boll returned to his desk. He pulled out the third sheet from top of the pile. He handed it silently to David. David scanned it, his face going ash pale. One glance was enough. The big bold letters were impossible to miss. For a moment he thought he was just having a bad dream. The ink was turning blurry, causing David to bat his eyelids. Please don't let it be true, he begged silently. But there it was in black and white signed by the colonel. Sixteen months, the same as Mann! He was banned from flying for sixteen months.

In plain English it meant David would never fly again.

CHAPTER 8

David was raging. "You are joking, aren't you?" David leaped to his feet and leaned with his hands against his captain's desk. He frowned down at Boll, who was back in his seat, like a bull ready for his fight. Breathing heavily, David snapped. "How could you let this happen?"

Boll elevated his arms in a defensive mode. "Listen, it wasn't me who made this decision. It has nothing to do with me," he replied in a conciliatory tone.

"Bullshit, you forced me into lying." David slammed his fist on the desk. He stopped caring about his attitude towards his captain. The last remaining bit of respect was gone. "It wasn't even me who caused it. Tell me why. Why are you doing this to me? I know it's down to you. You have a grudge against me." Boll returned David's gaze with a blank expression and shrugged his shoulders. There was nothing else to say.

David knew he was running against a brick wall. He swivelled on his toes and with the document of his flight prohibition under his arm, he aimed for the door. Before he opened it, he gaped one more time at Boll and growled. "Not with me, Captain. I won't give up that easily!" The walls began to shake as he slammed the door shut.

Furiously David headed straight to the major. David was trembling with rage as he swung his legs to the other side of the building, where Benjamin Kraft's office was situated. To reach it David had to pass the canteen. A roar of laughter was coming from the room. David placed it to his comrade Andrew Mann. For a split second he felt tempted to challenge him. A sixteen-month-long banning order was certainly not something to celebrate. And it was all Andrew's fault!

David pulled himself together and marched straight into Kraft's office. He didn't bother knocking. Kraft lolled against the filing cabinet with the phone squashed to his ear. When he spotted David he frowned at him with a dismissive gesture. David disregarded him. He moved closer and stopped right in front of Kraft. In comparison to Boll's office, this one was spacious. David widened his stance and crooked his neck to face the major. Kraft was almost a head taller than David. In fact he towered over most of his soldiers. Kraft lowered his eyebrows and patchy red blotches appeared on his cheeks. "Give me a moment," Kraft mumbled into his handset. Clutching it with his fingers, he dropped the handset to his side and glared at David furiously.

"How dare you, Sergeant Hunt? Storming into my office without the decency to knock? I certainly can't be dealing with you right now. I have other things to do! I am ordering you to leave my office immediately!"

Kraft's face began to beam blazing red. David took no notice. With a sharp movement he lifted up the piece of paper and held it right in front of Kraft.

"Sixteen months, Sir. I have been grounded for sixteen months for something I didn't do!" David pointed wildly, his fingers on it.

Kraft scowled at David and motioned to the door. "I asked you to leave. Now!" He entered David's space, with a menacing poise, forcing David towards the exit.

David's shoulders sank dauntedly. "So I guess you won't help me either," he asserted. Desperately disappointed, he began slowly to retreat. Kraft didn't reply. He indicated once more to the door and turned his back to David. David had no other choice than to leave.

When David was gone, Kraft put the phone back to his ear and said with a smirk on his face, "Thanks for the distraction. You called at the right time. He indeed showed up in my office. He behaved like a maniac. How did you actually know, he would come straight to me? Was it your sixth sense again?" Boll on the other line started to laugh.

CHAPTER 9

When David's shift ended he headed straight to an empty home. Lucy was staying at her mum's for the night. David was thankful for that. After such an awful day at the barracks, he was not in the mood to deal with Lucy right now. Their relationship had changed. They argued a lot. He knew it was mainly his fault. He was insufferable since that day in February. A piece of him had been taken away when they took his pilot licence. He was now constantly on sentry duty, part of his punishment. Something that David certainly hadn't visualised himself doing in his military career. Unbelievable! He had been lying for a peer, part of the camaraderie that was of great significance within the armed forces, and now it was used against him. Stitched up by his superiors! Sixteen months flight prohibition! David shook his head in incredulity. The biggest joke he'd ever heard in his entire life. He stood in the bathroom and hauled out his jeans from the washing machine.

Thank God Lucy hadn't washed them yet. Digging

out a slip of paper from one of the pockets, he made his way to the phone. Excitement was rushing through David's body as he glanced at the name and number displayed on the note. His front was swelling up just by reading her name. Not without reason. Being banned from flying had taken his self-esteem. But not when it came to his manhood. So he did what he could do best. Aware that this wasn't an excuse, he couldn't help himself. Women were one of his biggest weaknesses. It didn't take long for David to find what he was looking for. A tiny bit of guilt washed over him as Lucy appeared in his mind. He tried to shake her off. The female gender was his downside. He was addicted to sex. And unfortunately one woman wasn't enough for him. It gave him a sense of excitement and adventure having sex with more than one. And he needed it more than ever. After such bad news it was the only thing that kept him going.

An hour later, David, refreshed from a hot shower and only dressed in his black bathrobe, opened the front door with an erection in his pants. No surprise. The woman on his doorstep looked beautiful. She had thick, long, dark brown hair meandering in curves around her face. Fully erotic lips smiled at him and her sinuous body closed in on him. Her husky voice had a deep sexy resonance, particularly when she whispered perverted comments into his ear. He had known Sharon only for a month. Yet she already drove him nuts. It was pure sex between them and David was totally under Sharon's spell. "Come in, sexy," he murmured, wetting his lips with his tongue. She smirked at him provocatively. Her lips twisted upwards and she exposed one of her long tanned legs underneath her beige summer coat. David understood the meaning. He swiftly dragged Sharon by her sleeves towards his aroused torso and kicked the door shut with his bare foot.

Her heeled black leather boots scraped against the laminated floor. Groaning loudly with desire and full of verve he lifted her up. Sharon wrapped her legs around his buttocks. Her coat unfurled and he glanced down at her big firm breasts. She was completely naked underneath. Her toned tummy moved in and out with quick breaths as she clawed her long nails into David's biceps. David pushed her with his whole weight against the wall. His erect penis protruding from his bathrobe, pressed against her vagina. Sharon began moaning ecstatically. His hands clutched her bum, giving her a hard slap.

"Have you been waiting for me, my big naughty boy?" She bit his earlobe, and a silent howl escaped David's mouth.

"Of course I have," David growled and jabbed his tongue into her mouth, kissing her with such fervour she nearly struggled to breathe. Impetuously he swung around and carried his lover to the kitchen.

He approached the table and with one swift move brushed off some magazines from the surface. As he brought her down onto the table, for a split second he let go of her and greedily captured her nudeness. Satisfied with his prey, he bent forward and began sucking each of her nipples. His penis swept along her vulva, touching her sweet spot.

Sharon heaved a sigh. Unable to control herself anymore, she arched her hips, ramming it against his manhood and begged, "Oh please, David. Give it to me, fuck me now. Fuck me hard and fast." David didn't hesitate. He thrust his penis into her vagina and rode her fiercely. It didn't take long and both of them climaxed at the same time. Yet it wasn't the end. Several minutes later and after an intense blow-job David was ready for another round. He flipped his lover over and took her at the same spot from behind.

CHAPTER 10

David sat opposite his solicitor. He nervously shuffled in his seat. Within the last few days David had placed documents and correspondences, surrounding the incident and the aftermath, in chronological order in a folder. Paperwork had accumulated over the last few months. Not an insignificant amount either. Sadly it was all bad news including the official document unveiling the length of the flight prohibition. And to make matters worse an incredibly bad character reference received from Major Kraft. David had added to his collection a summary of the events in his own words. Receiving the evil news about his flight prohibition the other day prompted David to take up the courage to disclose the truth. He made several attempts to speak to the lieutenant colonel, yet he was ignored. Unfortunately the only way to arrange an appointment with a lieutenant colonel was through your own superior. But whenever he endeavoured, he was stopped either by Boll or Major Kraft. There was no light at the end of the tunnel.

David realised it was time to take the matter into his own hands. He arranged an appointment with his solicitor and here he was. "So, do you think I have a chance?"

He felt like a pupil in his head teacher's office, whose world depended on the next few words out of this person's mouth. Could he stay or would he be expelled? Not that he was ever close to getting expelled. Yet he imagined that it felt like this did right now. The solicitor tapped his pen against his mahogany desk whilst scrolling through the pages. David's gaze wandered off to the expensive art of Picasso and Van Gogh gilding the white walls. The office was situated in a big glass building along with other solicitors and barristers. It was appointed with expensive designer furniture indicating that business was going well for him.

The solicitor was dressed in a Hugo Boss suit that spoke for itself. It didn't come as a surprise. He had an excellent reputation. It was said he was one of the best solicitors in the area. Fortunately David had legal protection insurance otherwise he wouldn't be able to afford it. The solicitor flicked through the folder a second time. After what seemed like an eternity, he closed it and overlapped his hands on the front cover.

His head began waggling from left to right, clearly in scepticism. "I can't believe what I am reading here. For me it looks like somebody higher up has a grudge against you. Sixteen months is a really harsh punishment. Not so much for your colleague. After all he was the one who caused it. And the other pilot, hold on…" The solicitor skipped back through the first few pages, searching for David's summary that outlined all three flight prohibitions.

"Six months for Alex Feld, that's not so bad either. But for yourself, sixteen months? I struggle to trust my eyes. Have you upset someone?" He inclined his head.

"No, not that I know of." David shrugged. He spread his fingers on his lap and straightened himself. "I was trying to talk to my superiors. But they ignore me. They act as if I don't exist."

The solicitor furrowed his eyebrows. "Well, I don't know. Somebody seems to have a problem with you. And you are confident to be clear of any wrongdoing?"

David leaned back. "Positive. I have no idea what I've done wrong."

The solicitor thoughtfully scratched behind his ear. "Even if you have, this is not an adequate punishment. This is absolutely disproportionate. I would even call it disgraceful." David felt slightly better. Finally he was getting somewhere. Someone else shared his opinion.

"So what am I supposed to do next?"

The solicitor swivelled in his chair to free his legs and stood up. Seeing him in full length, David could easily imagine how he was able to grill somebody in court. David estimated him to be in his early forties. To his benefit the years had been gentle on him.

"Right now, I don't want you to do anything," he said. "Leave it in my hands. I will draw an appeal together and you will receive a copy via mail. I am confident we will see your licence back in no time. In the meantime please leave all your details with us and

I need a copy of the folder. My secretary should be able to sort it." David nodded as he moved back his chair to stand up. The solicitor endowed David with a reassuring smile.

"We should be able to get some of your flight allowance reimbursed. The army had no right to deduct it from day one. They should have waited for the official outcome. I will work on this immediately."

David was pleased with the good news. It would help to tide him over for a bit. The loss of the flight allowance had a big impact on David's lifestyle. The red numbers were steadily increasing. The first time since that tragic day in February, he began to have faith once again. David wiped his sweaty hands on his trousers and reached out. His solicitor met him halfway. They shook hands and David was seen off. On his way out David arranged the paperwork with the secretary.

David was whistling as he emerged from the glass building. He had made the right move. For the first time since this all began, he didn't feel alone. An elegant woman in a black suit dress slightly older than David collided with his right shoulder as she rummaged in her handbag. She muttered an apology and disappeared into the building. David licked his lips as he rotated to check out her bum. What a hot chick! He conquered the suppression of a groan. David made his way to the car. It was time to collect his children for the weekend. They lived with Emily, his estranged wife. Pity came up when he thought of Emily. She was sometimes too fond of the bottle. He blamed Emily's dramatic childhood experience. It was her way to deal with it. She failed to realise that alcohol just made it worse. She had to get her act together, for the sake of her children.

The last thing he ever wanted was to take the children from her. It would only break her heart. Still if she continued this way, he might have no other option. Once, Emily had tried to cut her wrists. The day was still fresh in his head. It was when David finally left her for Lucy. Another time, long after he'd moved out, Emily had another go. David had come to collect the kids. They began arguing about some bagatelle in the garden. He even couldn't remember what it was. Emily made a mountain out of a molehill. It escalated and they ended up screaming at each other, the children within earshot. Emily ran into the house. David remained in the garden, expecting Emily to eventually calm down. A piercing shriek from inside the house told him otherwise.

He followed the noise through the living room into the hallway. Thomas stood in the doorframe leading to the adjacent garage and stared at his mum's car, whilst screaming his head off. Approaching it, David understood why. A cloud of smoke was whirling through the air towards the inside. David reacted immediately. He grabbed Thomas by his shoulders, pushed him away and hurried down the two steps. The garage was filled with fumes and David quickly approached the vehicle with the driver's door wide open. He found a semi-conscious Emily on the driver's seat with her head slumped against the steering wheel. Emily had almost managed to take her own life. Not a nice death to suffocate like this. It had been David's fault. During their quarrel he had threatened to take the children away. He finally understood, that he was not meant to do that. She needed her children, as much as they needed their mum.

Thirty minutes later David turned into Emily's driveway. The house was located in a quiet residential area in the suburbs of Bueckenau. It was a semi-detached house, surrounded by lovely neighbours. Emily's car was nowhere to be seen. David assumed it was in the garage. He walked up the steps leading to the entrance. He still possessed the house key for emergencies. David knocked several times. When nobody answered, he went to unlock the door, but the door pushed inwards, telling him it was unlocked. He stepped in and promptly called out for his children. Again he was greeted with silence. It was the same when he shouted for Emily. With clenched teeth and his eyes narrowed he began to look around. He checked in every room, his face contorted in annoyance. Emily knew he was coming, so where was she? He made his way to the kitchen and was abruptly startled.

"Oh my god!" David blurted out. A cold shiver ran down his spine as his gaze was fixed on the ground. Blood was splattered around the floor tiles.

CHAPTER 11

On her way to the supermarket, Emily's thoughts were with David. Since their break-up she was going through a hard time. Yet life beforehand had been far from easy. To blame was David's infidelity. It began with his pilot licence. As a handsome pilot women lay at his feet. David rarely resisted. Their sex life had drastically reduced and she knew it wasn't entirely his fault. Emily didn't enjoy much sex. It was taken from her as a child. Glancing at her two children in the rear-view mirror, she knew she had to be strong. They depended on her. And although she and her husband had separated, she was confident he would always be there for them. When she married David her parents hadn't approved of it. David's family had a bad reputation; his mother was known for infidelity and his dad was a violent person.

Emily refused to listen. She had a burning desire to leave her parents' house as fast as she could. David felt the same about his childhood home. They had met when they were both only fifteen. Unlike David, who grew up in a big family, Emily grew up as the only child until her brother came along. By then Emily was already seeing David. In her childhood her parents allowed Emily to have anything she wished for. But not the one thing she needed most. Love! She grew up as an unhappy child. And then when she was only five, something happened. Her father began taking Emily with him to bed at weekends. He expected her to perform strange things on him. Emily hated these Sundays. Her mother knew about it, yet known for her chilly personality she played it down as innocuous.

Emily concluded that there was something wrong with her dad. He was definitely obsessed with sex. He had a passion for taking nude photographs of her mum and also of her as a child. He didn't touch her, oh no, but he loved exposing himself in front of her and worst of all she had to touch him. What happened in her childhood had traumatised her. Her dad took something from Emily, her self-esteem. Nevertheless, she loved him. Her feelings towards her mum were a different story. She thought of her as a cold woman. And then she met David. They fell in love. Emily saw her opportunity coming, a way to escape from her dilemma. So did David whose parents' house was shaped by domestic violence. He wanted to flee as much as Emily did.

When Emily was eighteen she asked for permission to marry David; her dad didn't give his consent. No way, Emily would wait until she was twenty-one. David felt the same. They decided to take fate into their own hands. And there he was. Thomas came along. Her parents felt trapped. A child born outside marriage was still a disgrace. Her parents, known as a very respectful family, had no other choice than to agree to the wedding to prevent a scandal. The marriage didn't last long. The things that had happened in Emily's childhood constantly lived with her. Emily had hoped she would get over it. And yet she didn't. It affected her whole life. The disloyalty of her husband didn't help either. Sometimes she looked too deep into the bottle. It soothed Emily, even if it was only temporary. It helped to forget. To forget that she was sexually abused as a child, to forget her husband's infidelity and now to forget that her husband had left her and moved in with another woman.

David had changed in recent weeks. Emily knew it was because of work. Not much did she know about the incident. Only that a colleague of her husband had flown into a power supply line and David was somehow involved in it. She knew he was in some kind of trouble. It didn't come as much of a surprise. When still together, David at some point even cheated with the wife of one of his superiors. It was when Emily was pregnant with her second child Zoe. He was quite in trouble that time. And the best part, when she told him that she was pregnant again, his only worry consisted of how to break the news to his new lover. As punishment David was transferred to another base. They had to move. As a soldier's wife she was used to living in different places. It was part of the game. On that occasion it was different. With this affair David had made himself quite a few enemies. They never spoke about it. And of course Emily wasn't supposed to ask. These were the moments she chose to numb her pain in alcohol, to shut her eyes to the truth.

A cry from the rear brought Emily back to reality. Thomas and Zoe rowing again was nothing new to Emily. Stressed and tired she pulled over, brought the engine to a stop and twisted her body to face her children. Zoe, glowing like a house on fire, pushed Thomas away. Tears spilled down her cheeks. Emily's attempts to appease her daughter were a waste of time.

She noticed she had stopped outside the local bakery and decided to get some bread. The bakery was filled with half a dozen customers. Emily ambled to the far end of the room to have a straight view to her children left inside the vehicle. "What can I get for you?" The oversized lady behind the counter glared at her. Emily turned to face her but her gaze halted at two young women on the other side of the room.

One of them stood out with her stunning long legs in stilettos. Her long auburn hair dangled in waves down her shoulders. She was dressed in a short black skirt with a matching black top and a tad too much make up. Her friend was the opposite. She was chubby with greasy blonde hair and her flabby tummy stuck out between her dull-coloured T-shirt and jeans. They sat, absorbed in a deep conversation, over a brew. Emily allowed herself a quick glimpse. She regretted it immediately. She recognised the stunning one, who now looked at her. An impudent smirk took shape on the woman's face. She whispered something to her friend. Her friend glanced at Emily's direction with a condemning smile. Emily blushed and averted her gaze.

She felt suddenly queasy. Flashbacks about this particular lady came back to her mind. The air abruptly thick with humidity, Emily's claustrophobia came back to life. Her head dropped to her chin. She felt moisture within her eyeballs. She skipped her order and ran out of the bakery with tears welling up. She couldn't stand it. Enough was enough. All the pain she had endured within the last few years, no, actually her whole life, was building up. Emily raced to her vehicle nearly tripping over an empty can of Coke. Plummeting behind the steering wheel she roared her car back to life and quickly hurtled off. Thomas and Zoe, who had stopped fighting and played a game together peacefully, gaped at their mum in astonishment.

CHAPTER 12

The next stop was the supermarket. With the children in tow, Zoe blithely sat in the shopping trolley whilst Thomas pushed it, Emily approached the alcohol section. The bitch, how Emily secretly described the woman from the bakery, popped up in her head. Emily had overheard the comment the bitch had hummed to her friend. It wasn't actually a whisper, it was loud enough for Emily to catch. Again, Emily was tearing up. What was the whole town thinking? That she was that stupid and naïve, who didn't know? She felt mortified by the encounter. Emily's rage towards David was rapidly increasing. She angrily wiped her eyes and fished a tissue out of her handbag. After blowing into it umpteen times until her nose was drained, she quickly grabbed a bottle of vodka from the half-empty shelf and placed it in the trolley. Emily finished the shopping very quickly and headed towards the checkout. Not long after, Emily found herself in front of her car hiding the vodka in the boot.

Turning into the driveway, David's Golf was sitting right outside their bright red coloured garage. Due to its paint it stood out from the whole neighbourhood. Emily clapped her hand against her forehead. She had totally forgotten about David. It was his turn to spend the weekend with the children. Emily was definitely not in any mood to see him right now. Not after the incident in the bakery. She rolled her eyes while cursing under her breath. She even had no words to describe how much she detested her husband. They rarely spoke to each other these days anyway. Only the bits that were necessary concerning the kids. Emily assumed he was waiting inside, most likely going through her cupboards to see if she was hiding any booze. It was time to take the house keys off him!

Zoe spotted her dad's car before Thomas. Abruptly overwhelmed with excitement, she shrieked, "It's Daddy! Daddy is here!" She leaped out of the car. With her favourite monkey clutched to her chest she sprinted into the house. Her long yellow summer dress dragged along the asphalt. Thomas barely acknowledged his dad's vehicle. Unlike his sister he wasn't thrilled to see his dad. He was old enough to sense it could mean a clash on its way. Like so many others he had witnessed between his parents. He had discerned his mum's reaction when she parked up. Indeed since she had emerged from the bakery she wasn't herself. He trudged to the entrance tensed up with his head down. Emily followed with the shopping bags dangling from each arm. The bottle of vodka stayed hidden in the boot.

David lolled in the armchair in the lounge. He tousled through his dark hair when he heard the door opening. Wrath was written all over his face. It eased slightly when Zoe bounced onto his lap, but returned the minute Emily stepped into the room. More than two hours had passed since he arrived. He jumped up and shouted, "Thomas, Zoe go to your rooms." The children obeyed. David then began railing at Emily furiously. After he had seen all the blood in the kitchen, he ran scared. He had been calling family and friends and even contacted hospitals.

Emily had completely forgotten about the blood. She had cut her finger when she prepared some sandwiches for the way. It had slipped her mind to wipe it off. To be honest she hadn't even noticed that blood had dripped to the floor. She frowned at her husband. Her mouth began to quiver and she crouched forward.

What had he been thinking? That she would do something to herself or the kids? Was he out of his mind? Emily was close to blowing a gasket. The replicate antique furniture, she usually was so proud of, was giving her an eerie sensation. David's reproachful gaze made it even worse. Emily finally lost it. She clenched her fists and lunged at him. She threw punches at his chest and screamed hysterically. The impudent smirk of the bitch was loitering continuously in her mind.

"You know how it feels going to town and people talking behind your back?" Oh yes, Emily had not missed the patronising comment as she murmured to her friend. 'Look at her! She is the wife of the soldier I told you about. The one I was shagging. Great in bed! Rumour says he has been cheating on his wife for years. I don't think they are together anymore. What a pity she is.' Emily repeated the comment in a yelling tone to David.

David's face went pale. He sank onto the brown leather couch, suddenly wallowing in self-pity. He wasn't so much bothered about Emily's emotions. She would get over it, no doubt about that. But what about him? Why was his life spinning out of control? A few months ago everything was perfect. He had been the happiest man on Earth. But now…? His elbows propped up on the glass table whilst he supported his head with his hands. What had he gotten himself into? His whole life was falling apart. Flashes of the incident following the aftermath were permanently on his mind. Why did they blame it on him? Being unable to keep on top of his debts added to his worries. And most of all he abhorred his current duties at the barracks. His military career had come to an end. There was no future anymore. His relationship with Lucy was suffering too.

David's head jerked back, his open palms falling onto his thighs. He glared at his wife and shrugged his shoulders. "I've had enough! I am going to top myself. It will be the best for all of us. I am just a pain for everybody." His desolated tone hung in the air. David pushed himself up, his hollow eyes bulging out.

Emily smiled at him ironically. "So you want to run out on your own children?"

David ignored the remark and quickly rushed past her. He headed for the exit, shutting the door with a bang. Zoe peeked out of her bedroom window. When she saw her dad bolting down the front steps, she darted down the stairs to go outside. The screeching tires of her dad's Golf met her halfway. Sadly she was too late. Her dad had left without her. A sudden deep pain entered Zoe's heart. Emily, who had followed her daughter, tousled through Zoe's thick blonde hair reassuringly. "Don't worry, he will be back soon." Emily then approached the boot of her vehicle and pulled it open to fetch the vodka.

CHAPTER 13

Andrew Mann fidgeted with the remote control. He still lived with his parents. They had gone to the theatre tonight. With no real perspective he switched the channels non-stop. His blank stare was directed straight at the screen. He struggled to focus, his mind wandering off to his captain. The bottle of beer within touching distance stared at him enticingly. He snatched it off the table and gulped a large amount of the cold liquid down his throat. Andrew shifted nervously on his sofa. He was immersed in the after-effects of the chaos he had caused. Many things had changed since then. So far he had the full support of his captain. He considered himself lucky. It could be the other way around. However, the phone call from his captain an hour ago unsettled him. Boll was on his way to see him. He called it a matter of urgency. Andrew was in the dark. Why on earth could it not wait until tomorrow when he was back on duty?

The doorbell rang and within minutes Andrew was back in his seat facing his guest equivocally. He pushed a bottle of beer towards his captain and nodded with his chin to help himself to it. "Sorry, mate, to turn up so late. But no way could it wait till tomorrow. It needs to be sorted now, face to face." Max Boll twitched his moustache. With an intent look he glared at Andrew. Droplets of sweat were visible on Boll's forehead. His shirt stuck to his clammy skin and two large blotches of perspiration were developing under his armpits. If Andrew didn't know better, he would think his captain had run a marathon.

"No problem, Captain. Is everything OK?"

"Yeah, yeah, it's all good. Just a bit stressed. The wife is keeping me on my feet, the usual bit." Boll chuckled. His handkerchief, crumpled in his hand, was brought to his forehead to rub off the sweat.

"So what's happening? I assume you are not here without a reason?" Andrew leaned back, his muscular shape brought to bear. Outwardly he appeared quite mature. Sadly it wasn't always the case. Occasionally he acted more like a young boy than an adult. As a child he never took things seriously. However, life in the armed forces coerced him to change. Still deep inside he felt the bloom of youth.

Andrew was aware of his captain's incidental cold-bloodedness. Individuals Boll didn't like, had to watch out for themselves. David Hunt was one of them. Boll had a grudge against David. It became clear after the incident. Andrew didn't know why. And to be frankly honest, he didn't care. Andrew was far from close to David. They were comrades, nothing more and nothing less. Luckily Andrew was on good terms with the captain. He was one of Boll's favourites. There was no doubt about that. His captain had bailed him out in the past. Not long ago when he flew into a telephone line, Boll had managed to sweep it under the carpet without any repercussions.

Unfortunately this time was different. Leaving the scene had been their big mistake. Andrew couldn't even explain why he did what he did. Did he truly believe his captain could sweep it under the carpet once more? How stupid of him. Particularly, as a whole village had suffered because of him. It was clear as crystal that Andrew would most likely never fly again. The licence would have ceased by the time the banning period was over. And no way would he redo the training. Boll was trying his best to get Andrew's licence back before the twelve months. Yet it was written in the stars if he had a chance. Also he still had to encounter his upcoming trial. Boll was working on Andrew's acquittal. It was one of the reasons why the flight order was changed in his favour.

"I have to ask you for a favour." His captain brought him back to reality. "It's about Hunt." Boll glanced down at his hands.

"About David? Okay." Rumours said David didn't accept the banning order. Andrew couldn't understand why. At the end of the day, all three of them had known they wouldn't get away with it. The chime of the massive cuckoo clock adhered to the wall emanated around the room. Andrew disliked the clock. It gave him the creeps. If he had his way, it would have long since found its way to the bulky waste. His parents clung to it. It was an heirloom of their ancestors.

Boll paused. The clock struck ten times. When the last strike faded, Boll drew a deep breath and proceeded. "Well, he is causing us a bit of a problem here. He doesn't want to accept the decision and the disciplinary action taken against all of you." Boll bent over and clutched for the beer bottle. "I know you are not close to him. Still, I suggest you stay away from him. If he badgers you, ignore him, walk away or whatever is necessary to stop him from bothering you. And if he asks you about the banning order, say you can't talk about it!" The sudden rise of his captain's voice made Andrew jump. His eyelids quivered in irritation.

"But why would he ask me?"

Boll rolled his eyes and censured, "I don't know if he will. I only know he is a proper pain in the arse right now. Listen, I am doing my best here. And it is in your own interest. Otherwise I might struggle to save your arse!" Boll downed the bottle in one swig and arose. "You know where I am coming from, do you?" Andrew, to some degree intimidated, nodded his head. His captain had never spoken to him like this before. For him it sounded more like a warning than a favour.

CHAPTER 14

First it looked good. David's solicitor was switched on. He put his heart and soul into it. The fact that his solicitor had managed to get David's flight allowance reimbursed spoke volumes. However, now, as David sat in front of him, he was not thrilled with his solicitor's advice. "Right now you have to wait and see. We've done what we could and now it's just a waiting game." The solicitor gave David a simper. "I know it's not easy. But you need to be patient." His solicitor had composed an appeal to challenge the decision. He suggested awaiting the response before taking another course of action. But David was sick to the back teeth. He had had enough of waiting for something to happen. It was time to take the matter into his own hands. With a plan already in his mind, he dashed home.

The other day when he ran out of Emily's house, he had no thoughts of harming himself. He had let himself down but managed to buck up. However, it had been a few months now since David last flew. It drove him up the pole. He felt he was losing time.

Lucy was still at work when David arrived home. He prepared some food and with a plate full of pasta and a hot cup of tea he rested on his handmade rocking chair in the living room. He had constructed the chair as a teenager. His first big project in school. He had fabricated many other items, such as tables, wardrobes and other bits and bobs. Most of it was forged. The living room was quite spacious. It was well endowed with a black leather sofa, two matching arm chairs and a glass table, also David's creation.

They had chosen the furniture together, him and Lucy. Lucy had incredibly good taste. A modern-style living room cabinet in black-painted wood, with a glass door on each end, was situated on the other side of the room. In the centre of the cabinet was a built-in shelf for their brand-new television. Yet the most important piece in the room, at least for David, was his hi-fi system. It was very dear to him. The rack was designed by David too and it carried a record player, a tape player, a radio and various vinyl from the Beatles to Abba. Massive loudspeakers flanked on both sides. Although David didn't play any instruments, music was his passion, mainly rock music. He finished his last bite of pasta and after moving the dishes to the kitchen he turned on the music and returned to his rock hair. Indulging in his favourite song from The Beatles, 'Let It Be', he gathered his thoughts about his next move.

Ten minutes later David had moved to the kitchen. He sat in front of his Vintage Oliver typewriter from the 1950s. He inserted two pieces of blank paper with a carbon one in between and began to write. He started with the incident and finished with the unfair treatment and the ridiculous flight prohibition. David went straight into details, not missing out a single bit. It was a summary of the events, similar to the one he had drafted before, however, this time he delved into particulars. He mentioned the altered altitude, outlined how he was pushed to lie and described how his captain pinned the blame on him, claiming David had been in charge that day when he was not. He ended up with two pages. He stuck the original one in an envelope and sealed it. The copied one found shelter in his folder.

David slipped a pen between his fingers and scribbled on the envelope, 'F.A.O. Lieutenant Colonel Schmitz'. He added the address of the barracks in Bueckenau and tucked it in a bigger envelope. Before sealing this one, he scrawled on another piece of paper, 'To my parents, if something happens to me send it off', and placed it in the envelope too. He scribbled his parents' address on it.

David's next mission was a letter to the service complaints commissioner for the armed forces. Usually the last resort if you were at your wit's end. It was the highest you could try in relation to complaints within the armed forces. Their task was to support soldiers who were treated unfairly. David kept it similar to the other one, a bit briefer and politer and in the form of a complaint. A copy of this one also landed in the folder. Feeling tones lighter than before, David went to the post office.

CHAPTER 15

"You got us into this shit, you get it sorted." Benjamin Kraft was fuming.

Max Boll was taken aback. He had never seen this side of his friend. He was right in Boll's face and Boll was forced to take a step back. Kraft's face was glowing like a bulb. His clenched fists ponded against his waist. They stood in Boll's kitchen, which was a decent size. Today, however, the kitchen equipped with rural appliances seemed small and crowded. Boll glanced worriedly at the knife rack. It was situated alongside the cooker and Boll halfway expected Kraft would reach out for one. When Kraft turned up unannounced, with a letter in his hand, Boll sensed it wasn't a friendly visit. His wife was out with her friends and the kid was in bed. However, with his friend behaving like a maniac, Boll for the first time in years, wished his wife was here. He knew the contents of the letter. He had read it several times just days ago.

Fortunately he had managed to stop it from reaching its recipient. All the more, he was astounded that Kraft had gotten hold of it. Boll had seen it coming the day David Hunt stormed out of his office. Hunt had tried to go above his head. It was up to him now to gain control over it. What had started with teaching a soldier a lesson was slowly escalating! Yet there was no comeback. They had to continue what they started. His aim to inhibit David Hunt from ever flying again, had so far worked out. It was some sort of revenge. And at the end of the day it was Hunt's own fault. If he had kept his dick in his trousers, none of this would have happened. When he came up with the idea to blame the incident on David Hunt, his friend and superior Benjamin Kraft had supported him.

There was no way Boll would have allowed Andrew to take full responsibility. Although Andrew wasn't a good pilot, Boll liked him. Andrew reminded Boll of himself before he moved up the ladder. When he was still able to act careless and before he had all those soldiers to take care of. When Andrew called him the same day as the incident occurred, Boll was dismayed. A mishap like this in such a short period could only happen to Andrew. Boll had to think fast. His first thought, *Not again*, was quickly replaced by the idea to finally seek revenge. There was no way he was able to make it go away this time, not with a whole village left without electricity. Someone had to take the blame. And in this case it was David Hunt. Boll had hoped Hunt would eventually accept his fate. However, it wasn't meant to be. Instead of finding Hunt's resignation on his desk, he'd received an appeal from David's solicitor on the grounds that a punishment of sixteen months' flight prohibition was unacceptable.

And then Hunt had the audacity to write to the service complaint commissioner of the armed forces. Beyond belief! Luckily before it could be passed on, the bureaucracy within the armed forces had to go first through the admin in the barracks. Boll watched Hunt's movements very closely, particularly his correspondence. The other day when he saw the letter in the out tray, he took it into his possession. His intention to keep it quiet from his friend, had failed. Kraft confirmed that he had found it, when searching for some staplers in Boll's drawers. Now it was up to Boll to explain why he hadn't mentioned the letter to Kraft.

"You can't keep things like this from me. Not even for my own protection. Too many documents are displaying my signature." Grinding his teeth, Kraft swayed back and forth. He squinted his eyes exasperatingly at his friend. "Promise you won't do it again."

"Of course not, I wasn't thinking straight." Boll mouthed an apology.

Even though Boll had managed to stop the letter, it was clear they were in deep shit. If the truth ever came out Boll's career would be over, perhaps he would do some time too. It wasn't only his future at stake, it was Kraft's too.

"Why did I ever say yes to your plan? I even didn't know the full extent of your purpose." Kraft snorted with rage. He was so furious at his friend. Right now he was subdued by the lust to kill Boll. If he had known the full scheme, without question he would have never agreed to it. "Is it worth it? Tell me, is it worth ruining our lives, just because of a bit of revenge?"

The word 'yes' was on the tip of Boll's tongue, but he repressed it. Still the smile on the face of his wife stayed with him. The one she had bestowed to David Hunt, when he fitted Boll's sauna. And the sudden change of his wife. She never had been the kind of woman to dress up or wear make-up at home. However, the days when Hunt came to their house, she did.

Max Boll would never concede to it, but he was jealous of David Hunt and wished this man out of the armed forces. Nevertheless, he finally realised his mistake. He understood the only way out of it was to stop Hunt. It was only a matter of time until Hunt found out the truth. The million-dollar question was how? Just the thought of the ramifications gave him a headache. Then it wasn't just him or Kraft whose names were showing on various documents. It was the colonel's name too, the person who was in the dark and had no idea that his name had been wrongly used.

Absorbed in his thoughts Boll cringed when Kraft abruptly jolted him by the shoulders and hissed, "You need to get this sorted before it's too late. I don't care how and please save me the details, but straighten it out. You brought us this shit, so deal with it. And any more letters from Hunt and you will let me know!"

Boll answered with a nod. Unfortunately there was only one way to fix this mess.

CHAPTER 16

"David, are you listening?" Lucy wailed as David mooched about in the bathroom. It was only big enough for one person. Her freshly painted fingernails trembled against the door frame. She was losing her patience with David. Nowadays they rarely spoke to each other. If they did nine times out of ten it ended up in controversy.

David was absorbed in his thoughts and totally oblivious to Lucy. The conversation he had overheard in the barracks the day before, was bothering him. When he had walked past Boll's office, the door left ajar, he heard his name mentioned. Boll's voice had sounded agitated. He overheard some remark about David's flight prohibition and some documents he needed to track down before it was too late. As no one else could be heard, David assumed Boll had been on the phone.

It gave him a feeling of unease. Was his captain already aware of his complaint to the parliamentary commissioner? And what documents had he been referring to? Was the captain suddenly on his side? No, he couldn't imagine that. Something was off. He just didn't know what and who he could trust.

"David, I am talking to you!"

David jerked by the sound of Lucy. For a moment he had to refocus where he was. Turning back to the mirror to apply the razor to his skin, he spotted his hollow cheeks. His appearance had changed in recent months. He'd lost about a stone and a dark shadow was permanently towering above him. Would he ever be happy again? "Apologies, I was miles away. What did you say?" Lucy wasn't even supposed to be home yet. When she turned up four hours prior to her shift ending and explained that she had taken a half day of leave, so they could spend the afternoon together, David felt trapped.

With other plans in mind, he was in a quandary. It was a delicate situation. Clearly he didn't want to upset Lucy. Forming all sorts of excuses in his head, David didn't know how to go about it. When David didn't greet her with a sense of delight Lucy's mood had changed drastically. And doubtlessly he didn't want to make it worse. He let go of the razor and with some foam still stuck under his nose, he pulled the towel from the rail. He meant to take his new lover Sharon on a boat trip. And no way would he call it off. He had been looking forward to it all day.

Drying off the last bits of foam, David turned to face Lucy. A lame excuse was on his lips, when Lucy said, "I am going quickly to run some errands. I will be back soon." She aspirated a kiss towards him and left the flat.

Dumbfounded by Lucy's sudden resolution to run some errand, David raised his shoulders. He had no idea what to think of it. Still, it was his opportunity to jump at the chance. With a piece of paper already in his hand, he smoothly jotted down some notes. Not knowing when Lucy would return, every minute counted. David was dressed in no time. He grabbed his wallet, his car keys and his folder, just in case as he liked to call it, and vacated the flat. As he stepped outside, the bright sun shone into his face. He had to cover his eyes with his hand to find his way to his Golf. David swiftly backed his car up and hit the road. The song 'I Get Around' from The Beach Boys was blaring from the radio. It put him in an excellent mood.

On his way out of town David stopped at a florist and purchased a bunch of pink roses. Back in his car, he steered out of town towards Schossener Lake. Finally he was on his way to Sharon. In his mind he imagined Sharon in sexy red lingerie. With a watery mouth he slid his hand down to touch his crotch. His jeans began to swell up. Sharon was like a magnet to him. He was unable to let it go. The thought of her curvy figure possessed his sanity. Overwhelmed with eagerness, David put his foot down. The weather was perfect for a boat trip. It was warm, not too hot, thanks to a gentle breeze wafting from the North. But before the boat trip, he was desperate for a good fuck. And perhaps they could have another round on the boat…? David, too preoccupied with sexual thoughts, picturing himself with his lover in various positions, never noticed the small blue Fiat trailing him.

CHAPTER 17

Lucy was trying hard to keep up with David. As usual he had his foot down, ignoring any speed limits. At one point Lucy was even forced to jump a red traffic light to avoid losing sight of David's vehicle. When she had returned from work and saw David lingering in the bathroom, she sensed that he already had plans. Running some errands was an excuse for Lucy to leave the house in order to find out what David was up to. She parked her little car, a Fiat which she had named 'Nancy', around the corner and bid her time. Half an hour elapsed and David at last made an appearance. She began following him.

When David stopped at a florist, a modicum of hope awoke in Lucy. David was buying her flowers, how sweet! And she had secretly accused David of cheating! She shook her head ashamedly. With a guilty conscience, Lucy began backing onto the road to head back to their flat. She wanted to get home before David could surprise her with a bunch of flowers. She was just about to roar off, when David emerged with a bunch of pink roses.

Lucy paused. She hated the colour pink; not only the colour, she also disliked roses. It slowly sank in that the flowers weren't meant for her. She frowned. So she was right. David was on his way to his lover. If it wasn't for her, for whom else would he buy flowers! With a sour expression, Lucy observed David's face beaming with joy as he hopped into his Golf. Sadly she discovered that she had been unable to raise a smile like this out of David for months. David hurtled off and Lucy was on his tail.

As she followed David from a distance, she was preoccupied with thoughts. The first six months of her relationship with David had been great. They had so much fun together. She recalled the times when he smuggled her to the barracks in the boot of his car. Still the secret rides in the chopper had been the best ones. Only a man like David was able to get a woman surreptitiously into an army helicopter. She pondered if he would take his new lover up to the sky too; as soon as he was allowed to fly again.

Lucy broke into a sweat. She rolled up the sleeves of her blouse one after the other, with one hand still in control of her steering wheel. The sun gleamed through the windscreen generating a suffocating heat inside her car. Besieged with a sudden loneliness, Lucy snuffled to choke back her tears. She no longer knew the man she fell in love with. David's problems in the armed forces had changed him dramatically. And instead of speaking to her, was he trying to find his luck in other women? Did he feel ashamed about what happened? Why did he not talk to her? How could she help him, if he didn't trust her? Lucy had tried so many times to have a reasonable conversation with him. But David turned his back on Lucy. Today she would definitely be wiser. And if David was indeed cheating on her, it would be the end of their relationship.

Doubting herself if she was actually doing the right thing by spying on David, Lucy struggled to avoid the temptation of turning back home. As they were on the road for more than twenty minutes heading north, Lucy suspected David was setting out for Schossener Lake. It was the third largest lake in the North of Germany, famous for water-skiing and other sport activities. The lake had a size of about forty square kilometres. Over the years it became one of the largest tourist attractions with numerous hotels constructed around the water. The lake got its name from the nearby village called Schossen. David's motor boat, one of his gadgets, had its place there. When they first started dating, David often took Lucy out on boat trips. Unfortunately these times were gone. He rarely did it now.

Lucy was abruptly charged with hope. Could it be possible that David's destination was his boat and not some random lover? She took a big sip of the water that she always carried with her. The image of the pink roses dashed her optimism. He was most likely taking his lover on a boat trip. Not long and Lucy's suspicion was confirmed. They reached Schossen and instead of driving to the harbour, David turned into a side road. Lucy captured the road name. Lake Road, an easy name to remember. Lucy stopped and parked half on the kerb before the turning. She quickly alighted from her Nancy and peeked around the corner. The road was in a residential area and David came to a halt outside number 11. It was a big white house with a large front lawn enclosed by a one-metre-tall hedge.

She moved closer and found cover behind a skip. With a clear view she watched David strolling towards the porch of the house. Besides the roses in his hand he was carrying something else. Lucy blinked her eyes. She focused her gaze on it only to be met with bafflement. Why did he clutch a folder to his chest? Certainly not something you would bring to the doorstep of your lover! The door opened, yet Lucy's position didn't provide her with a clear view of the entrance. David vanished into thin air. She dithered over what to do next. David might spend hours in this house. Perhaps he would remain there for the night. Yet she had come that far, she wanted to know. Lucy chose to wait inside her car. She moved Nancy into Lake Road, three houses away from number 11 behind a black Ford. From here she had good visibility of the house.

As she made herself snug in her Nancy, a big yawn escaped from her mouth. She hadn't slept much in recent days, all down to her heartache. David was her big love. The relationship now in debris spawned her lots of sleepless nights. This part of town was a quiet area. Ahead of Lucy to her right was a farm with a large field behind it bordering a forest. A few young boys sat on their bicycles outside one of the houses engaged in a deep conversation. Lucy wound down her window to cool herself down. She took a deep breath, inhaling the fresh country air. It reminded Lucy of her late grandparents. They had owned a farm, not far from Hanwau in a nearby town called Zelgen. As a child she had loved spending her summer holidays with them. The scent of her gran's fresh baking infiltrated her head.

Lucy glanced at her watch. More than thirty minutes had gone by. She felt slightly on edge. Tempted to knock at the door, she jiggled her left hand towards the door handle. The abrupt thought of David opening the door in the nude with his lover behind him, stopped her in time. She gave it another thirty minutes and was soon remunerated. David's face surfaced in the opening. A young brunette followed and pulled the door shut. She was carrying a basket and the neck from a wine bottle obtruded. Lucy's heart slid down her legs. Deep inside her heart, she had known it all along. Still a glimmer of hope had stayed with her, wishing the occupier of the house would be some male friend or elderly lady. She observed David placing his arm around the brunette's shoulders as they ambled giggling to his Golf.

The girl was around Lucy's age, not older than twenty-two. She had a curvy body dressed in a short red skirt. Her white top was exposing too much of her boobs. Her white stilettos were far too high. Lucy wondered how she was able to walk in them. Her face, covered in too much paint, was glowing in the sunshine. Although David had lost weight in recent weeks, he still looked good. With his dark brown hair and blue eyes, women were at his feet. The white shirt and the black slacks David was wearing today, gave him a casual sexy look. He still had the folder in his hands. Had he clutched to it as they fucked? Lucy wasn't dumb. She knew exactly what they did inside the house. David's cheerfulness felt obnoxious to Lucy. Why could he not be like this with her anymore? It was a stab to her heart. Sadly she came to terms with the fact that her times of making David happy were long gone.

Watching them both driving off, Lucy had seen enough. No way would she follow them. Wherever they were heading to, she didn't need to know. She slumped onto the steering wheel, her hands angrily gripping at it. Inflamed with rage and disappointment she began banging her head against the wheel until the pain became too severe. A gush of tears exploded from her eyes.

Not far from Lucy on the other side of the road two men, occupying a black Mercedes, were watching too. They weren't interested in David's cheating. No, not at all! They were far more intrigued by David's folder. The one David had clasped like a child that was afraid of somebody stealing his teddy. And unlike Lucy who was oblivious to the Mercedes and ceased her espionage, the black Mercedes kept a trail on David's car.

CHAPTER 18

Surrounded by white walls and white wooden doors, Emily ran down an empty corridor. The floor was covered in pitch-black tiles exposing a slippery surface. Emily wasn't sure where she was or how she got here. She peeked down at her body and realised that she was barefooted and only dressed in her nightgown. She tried to push open every single goddamn door. She began to scream like a lunatic for somebody to answer her prayers. When no one replied, Emily gave in. She struggled to remember her last movements. What kind of building was this? Was she in a hospital? It certainly looked like this. Where were Thomas and Zoe? She began shouting their names, but only her own echo came back. No soul appeared to be around. Not even from behind the doors.

Her eyes were white and shallow. Her torso was trembling madly. Her windpipe felt blocked. She desperately began to gasp for air. All at once a creaking noise reverberated from behind her. Emily slowly rotated, with her hands pressed against her heart. Pure anxiety spread from her eyes. She leered at a large black metal door towering over her body. She hadn't seen this door before. She drew closer, still with her palms jammed to her upper body. Her eyeballs darted wildly from left to right. When the door began to open inwards, Emily stopped abruptly. With a fearful expression she observed a large hand stained with blood crawling alongside the lock. The door slammed wide open and Emily began to shriek her lungs out. Covered in blood, David appeared from the other side of the door. He had a smirk on his face.

Emily slapped herself across the cheeks until she woke up. She was lying on her back. Her sticky nightgown was adhered to her skin. She drove herself up into an upright position. A big sigh of relief streamed from her mouth as she realised that she had been plagued by a nightmare. Wondering if she had screamed for real or only in her dream, she glanced at Zoe. Her daughter must have sneaked to her bed during the night. Zoe lay fast asleep in a foetal position. Her chubby cheeks slightly bulged whilst wheezing. Emily's eyes dashed to the alarm clock. It displayed one o'clock in the morning. Thomas was next door in his own bed. Emily recalled the creaking noise from her dream. It sounded so real that she wondered if it had come from inside the house. Emily roamed to the window. It faced the driveway and part of the road. She glanced right into the beam of the street lights. David's car was on the driveway. The root of the noise in her dream became clear. David was causing it.

David unlocked the front door. He set foot quietly

into the house. The last thing he needed right now was a confrontation with Emily. The folder tight in his hand, he walked past the kitchen, straight to the living room. The dripping noise from the tap in the kitchen somewhat unnerved him. How many times had he told his wife to turn off the tap properly? He shook his head in disbelief. Emily would never learn. He pulled lightly on his wet shirt, separating it from his skin. He was soaking wet and would do anything right now for a set of fresh dry clothes. He was fortunate to still be alive. So was Sharon. Tremendous, how the day had turned out. Sharon wasn't even sure anymore, if she wanted to see David again. She was shaken up when he dropped her off.

It didn't surprise him. What was supposed to be a nice boat trip on the lake ended with pure horror! David made a beeline for the living room. He turned on the lights and approached the cupboard. It was made out of walnut wood with several shelving units, a mirror and even a bar cabinet. He swivelled around with one more glance towards the door. Satisfied that he was alone, he opened the top compartment and reached behind a pile of tablecloths. He then slid the folder into a slot between the mirror and the panel facing the outer wall. David was confident that the folder was safe in there. Only if someone wanted to take the cupboard apart, would they be able to find it. He left the house in silence.

Emily, who chose to stay in her bedroom to avoid an argument, observed David from the bedroom window. The security light on the front porch was triggered by David surfacing from the house. She took a closer look at David and puzzled over his clothing. Wondering if her eyes were playing a trick on her or if David was indeed soaking wet, she scrutinized him as best she could. Was it raining? The dry surface on the road told her otherwise. And the weather had behaved all day. The engine began to rumble as David brought his car back to life. Emily stepped back. What was that all about? Why did he come to the house in the middle of the night? And worst of all, why was he soaking wet? First Emily had assumed he came to get his head down. But not even five minutes had he lasted in the house. Curiosity took over and Emily scurried downstairs. She went to every room to check if anything was missing or out of place. Everything was still the same.

CHAPTER 19

Lucy was tossing and turning around in the big bed, unable to doze off. She pictured David and the curvy brunette fucking their brains out. The image of them wouldn't go away. The cream-coloured satin linen filling the duvet lay heavily on her body. Her head rested against her red cushions. Brightness filled the room as she pressed the light switch. She glared at her reflection in her mirrored wardrobe. Her heavy tear sacs, caused by too much sobbing and sleepless nights, stared right back at her. The bedroom used to be her whole joy. Unfortunately that had been taken from her. When she first moved in with David, she had spent days decorating it. She had chosen the wallpaper bordering the headboard in black and white colours with a pattern of dark grey patches and red tangled roses. The rest was painted in a light grey colour. The black and red furniture added to the cool, but sexy atmosphere.

Lucy had put a great deal of effort into making the room look sexy. Sex was very important to her, for

David even more. A man like him could never have enough. The aspiration that a sexy bedroom would keep their relationship, especially their sex life, intact for a long time had been Lucy's purpose. How wrong had she been? When David first caught a glimpse of their newly decorated bedroom, he had a shocked expression on his face. It wasn't because he didn't like it. It was more the fact that he hadn't expected it. The creative side of Lucy was new to him. He began to love it and for the first few weeks they spent almost every free minute in their bedroom. Those times had disappeared. It seemed that nowadays David rather preferred to pass his time in other beds than his own.

Lucy allowed herself to peek at the clock. It was now 1am and David was still not at home. Tears burned her eyes as she failed to suppress a sob. She found it very difficult to accept the fact that he most likely would not turn up before morning. Perhaps it was better this way. What other proof did she need of his adultery? After she had watched David with his new lover driving off, she decided to move on. She went back to Bueckenau and bought several newspapers from the local shop. At home, she scanned through the job market in Hanwau. It looked promising. She noted several interesting job vacancies that appealed to her. The first few months, until finding her own place, she would stay with her mum. As it had been too late to ring, she put in on her list as one of her first tasks in the morning.

Lucy was ready to give repose another go and dimmed the room. Once again she was writhing around from one side to the other. After an hour she surrendered. Unsure how to survive another day at work without any sleep Lucy leaped from the bed. The white fur rug, protecting the laminated floor was tickling her feet. She crept in the dark to the kitchen. Her big white shirt that once belonged to David dangled off her shoulders. She was smitten with wearing his shirts at nights. It gave her a feeling of comfort. One of the many things she would miss about David. She grasped a glass from the kitchen cupboard and filled it with tap water. The sudden bang of a car door, made her wince. Convinced it was David, Lucy patted her dishevelled hair in one direction and polished off her drink. The house door opened with a gentle creak. Lucy moved to a forward leaning position, her palms propped up against the small kitchen table.

One of David's habits was aiming first for the kitchen. He turned the lights on and cringed. The sight of Lucy in the middle of the night standing in the dark was the last thing he had anticipated. The last bit of space left in the kitchen was now crammed with his presence. Lucy's tear-stained, puffy eyes stared at him reproachfully. She went blue in the face and bristled with anger. David silently fumed. He had hoped to find her fast asleep and wasn't up for a fight right now. With a nervous gesture, he combed with his left hand through his hair and asked innocently, "Why are you still awake?" Lucy's eyes narrowed to slits.

"Pardon me. You are asking why I am still awake? You must be joking." Lucy was frothing at the mouth. "How about if I am the one asking the questions here! First of all, where have you been?" Lucy accusingly pointed her right index finger towards his face.

"On duty. I left you a note. Did you not see it?" David fibbed. He motioned to a piece of scrap paper on the table.

Lucy hadn't seen it. She glanced down and briefly scanned the contents. The note read 'I am on call duty. They called me in. Don't wait for me. I most likely finish late.'

Lucy was beyond words. She shook her head furiously. "I don't believe this. How dare you lie to my face like this? Do you really believe I am that naïve?" David moved forward. He extended his arm to touch Lucy's face in an attempt to soothe her, but she withdrew.

"Call the barracks. Check if you don't believe me." David knew she wouldn't do that. Usually Lucy took David at his word.

Lucy frowned. A bit more respect was the least he could give her. But no, David continued lying. Unbelievable! She was about to tell him where to get off, when she noted his wet clothes. She arched her eyebrows scornfully and outstretched her chin. "Is it part of your duty to get wet too?"

David's lips began to form an answer. He was stopped by Lucy's sudden outbreak. Tears spilled down her cheeks beyond control. The last bit of her self-esteem flushed down the river. She plopped onto one of the stools and pounded her fist on the table. "David, stop it. Enough is enough! I know where you've been. I followed you. You are the biggest liar and cheater I've ever met." Her voice broke and more tears streamed down her cheeks. She covered her face with her open palms and hid beneath it.

David was perplexed. He hadn't seen that coming and clearly struggled for words. The thought to whitewash the situation played in his mind. Yet he realised it would be a waste of time. At the end of the day Lucy was right. He was cheating. Whatever he said wouldn't change a damn thing. He still had to come to terms with the fact that Lucy had spied on him. Playing it down, he began. "Listen, it's not like it seems." He cleared his throat. "Yes, I was telling porkies. I wasn't called for duty. I went to see Sharon, because I had promised her a boat trip."

"Oh, Sharon is her name," Lucy interrupted with an acrimoniously smile.

"Yes, Sharon is her name. She was only available today. And I had it promised for ages. She is just a friend. No more and no less. Nothing happened, believe me. It was just a harmless trip."

Lucy jerked her head back and sprang to her feet. Tired of his lies, she yelled, "How dense do you think I am?" Her lungs were on fire. Her lips quivered in outrage. "You've been more than an hour with her in the house and still you are trying to tell me nothing happened? Are you out of your mind?" She tapped her forehead at him. David gave up and kept quiet. He had no more excuses left. His silence was enough proof for Lucy. Sharon was his lover. Tears welling up again, Lucy couldn't bear to be in the same room as David a second longer.

As she stormed past him she howled, "That's it, David! I am sick to death of you. I am leaving. I will be gone first thing in the morning!" As she brushed past David and touched his shirt with her naked arm, she was reminded of his wet clothes. In spite of everything Lucy still held her curiosity. She paused and demanded, "What happened to your clothes?"

David advanced to the fridge and took a small bottle of beer out. He opened it and drank the whole bottle in one go. Lucy impatiently tapped her toes against the floor. "I had an accident. Like I said we went for a boat trip, but it sunk. I lost all my documents!" He shrugged his shoulders. "Everything is gone, right down to the bottom of the lake."

Lucy looked sceptical. "What are you talking about? What documents?"

David was too tired to explain. One way or the other it didn't matter anymore. Their relationship was over. He knew that. He glanced at Lucy with a doleful expression and disappeared into the living room. Lucy went to follow. She hesitated when she heard the click of his shotgun. First she was rooted to the spot, but her sanity returned quickly. She sped to the living room.

David was right in the middle of loading his chamber. "What are you planning to do? Surely you are not going hunting at this time of night?" she asked sarcastically. David disregarded her remark. He gripped his gun and headed for the bedroom. Lucy's perplexed gaze followed him. When she heard the turn of the key from inside the room, Lucy began to panic. She ran to the door and throbbed against it. "David. What are you doing? Please open the door!"

The thought of ringing the police entered her mind. But wouldn't it be too late when they arrived? She mulled over it long enough for David to unlock the door and resurface. He was in a set of fresh clothes, his favourite grey hooded jumper and jeans. Lucy didn't want to admit to herself, but he looked as handsome as ever. His facial expression, however, was a different story. It gave Lucy shudders down the spine. Haunted and melancholy eyes with cheeks as white as a sheet faced her. The silence was the worst part. Whatever Lucy said, David refused to reply. He stepped into his trainers and crouched down to lace them up.

When David arose, he finally broke the silence and muttered, "I know I am a right pain in the arse. I have caused you so much pain. I promise I will end it tonight and you will be happy again." A gasp of relief escaped from Lucy's mouth as he finally started talking again. Too late she realised, that it wasn't the kind of words she had wished for. David was gone by the time it dawned on Lucy what he meant. And the shotgun went with him.

CHAPTER 20

Uncertainty sidled through Lucy's mind. For the last ten minutes she had sat on the bed, pondering what to do about David's threat. She hadn't known him long enough to say if he meant it seriously. She discarded the option to call the police. What could she tell them anyway? She had no clue where David had gone. Even if he was in earnest, where would he commit such an act? In his car? As far as Lucy was concerned it could be anywhere. The aim of going back to bed had gone straight out of the window. No way would she be able to find any sleep now. She slipped into some jogging bottoms she had found at the rear of her wardrobe, and sagged on her bed. Supported with her elbows in her lap, she dropped her head into her open hands. With sudden vehemence her head spun upwards. He might have gone to the barracks? But no, she didn't think so. Potentially he was on his way back to his lover, and the suicide threat was just a bluff.

Lucy also considered the possibility that David had

gone to his wife. Perhaps she should ring Emily to find out for herself? Or Emily might have an idea where he would go? David still possessed the keys to her house. Lucy knew that and had no problem with it. He kept it because of his children, to see them whenever he wished. He often worried about Emily, too. Just in case, he used to say. Lucy wasn't concerned that David would go back to his wife. It was long over between them. Anyway it didn't matter anymore. She had made up her mind. In a few hours' time she would hand in her resignation. And who knew, with all the holidays she still had left, she might be able to go within days. Not one day longer than necessary would she stay in Bueckenau!

Lucy grabbed the phone book from her bedside table and searched for Emily's phone number. It didn't take her long to find her finger on it. She moved to the hallway to grab the phone. As she dialled Emily's number, she was tempted to abandon it. Perhaps it wasn't such a good idea to ring a stranger in the middle of the night. Especially when it was the wife of your partner, or now ex-partner! She also imagined Emily not to be pleased either. She had never met or spoken to his wife. And of course Emily had every right to be angry at Lucy. Although the marriage had come to an end before they even met, David had left her for Lucy. On the other hand if David really committed some harm to himself, how would Lucy ever be able to forgive herself?

She went ahead with it and broke into perspiration, when after God knows how long, Emily picked up the other line. Lucy felt edgy. Her knees began to buckle and she steadied herself against the wall.

Down to her nervousness, she rarely managed to introduce herself. Emily sounded very grumpy. She made it clear that she wasn't happy about her call. Lucy tried to pull herself together. Her hand shook badly when she spluttered the reason for it. Emily corroborated that David wasn't present. The disdainfulness in Emily's voice was unmistakable. Yet she sensed something else in Emily's tone. Did David go to see Emily earlier on? It wasn't that she didn't believe Lucy. Still, when she mentioned the boat accident, Emily didn't seem surprised at all, like she had known it all along.

She told Emily that David had left with his shotgun and threatened to kill himself. Emily was of no help. Lucy formed the opinion that his wife wasn't bothered at all. She even said, "Don't worry, he will be back in no time."

Still, Lucy couldn't let it go. She finished the call, grabbed the car keys and left the house. Fifteen minutes later she turned into the car park of the barracks. She parked outside the barriers and approached the soldier performing his duty on the gates. When asking for David, the soldier confirmed that no one had come in since 10pm the previous night. Hope was fading. Lucy wasn't sure where else to look. Their favourite place came into her mind. It was just up the hill not far from where they lived. It was a spot they both discovered and loved, a parking bay overlooking the city of Bueckenau with a great view of the medieval castle. It was residence to the Princess of Tronau. Although the family had ceded political power in 1890, the family still inhabited the palace. Part of it was open to the public as a famous tourist attraction, best known for its architecture and mausoleum. As it turned out, David wasn't there. Lucy grew desperate. She had exhausted all possibilities she could think of. David didn't have many friends. Since his separation from his wife, David had withdrawn contact with their mutual friends, leaving them for Emily.

He wasn't close to his comrades either, not since the incident. So where could he have gone? After two hours driving around with no luck, Lucy returned home. Full of optimism that David may have seen reason, she turned into her road. Her hope was destroyed in a trice. David's car was nowhere to be seen. Disappointment but also fear crawled into her body. What if he really harmed himself? Could she ever forgive herself? She shrugged it off.

In the flat, Lucy pulled her suitcase from underneath her bed and gathered her belongings together. On and off David gnawed on her conscience. In these moments she assured herself over and over again that David most likely was back in his lover's arms. The thought encouraged her to pack even faster. Everything reminded her of David. It saddened her. No way was she in the mood to attend work in the morning. She would throw a sickie and head straight to her mum's. Her mum would understand.

An hour later, the sun already rising, she put pen to paper and scribbled, 'I am sorry David. As I've told you, I am not able to carry on like this. I am going back to my mum's. It's the right thing to do. I will be back soon to collect the rest of my belongings. Take care, Lucy.' Watery eyes blurred her vision as she placed the note on the kitchen table and proceeded with her luggage to the door.

PART 2

NOW

CHAPTER 21

The folder stared at me, screaming, "Read me now!" Positioned in my lap and unsure what to do next I began dog-earing some of the documents within the folder. A sign of my jumpiness! I was currently living with my mum. After breaking up with my boyfriend and then one year backpacking around the world I had temporarily moved back home. Eventually I would look for my own place. My mum was at work and I hand plenty of time on my hands to concentrate on the task in front of me. After taking possession of the folder, I had dumped it in the far end of the corner of my wardrobe. First I was afraid to look at it. Why? I don't know. For so many years I was craving for an insight into my dad's live. To understand why he did, what he did. To be closer to him, and not just blaming him for leaving us behind!

And now finally taking it on board, I started to hesitate? Did this even make sense? Was I afraid of what I would find out? Perhaps it wasn't such a good idea to poke in the past. Possibly I would discover things about my parents I wasn't supposed to know? On the other hand I was quite confident that I knew most of it anyway. Nobody had ever made a secret about my dad's cheating or that he had left my mum for another woman. I was also aware that my dad had taken the punishment that followed after the helicopter incident to heart, but nothing precisely. And the last thing I knew, my dad had put his shotgun to his head and fired. My past sounded tragic and indeed it was, especially what my mum went through but also us kids, Thomas and me. So what worse could I find out?

I slapped my hand with my other to stop the dog-earing and began skimming through the pages. The incident my dad was involved in occurred on a cold winter day in February 1983. It said my dad was flying through a valley with two other choppers behind him. My dad was leading, followed by his colleagues Andrew Mann and Alex Feld. They flew back to their base after they had completed their assignment. They were instructed to fly a minimum of 400 feet. In fact they flew below that. That's when Mann hit a power supply line. It was running through the valley providing the nearby villages with electricity. He steered straight into it. Subsequently Andrew Mann landed the helicopter. All three pilots including a technician, who had been on board with my dad, checked the machine. Fortunately it was only minor damage. However, the rules were that any military machine involved in any kind of incident had to be checked by an examiner before setting off again.

As it happened late on a Friday afternoon, with all of them looking forward to their weekend and no examiner available at this hour, they decided to fly the damaged machine back to the base. And with the military aircraft grounding at weekends, it would have been necessary to deploy a soldier at the scene until Monday. Bear in mind the aircraft landed in a valley full of high snow, impossible to reach with a vehicle. Andrew Mann also panicked. He had caused a similar incident just a few months prior to this one and feared the consequences. Still, what difference would it have made? The implication would have come anyway, or did he really think he could just sweep it under the carpet? Perhaps he did. At this point the pilots didn't even know that a whole village was left without electricity, that indeed Andrew Mann had damaged all three wires of the electricity mast. My dad first doubted the decision. But because of the circumstances he agreed with the others, which led to the failure to report it there and then.

The next document elucidated that the pilots involved in the incident were not allowed any aviation until further notice, signed by Major Benjamin Kraft. As I leafed through the next pages, the character reference of my dad caught my eye. I shifted in my chair nervously. Reading the following points, also signed by Major Kraft, I was utterly in shock. My dad was described as an indecisive, untrustworthy soldier with no resilience when under pressure. Furthermore, it stated that he was in need of strict observation in the air traffic and was short of leadership skills. He lacked the necessary characteristic maturity and ability expected of a military officer and therefore was not able to fulfil the task within the role. Thus, it was recommended to dismiss him from his career path as an officer.

I felt dumbfounded. My dad was described as a total loser. I found it hard to believe. My dad's reply to this was pure defensiveness. He explained that he had never done anything wrong leading up to this day. He had always followed instructions and fulfilled orders in the correct procedure. Indeed, he was never given the opportunity to show any leadership skills. In fact my dad protested if he had been selected that day as the one in charge he would have reacted differently. Enraged by what I was reading, I was suddenly so much in need of a cigarette. I stepped outside. I actually had given up smoking a year ago. However, I still liked the occasional one, particularly when stressed. Today was one of these days.

Five minutes later, fully recharged and much calmer, I settled back in my room. With the folder on my knees, I continued where I had left off, only to be confronted with the next blow to my face. In front of me I was facing the truth, the duration of my dad's flight prohibition. It changed everything. The document was dated two months later in April signed by the colonel. Lacking in comprehension, I gazed at it in disbelief. It felt like facing my dad's death sentence. The colonel had decided to revoke my father's pilot licence for a total of sixteen months. As my dad elucidated on one of the pages, the meaning of it was fully clear. His licence was gone forever.

If a pilot licence was revoked for more than twelve months, the whole training had to be redone. And no chance my dad would have been given this opportunity again. Not after receiving such a bad character reference. It was indeed a very harsh decision. If my dad had been the one causing the incident, I would have understood. But it had been his comrade. So why such a severe punishment? Scrolling through the rest of the folder which comprised documents between my dad's solicitor and his superiors, court warnings and other documents, I found myself gaping at a summary of the true events written by my father. It was sent to the service complaint commissioner of the armed forces. It narrated the day of the incident and the aftermath.

My dad depicted how he was asked by his captain to lie for the benefit of Andrew Mann. They feared serious consequences for him, owing to the incident in the past. Unfortunately my dad agreed to lie, grasping too late that his captain had something else in mind, to blame my dad for the whole thing. After realisation hit ground my dad made several attempts to speak to his superiors. Sadly in vain; he was ignored. It was one of the last writings in the folder. Two months later my father was found shot dead in his bed, his shotgun beside him.

Abruptly I was possessed with fury. My stomach began to tighten and with cramped fingers, I desperately began to search for a reply from the complaint commissioner. I was pretty sure they were obliged to reply.

First I couldn't find anything. I started pondering if they'd ever received the letter. And then I located it, a reply to my dad's complaint. My heart embarked on a rampage, primarily because I hoped for good news. But if it had been good news, wouldn't my dad still be alive? My eyes adjusted quickly to the brief contents and my heart dwindled. It was only an acknowledgement of the receipt of the complaint with a brief explanation that they had to wait for the outcome of the appeal that had been filed by my dad's solicitor before taking any action. And that was the end. There was nothing further from them or my dad's solicitor. Overwhelmed by disappointment and sadness, I closed the folder.

Clearly, my dad involving a solicitor had gotten him somewhere. His solicitor had even managed to get some of his wrongly detracted flight allowance reimbursed. So why did he kill himself two months later? He put so much effort into it and then he shot himself? It was beyond me. Boiling with frustration and wrath, I grabbed a piece of paper and jotted down some notes. After reading my dad's folder I was unable to leave it like this. I could sense there was more to it. The folder was crying out loud to me, telling me a different story. My dad had been stitched up, bullied into his death, I was sure of that. I was aware it wouldn't be that easy. But despite the fact that my dad had been dead for more than twenty-five years and some of the persons involved were possibly deceased by now, nothing could stop me.

CHAPTER 22

The next day I arrived at Sally's house very early. The way from Brielen, where we lived now, to Mitzen took more than forty-five minutes. To blame was the rush hour. Wearing jeans and a green sweater Sally greeted me at her front door. She had her own flat in her parents' house. A few years ago they converted the attic into a two-bedroom flat for Sally and her boyfriend Sam. She was born and bred in Mitzen. Unlike me, I was a bit of a globetrotter, she would probably stay for the rest of her life in this town. Sally and I had known each other since high school. We were best friends. Once, as teenagers, I plucked up my courage and told her about my dad's suicide. Quite often she was a witness to the disputes between my mum and brother and I felt the need to explain the reason behind it. To unburden myself felt so much better too.

Last night I rang Sally to inform her about my discovery. She was all ears, virtually almost more excited than me to look into the past of my dad. We arranged to meet up and to head first to the city where my dad had last lived and passed away. She suggested starting with the police to see if they still had a file with regards to my dad's death. I agreed and now we both sat in my car on the way to Bueckenau to the local police station.

"Wow," Sally spluttered. My dad's folder was lying open on her thighs as she made herself comfortable in the passenger seat. Her short dark hair appeared spikier than usual as she thumbed through my dad's folder. Several gasps escaped from her mouth covered in red lipstick, whilst she muttered under her breath, "Your dad was in deep shit. It looks like to me he was proper set up!"

I threw a brief glance at my best friend and sighed with relief. It was good to hear it from Sally's lips. I had been slightly concerned that I was the only one to think like this. It was always good to get an opinion from an outsider. A person not personally involved in it, saw things clearer. With my eyes back on the road, I spotted the dark clouds fast approaching our direction. It was mid-June and although the day had started with bright sunshine, the strong wind had foreshadowed the sudden change. It was only a twenty-minute ride and as I parked outside the police station, Sally and I were still engaged in a deep conversation about the folder. We racked our brains with questions such as why and what the f… it was all about, until Sally came to the conclusion, "Your dad must have pissed somebody off!" She now glanced at me enigmatically and arched her eyebrows.

I couldn't agree more and nodded. His affairs came to my mind. According to my mum my dad had seldom resisted any pretty woman. It all started when he began his training as a pilot. I gave Sally a poke and we made our way into the building. The visit to the police station turned out to be a waste of time. But at least I was directed in the right direction. The file was kept at the district court which was in the same town. The middle-aged police officer didn't hide his astonishment. He was clearly surprised by my request after more than twenty-five years. I didn't provide him with an explanation. I didn't care. It was none of his business. He surely must be used to more preposterous inquiries. I was given directions and ten minutes later Sally and I stood in front of a huge reception desk in the court building. The friendly receptionist organised an appointment for me for the following week. It was with a judge to allow me to view my dad's death file.

I had imagined it to be catchier and was very grateful for it. The next stop on our agenda was a bit tougher for me. It was the flat my dad had resided in before his death. The place he had shared with his partner Lucy, the woman my mum detested so much. And the place my dad had breathed his last before aiming his shotgun against his head. With the assistance of a local map we located the house without any problems. Although I had been there as a child, there was no chance that I would have known the way. I was only three years of age when my dad had made the decision to leave us. Charged with emotions I struggled to hide, I veered my vehicle into Honkgasse, my dad's old road. My fingers began to tremble against the wheel and Sally cast me a mollifying look.

Sinister clouds were looming right above us now.

Any second and we would be hit by a downpour. After parking my car half on the road and half on the kerb outside my dad's old flat, I gazed at the two-storey building painted in a creamy colour. I lowered my head and scanned my notes once more to ascertain that I had the right place. I wasn't plagued with any sudden childhood memories or any other reminiscence of the past. Not that I had expected any. I was aware I had been too young. On the other side I'd heard stories of people who remembered their childhood from a very young age. It wasn't the case with me. I exited my car and approached the building with wobbly legs. Sally, who had followed me, squeezed gently in my shoulder blade. I locked the car with the key fob and dropped it into my shoulder bag.

I stopped at the front door and raised my eyebrows. The three buzzers labelled with different surnames on the outside wall, didn't mean anything to me. Still consecutively I tried all of them. I pressed several times with no reaction. I glared at Sally dauntingly. Seriously, what had I expected? After all these years did I really believe I would find someone who could bring me closer to the truth? I wasn't even sure what I was looking for. With no names to go with and no knowledge of my dad's former landlord or landlady I was in a very difficult position. Still, here I was, hoping to find some answers. I had aspired to see if any of the neighbours would remember my dad. Events like this, when somebody committed suicide, people tend to remember. The hope to find some elderly person who had lived here their whole life slowly decreased. Disenchanted, I span round on my heel aiming for my car.

CHAPTER 23

Sally stopped me in my tracks. She gave me a nudge. "Come on, Zoe. Don't give up. Let's try over there." She pointed to the house next door. It was the same kind of house, but in white. She gestured to follow. Sally led the way and I stumbled behind her. We walked past the front lawn that was planted with beautiful flowers in a zigzag pattern. We reached the porch and unlike the house my father had lived in, this one was inhabited by merely one family. I jingled and the door was opened by a chubby female in her mid-sixties with short grey hair. Her front was covered with a white apron adorned with some kind of fat stain, suggesting that I had interrupted her cooking. An enticing aroma of some homemade stew swirled in my direction. I slowly and discreetly as possible inhaled the scent into my nose. My stomach growled in response.

The woman wiped her hands clean by using her apron and cocked her head with a puzzled expression. Perhaps she thought we wanted to sell something. I expected to see the door slammed in our face at any second. But before the woman had a chance to react, a croaky voice belonging to a man shouted, "Love, who is it?" I could hear footsteps heading our way. A stocky built man with a grey beard appeared next to the aproned woman. He was in the same age group. I assumed he was the husband. "Who is that?" He glanced at the woman, who shrugged her shoulders. "What can I do for you?" He turned his attention to us. A half-smile crossed his face.

"I am sorry for disturbing you," I started. "However, I was wondering if you could help us." I introduced us, so did they as Mr and Mrs Donner. I spluttered some explanation for our presence.

"We have lived here for more than thirty years. And I remember everybody in this neighbourhood. Come in. I am certain I can help you somehow."

Bingo, I cheered silently and my face lightened up. With Sally on my tail, I followed the Donners to the interior. The hallway was huge, with a variety of animal horns and hunting certificates displayed on the wall. The love of this kind of sport continued through to the lounge. The couple led us through to the garden. The dark clouds were still visible, only at a distance now as they had moved on towards the north. Thankfully we had escaped the rain. Like the front lawn the rear garden was covered in a beautiful flower bed from roses to sunflowers. We were offered some coffee and cake and made ourselves homely in the garden furniture. Sipping on my cup of freshly brewed coffee, I began my story. The couple's eyes hung on my lips whilst I chatted away. I peeked at Sally and she batted her eyelids.

I finished my story and my eyes were beaming with hope to find some answers. And indeed my wishes came true when Mr Donner replied, "Yes, a young couple had lived in the ground-floor flat around that time. I remember your dad. Wasn't he in the army?"

"Yes he was," I confirmed. At first not sure how to ask, I managed to mumble, "Did you know that he committed suicide?"

Mr Donner shook his head in astonishment. He turned his head slowly towards his wife, who appeared to be even more baffled. "We knew something had happened. But we didn't know what. Rumours were going around in the neighbourhood, yet nothing concrete. It was odd, from one day to the other the ground-floor flat was empty. Not long after that somebody else moved in." Mr Donner cleared his throat. "I remember asking Carla Sturm, the landlady, about your dad and his partner. However, she was reluctant to give any information. So I never pressed further."

Raising my eyebrows, I asked, "Do you have her phone number? Perhaps I could contact the landlady myself to find out what she knows."

Mr Donner shook his head. "I am afraid she passed away ten years ago. Her sister is still alive though. I will give her a quick ring to see if she knew your dad."

I nodded in agreement, glad that this was taken off me. Mrs Donner scurried inside to fetch the phone. Within seconds she reappeared on the patio. One hand was clutched to the phone whilst the other was swinging a phone book. Locating the phone number instantly, Mr Donner quickly pressed his fleshy index finger into the keypad. He presented me with a heartening smile. I grinned shyly back and found myself sat in a fierce position, unsure what to expect. We didn't have to wait long. The other end was answered promptly. All three of us focused on Mr Donner's words, trying to unravel the conversation he had.

My eyes wandered off to their flowerbed. I began visualising my mum in my first childhood home planting sunflowers. It was one of her favourite flowers. Instantly I sensed Mr Donner's gaze on me. I glanced up and noted his pursed lips with a light frown. "Really? That's interesting." I tensed up.

Clearly Mr Donner's face told me something wasn't right. I rubbed the sweat of my palms on my jeans as I felt slightly uneasy. Mr Donner exchanged a few more words and then hung up. Sally and I looked at him impatiently, waiting for him to speak. Even Mrs Donner grouched at him, "Stop torturing us. Tell us what's going on!"

Still Mr Donner took his time and I was not far off from going *pop*. Eventually he looked at me and scratched his beard in a slow motion. I conjectured it to be a habit when he was engrossed in thoughts.

Finally he began, "You won't believe what the sister just told me." Mr Donner averted his gaze to his wife. He turned his attention back to me and continued, "Before Carla Sturm died, she confided in her sister. She said to her sister that she needed to get something off her chest." He now turned his head to Sally, satisfying himself he had the full attention of his audience, like a narrator in a TV show.

"Please, what did she say?" I began pleading with Mr Donner.

He spun towards me and locked eyes with me. "The next morning after your dad had killed himself, your dad's captain, a man called Max Boll, paid a visit to your dad's landlady. He demanded her to keep the suicide quiet and offered Carla Sturm a fair amount of money for her silence. Apparently he feared the press would get hold of it. He was trying everything to prevent this from happening. She accepted the money."

CHAPTER 24

Tina Sturm put the phone down. Dumbfounded by this call, she brushed with her fingers streaks of her grey hair behind her ears. Why after all these years was the daughter asking about her father? Tina proceeded to the window and watched a wasp trying to find its way in. She lived alone in a small two-bedroom flat and apart from her nephew, his wife and two children she had no family left. Her sister Carla Sturm had died of cancer a decade ago and Tina had no family of her own. She still reminisced about the day Carla passed away. She remembered when her sister told her about this night. She had always known that Carla had kept something from her. Something had been bothering her. When her sister was diagnosed with terminal cancer, she decided to get it off her chest. Tina remembered as she sat in a chair next to Carla's death bed. Her sister clutched her hand and whispered, "Please God, forgive me for what I have done." So Tina had listened in silence as Carla poured her soul out to her.

Perhaps she should have not revealed it to Mr Donner. She knew he was a very curious man. Her sister had mentioned her neighbour on numerous occasions. He was one of the people who liked to stare out of his window all day long and nothing would escape him. On the other hand Tina believed the daughter had a right to know. And if it helped the girl to get closer to her late father, then so it should be. She glanced at her sister's picture that hung above her desk in the living room. It was a huge one kept in a golden frame that spread a lively atmosphere to the barely furnished room, which was mainly decorated with ornaments of Jesus and other religious objects. A tear escaped her green eyes and the stabbing pain she inevitably felt when thinking of her sister, reminded her how much she missed Carla. They had been very close and her nephew was all she had left from her beloved sister.

Carla had been forty years of age in that photograph. She looked younger in it. Her pretty face surrounded by long dark hair showed to her advantage. It was taken on one of their holidays in Italy together. That must have been the age when Carla took the cash she had been offered by Max Boll for her silence. She knew why Carla had taken the money. She had been a good woman. Yet she had struggled to scratch a living. After all, the father of Carla's son had walked out on her when he learned about her pregnancy. She was left to raise her child on her own. Carla also had to cope with a certain degree of profane language from local people on grounds of having a child born outside marriage. The big house she had to maintain was an additional burden. The takings she made from renting out the ground-floor flat were not enough. In the end she had to sell the property as she couldn't afford the mortgage anymore.

But it wasn't just this, that had kept her sister silent. Boll, who was quite well known in the area, had a reputation for being a very contentious person. He was not a person to mess with. And to rebel against the army did not seem a good idea either. Many years ago, not long before the soldier's suicide, a rumour had been going around. Someone had upset Max Boll. This specific person had to pay a high price for it and was never seen again after that. Gossip said he moved away of fear. In plain language, Carla had been afraid of Boll. So she took the money and kept quiet. Tina didn't blame her sister. She would have done exactly the same. Still Tina mused deep into the night about the phone call of Mr Donner. Being a very religious person, Tina even began to pray for the soldier's daughter. Just in case, as she liked to think.

CHAPTER 25

"Max Boll. Why I am not surprised!" Mr Donner scoffed. He pressed his fingers against his chin and shook his head as if he had known it all along. "He has a bit of a reputation here in the area, known for dodgy things but also as a respected businessman in the area." Mr Donner's grey beard stubbles projected from his skin.

Sally and I glared at each other. Did my mum not mention the name before? My mind began to race in a desperate attempt to recall the words my mum had used. Something about some disagreements with his captain…? They used to get along and then it stopped…? I chewed it over and over again, still nothing else came to my head. It was a shame that the landlady had passed away. Otherwise I would be able to ask her myself about that day. Kneading with my hands under the table, I glimpsed at Sally who returned my gaze with a shrug.

"Why don't we ring him and see what he has to say?" Mr Donner suggested and his eyes brightened up.

"Not sure if that's a good idea." I gulped. I would have rather preferred to be prepared for it. Then again why not? Let somebody else do it. Max Boll would be made aware that more people knew about it. I even had no time to protest. Mr Donner's stoutly fingers swept along the pages of the phone book. In no time his index finger was pressed against some numbers and with the other he pushed the key buttons of his phone.

Once more Mr Donner had a chat with the other person on the line, outlining the reason for his call. Wow…! He was really good at that. The way he was taking to it like a duck to water. A stranger would believe it was about his dad. He even mentioned the folder that I had brought along. As he jabbed away, Mr Donner's free hand wandered to the receding parts of his head. He began to pat it. I had no clue who he was talking to.

It didn't sound like Boll. "Oh, I see. OK, hold on." Mr Donner's eyes attracted my attention. He gestured towards the handset and uttered to me. "That's his wife. Mr Boll is currently in the USA on business. He will be back in a few days. Mrs Boll would like to take your phone number, so he can ring you when he is back in the country."

I nodded and pouted. Frustration unfurled inside me. I had anticipated Boll to be at home. I would have loved to see him today. I had so many questions for him and wanted to get them out now. Dispirited, I passed on my phone number.

When Mr Donner hung up, he gaped at Sally and me and divulged. "That was his second wife. He had been married before. This one didn't know your dad.

He married her after your dad passed away…" He paused and rubbed his chin. "Still, when I mentioned your dad's name, she knew straight away who he was. It surprises me. It seems to me that Boll has spoken about your dad to his current wife."

"That's interesting!" Sally interrupted. "Why would he mention your dad to his second wife, if she didn't know him? Not without reason, I tell you." I concurred with Sally on this one. It was odd. Why would he do that? I was still pondering about it, when Sally and I decided to take off. We thanked them for the hospitality and on our way out, Mr Donner tapped me on my back.

"Be careful when you speak to him. From what I've heard, he is not a man to mess with. Look after yourself and good luck." Again Mr Donner's gaze was caught at my folder that was clamped under my arm. His constant curious glances spoke volumes. He inconspicuously had tried to see the contents of it. I didn't let him, neither did I relinquish the contents. The only part Mr Donner was able to see was the label unveiling 'Helicopter incident February 1983'. That was enough. He didn't need to know more.

Disappointed, I ambled alongside Sally to my vehicle. It seemed like an eternity to wait until Boll was back from his trip. He might not ring at all. Or his wife may fail to pass on the message. His wife would most likely have forgotten about me by the time her husband got back. Sally, sensing my bad mood, opened the driver's door. A funny grimace appeared on her face. In an attempt to cheer me up, she said jokingly, "Come on, Majesty. I am sure he will call after his trip. Let's see what's next on the list."

Inside my car she poked me in my hip. She pretended to imitate me by pulling a face.

A smile escaped my lips. I gathered my 'to do' list from my purple handbag when suddenly the voice of Plan B with 'She Said' erupted from my phone. I peeked at the screen. Confusion plastered all over my face when I didn't recognise the number. It showed a foreign number that I had never seen before.

Debating with myself if I should answer or if it was not worth my time, possibly being some sort of scam, Sally jerkily grabbed the phone from my hand. She pressed the green button, placed it to my ear and flourished to answer. I managed a curt 'Hello'. I was greeted by a high-pitched male voice, I had never heard before. I felt queasy. And when he introduced himself as Max Boll, my dad's former captain, I nearly dropped the phone.

I pointed franticly with my finger to my mobile hinting at Sally that my dad's former captain was on the other end. Incredulity cropped up in her face. I was as perplexed as she was. Not even half an hour had gone by since Mr Donner had spoken to his wife and he already rang me? Wow, did he have a guilty mind or what? Not in a million years had I seen that coming. His wife must have contacted him immediately. More than twenty-five years had passed since my dad's suicide. Boll reacting to my call instantly threw me totally off course. Just a few minutes ago I even thought he would never call at all.

CHAPTER 26

Max Boll was scanning the conference room swiftly when his mobile phone began to vibrate. He was in the middle of a business meeting in a Hilton Hotel in Manhattan. The meeting had just started and he was already interrupted by his annoying wife. He heaved a sigh. His wife was aware that he was in a meeting right now, so when he saw that home called he became slightly concerned. Sweat pouring out of his forehead, he apologised quickly to his counterparts. Even chubbier compared to when he was young, he moved his sixty-year-old body to the door and left the room. His business was going well so far. The trip was paying out. As the proud owner of a construction company back in Germany, which he had expanded over the years across the continent, he was travelling a lot. After a successful career within the army, he finally settled in the construction business. Owing to his cold nature, he was a successful businessman and didn't care about others.

Boll leaned with his back against the wall and

answered the call. He rolled his eyes, when he heard the excited voice of his wife. "Max, guess who I had on the phone just now," she spluttered. Boll breathed out a sigh of relief, mixed with a tiny bit of annoyance. Did she call him out of a business meeting to tell him the newest gossip?

"Did you seriously call me to tell me who you had a small talk with?" Boll objurgated.

"I am sure you'll want to know this one." His wife's defiant undertone didn't escape him.

"OK, go on then."

"It was a former neighbour of David Hunt, the soldier you mentioned to me years ago."

Boll's blood drained from his face. It always did when he heard the name he hated so much. He cupped his neck as if trying to remove an invisible hand strangling him. He took rapid shallow gasps and his body began to tremble.

Pushing off the foreboding, Boll told himself that it had been more than twenty-five years and this phone call had probably nothing to do with the past. "What was his name and what did he want?" he demanded and pushed himself off the wall.

"Donner is his name. He asked for you, wanted to know if you remembered David Hunt who had killed himself in 1983. The daughter of Hunt sat next to him. She was sniffing around, wanted to know what happened all those years ago. Apparently she had some papers with her, some documents from the army. She insisted his death had something to do with the helicopter incident you once told me about."

Boll could feel his hair standing up on the back of his neck. Glad that nobody was around, Boll snatched off his tie and unbuttoned the top part of his white shirt in a desperate attempt to get some air down his throat. His suit pants were glued to his sweaty legs and he began fumbling with his fingers on the fabric.

The lift on the other side of the corridor made a jingling noise. The door opened and a middle-aged woman in a pink blouse and a grey skirt stepped out. She walked past Boll and wagged her head when she noticed the hairy chest protruding out of his shirt.

The woman cringed and accelerated her pace when Boll began to swear into the phone. "For fuck's sake, what did you say to him?" His face was glowing like a tomato. The woman disappeared quickly to one of the other meeting rooms. Boll hadn't foreseen that. For years he had been worried that somebody would look closer into Hunt's death. Then after many years without anything happening, he stopped agonising. But now the past was catching up.

The voice of his wife brought him back to earth. He realised that the past would haunt him for the rest of his life. "I didn't say anything. I only took the phone number of the daughter and said you would call her," his wife whimpered, clearly upset by her husband's outburst.

"OK, no worries. I'll sort it. What's her number?" She passed it on and Boll ended the call.

His wife didn't know the whole story. It was for her own good. She only knew a brief version of the incident followed by Hunt's suicide. He once told his wife about it, so she was prepared if ever anybody mentioned it. His wife had never met Hunt herself. Boll slid his phone into his pocket and brushed his sweaty fingers through his hair. He began bustling about, the phone number crunched in his fist. Should he call right away? But what would it change? He slapped his fist in his palm. His inner voice told him otherwise. What if Hunt's daughter talked to the wrong person? He had to stop her from talking to others. Straight after Hunt's suicide, Boll had taken the majority of the documents home out of fear they would end up in the wrong hands. Of course some of it he had left there to avoid any suspicion. Nobody had ever noticed. If everything came out now, oh dear! He couldn't let this happen. He had to call her right now. If he left it too long, things would get out of hand like they did twenty-five years ago. He couldn't risk that again and began dialling the number.

CHAPTER 27

"I am sorry about your dad. But you have to know I tried everything to help him."

I was conspicuous of the edgy tone in Boll's voice. "Pardon me. What do you mean you tried everything to help him?" I queried in confusion.

"I mean the aftermath of that tragic day. I assume you know what I am talking about?"

I cleared my throat nervously. I wanted to make sure I was asking the right questions without giving too much of what I knew away. "Oh yes, I know about that, not much though." I lied. No way would I mention anything about the folder. Oh shit, hadn't the neighbour said something to Boll's wife about some documents? But then it could be anything. "I was hoping you could tell me a bit more. I believe his suicide is related to this." I felt Sally's gaze on me as I stared out the windscreen and simultaneously began wiping some dust off my dashboard.

A deep drawn sigh escaped from the other line.

"Like I said, we tried everything to help your dad. You have to know, he was a good-looking man. Women made it too easy for him. And your dad took advantage of it. It caused problems." He paused. I was wondering what all this had to do with his death. Uncertain how to respond, I said nothing. "Listen, I will be back the day after tomorrow. I think we should meet. Would you be able to see me straight after my return? I have everything you need to see, all the documents surrounding the incident. I can show them to you and explain."

His desperate tone set my suspicion on high alert. I glanced at Sally and distorted my face. Clearly something bothered him. Was he afraid? What was he hiding? And why did he keep military documents at home? Was he even allowed to do that? Sally raised her eyebrows and focused back on my dad's folder.

"I assume you are intending to speak to former colleagues too?"

I flinched at the sudden question, particularly at the hint of resentment in his voice. "I am not sure yet. Why are you asking?" It was certainly none of his business.

"I am sure you will. But I am begging you, don't speak to Lech!"

Who is Lech? I had never heard of him before. Max Boll didn't give me any time to muse about it. He went on. "You have to know your dad left some suicide notes behind. In one of them he blames me for what happened." I shifted uneasily in my seat. Suicide notes? I was taken aback. It was the first time that I heard of suicide notes.

"Do you know where these letters are now?" I asked. I didn't let on that this news came like a bombshell to me.

"Well, I don't know where the one is in which your dad blames me. I think he asked someone to send it to the barracks. I have actually never seen it, not been questioned about it either." He sighed. "Like I said, I didn't do anything wrong. I was trying to help your dad, although he saw it differently. I guess the other ones must be with your family."

Not even one person in my family had ever mentioned any suicide notes. It had always buggered me, why my dad hadn't left anything behind. And now after all these years had passed, some stranger told me about some suicide notes? I was speechless.

"So when can you come to see me?" Boll asked impatiently.

"Whenever is best for you!" I said bluntly. I was still baffled and sensed Sally's side glance. I purposely kept my stare out the windscreen to focus purely on the conversation. The dark clouds had returned and now fully overshadowed the sky. I was positive it would start raining any minute.

"I am flying back on Wednesday. Come Thursday afternoon, let's say three o'clock, and I will have everything ready for you." I agreed and groped with my hand towards the glove compartment. I pulled the handle and began nervously rummaging for a pen and paper.

Sally leered and produced a pen and paper from nowhere. I snapped it from her hand and scribbled Boll's address on the chit of paper. I also wrote the name 'Lech' with some exclamation marks and underlined it. The fact that Boll didn't want me to meet this person, obviously gave me more reason to do so. It moved now to the top of my list! I had one more question on the tip of my tongue before ending our conversation. It was weighing heavily on my mind and couldn't wait until we met. I took a deep breath and asked, "Who found my dad?" In my family my father's death had never been a subject, therefore I had no details about his death. And as it seemed that Boll knew more about it than my own family, I was pretty confident he would be able to answer this question.

"Of course, I found him. Your dad was supposed to be on duty that night. He never showed up. So I went to see him and found him dead in his flat with a gunshot to his head."

CHAPTER 28

The next day I was on my way to Lech. After I had dropped off Sally, I went back home, sat behind my laptop and brought the search engine up. Luckily Lech was a very rare name. It didn't take long to dig out his phone number. His first name was Paul and he lived in Mitzen like Sally. As no other Lech came up in the local area I was confident I had the right person. And indeed when I rang he confirmed to be a former colleague of my dad, but of no degree was he pleased about my phone call. He was very reluctant and questioned several times how I had found him. Based on the fact that my dad's former captain didn't want me to talk to him, I had hoped for a different reaction. I told myself to be patient. Probably Paul Lech would be a bit more forthcoming when I actually met him face to face. After all, he agreed to meet and invited me to his house the following day.

Now as I was driving through Mitzen, I found myself overwhelmed with memories. Mitzen had a population of about 80,000 people. It was situated about thirty miles from Brielen. It was the city where I went to school, the city we moved to after my father's death until we moved again and also the city where I met my first love. Lech resided in the suburbs. I found his place instantly. He lived in a quiet road, not far from the barracks. An elderly couple strolled along the pavement. The house number he had given me belonged to a big detached house with an adjoined garage. I pressed the buzzer and a woman in her mid-fifties with a stern face invited me in. Her mousy hair displayed a trail of grey streaks. Her almost too skinny body made strange movements as she motioned to walk behind her. "My husband is already waiting for you." I trudged behind her through the kitchen into the garden.

The sun was taking control today and the sky was clear of any clouds. The heat was almost unbearable and I wished I had gone for a skirt instead of jeans. The first thing that met my eye was a small wooden summer house right in the middle of the lawn orbited by plants. It was somehow out of place, perhaps because of its location. Lech sat at the garden table with a cup filled with black liquid, presumably coffee. A daily newspaper lay in front of him. With frayed nerves I glanced at him. He looked over the top of his reading glasses right into my eyes. A tiny smile, that didn't reach his face, showed on his lips. With an oblique head, I scrutinised his face which was embellished with a moustache. I was hoping to recognise him from any of the pictures I had found of my dad and his comrades. He didn't resemble any of them. Perhaps he had been with a different unit.

Lech stood up; he was a head taller than me, and

his small pot belly didn't escape me. I shook his proffered hand and we both settled in our chairs. "What can I do for you, Miss Hunt? I assume it is still Miss?" he drawled.

"Yes, it is." I folded my hands, placed them on the edge of the table and began my story. His wife appeared in between and offered a cold drink. I gratefully accepted. "Well, as you know, my dad was involved in this incident, which his colleague Andrew Mann caused, and six months later he killed himself. My dad kept a folder with some documents about the incident. It shows that he was made responsible for the whole thing. And then they grounded him for sixteen months, basically forever." I paused to gasp for air. I had this annoying habit of talking too quickly when I was agitated. Lech's interrogative look made it even worse. There was something creepy about him.

"What makes you think that?" He frowned, his grey hair glowing in the sunshine. His reaction annoyed me. I formed the opinion that he didn't like what I suggested.

"The documents and summary of my dad – it clearly shows he was bullied!" I said, defensive, and felt my cheeks going red. I leaned back and crossed my arms. A dislike towards him developed inside me.

Mrs Lech returned with a glass of sparkling water. I was glad for the interruption. It was an opportunity to gather my thoughts. I avoided Lech's scowl and took a big sip. I wasn't daft. His intention was to alienate me. It was obvious, he didn't like the fact that I was rummaging in the past. Mrs Lech went back inside. Lech didn't avert his gaze. He continued staring at me and said nothing. I had enough of it. I wasn't this kind of person, who was easily intimidated. But I had to say, he was nearly succeeding. I didn't let on, braced myself and continued.

"Nevertheless, my dad got a solicitor involved. With the help of him, he was appealing against the decision. In fact he was slowly getting somewhere. My dad even wrote to the complaint commissioner for the armed forces. And then all of a sudden he killed himself. It just doesn't make sense to me."

The sudden buzzing of a wasp made me jerk. The wasp was right in my face. I raised my arms and waved them wildly around. I was terrified of wasps. I had a bad childhood experience, where I was stung by one and a terrible allergic rash arose from it. A spiteful smile escaped Lech's mouth as he saw me suffer. The wasp finally gave in and disappeared into the air. Lech rubbed his chin in a cogitating gesture. He still loured at me. It began to irritate me. It wasn't like I was accusing someone of murder. I just wanted to know what happened. The thought that Lech must have been a good-looking man when he was young entered my mind. His tallness and bright blue eyes spoke volumes.

He finally grunted, "What are you trying to do here? Are you looking for justice?"

He was clearly challenging me now. It was the last thing I had anticipated. I had hoped he would be on my side, but it was the opposite. All I was getting was an arrogant look and sniffy remarks. He was acting in such a cryptic way which didn't make sense to me at all.

"After all these years, why all of a sudden are you poking in the past?" A hint of exasperation was in his voice.

"I was actually hoping you could give me some answers. That's the reason why I came to see you. As I told you over the phone, I have spoken to his former captain. He was the one who gave me your name."

"Which one?" he snapped.

"Max Boll!" I replied.

That caught his attention. Finally I could see some movements in his face. I certainly piqued his curiosity. "What did he say?" He straightened up.

"He wants to meet me. Apparently he kept all the correspondence from the incident at home. He wants to show it to me. I will see him the day after tomorrow. But he also begged me not to speak to you. I was wondering why and thought I could get some answers from you!"

Lech didn't look impressed. He rolled up his sleeves and folded his arms. "I can't tell you anything! Your father secluded himself after the incident. He lost trust and didn't let anybody come near him. Of course in these circumstances it didn't come as a surprise," he said curtly. "I am sorry but there is nothing else I can tell you."

He sounded a bit friendlier. Still, I was asking myself if he was trying to chuck me out. I was pretty sure that there was more to it than met the eye. Yet he was clearly not willing to give me any more answers. I arose from my seat. "Well, I won't keep you any longer then." Lech escorted me out.

As I gripped the door handle to exit, he pestered, "I still don't understand. What are you hoping to find out? Tell me!"

I nearly blurted out that it was none of his business, but thought the better of it. Did he think I was after revenge, trying to blame some of his former colleagues and perhaps get some compensation? I turned around and crowed, "Listen, it is not what you think I am after. I would like to rehabilitate my dad, that's all! As it stands people think he was a coward for taking his life and leaving two small children behind."

I spun around and opened the door, when I suddenly felt a hand on my left shoulder. "Before your dad killed himself, he came to see me. He told me he was put under pressure."

I stopped in mid-stride. Facing him, I glanced at him dubiously, waiting for more to come. Finally we were getting somewhere.

"That's all I can tell you!" he added and promptly removed his hand from my shoulder, dashing my last hopes.

Still, before I left I had one more question. "Did you know Lucy, my dad's new partner? Apparently she worked in the admin at the barracks?"

He shook his head. As he shuffled me out of the door, he hissed, "I only can give you one bit of advice, leave it alone. And be careful when you meet Max Boll. He is not a man to mess with."

CHAPTER 29

After Zoe had gone, Paul Lech who was known to everyone mainly by his surname, fetched his mobile phone from the kitchen table. With a lame excuse to his wife he disappeared from the house. He had no intention to let his wife in on this. The less she knew about it so much the better. His wife didn't ask any further. She understood when to keep quiet. She wasn't blind. Her husband was clearly choked up by their recent visitor. She had met her husband after he had left the armed forces. Still, one night they both had too much booze, he made a strange remark about something he had done in his military time that could destroy their lives. At the same time, he said that even if he could turn back the time, he would do it again.

When she queried further, he replied that it would be in her own interest not to know. She never pressed again. Now his wife was wondering if it had something to do with this girl asking about her dad. Perhaps her husband was right and it was for her own good to shut her eyes. They had a nice life together.

They had two grown-up children they could be proud of. They had enough money to enjoy their retirement soon. And for nothing in the world would she want to change her life. So if the secret her husband was hiding from could destroy their lives then she rather preferred not to know. She began clearing the dishes from the garden table.

As Lech set foot outside, he took a big breath to inhale the fresh summer air. He veered towards the stream that ran parallel with his street. The footpath was beleaguered with branches and mud from the previous days. The summer had started with weeks of rain and strong winds. Finally the weather forecast changed its mind and promised weeks of sunshine and blazing heat. And today it was showing its first signs of improvement. Lech stomped along the narrow trail. He instantly began to regret his route. Swamped by mosquitoes hunting for blood he swivelled around. He changed his direction away from the bushes and entered an open field.

From a distance he could see a tractor harvesting the wheat. Once more he altered his route and ambled to the pavement of a busy road. Under no circumstances did he want to get caught in the fields by a farmer. Farmers could get quite cross if you invaded their space. Rapt in the conversation he had led with David Hunt's daughter, he wondered what else he could have said. Lech had tried his best to deter Hunt's daughter from churning up the past. Yet he doubted she would cede. She had the same determination in her eyes her father used to. It frightened him.

The whizzing traffic blared in his ears. Lech

dithered over how else he could stop her. He wasn't willing to make the phone call just yet. He didn't want to spread panic. Still, what other choice did he have?

He turned around towards home and when he found a quiet spot around the corner of his house, he dug for his mobile. He began dialling the endless number he so much wanted to steer clear of. When the other end was picked up, Lech said only three words. The person on the other line didn't need any explanation. He understood.

CHAPTER 30

Two days later I glanced at a big white house with a double garage slightly on the hill. The rear of the house was facing the blooming meadow. I only could imagine the beautiful view from the other side. It was in a suburban area of Bueckenau, one of the nicest parts of town. I parked my car opposite Max Boll's house close to a hedge. I was still recovering from my deeply disappointing meeting with Lech. Today I expected it to be a better day. I had taken my dad's folder with me, just in case. I had no intention of actually showing it to my dad's former captain. I left it in the boot of my car. I departed from my vehicle, crossed the street and entered the driveway. Gravel crunched underneath my sandals as I proceeded to the entrance. The front door abruptly opened. My heart began to throb madly. I feared the middle-aged short man, who now stood right in front of me and introduced himself as my dad's former captain, was able to hear it.

Boll was bulged around his front. Even without an

introduction I would have recognised him straight away. I had a photograph of my dad and his captain at a flight ceremony, held in honour of my dad for completing 1,500 hours of flying. Apart from turning older, Boll didn't change much. On some parts of his head his thin grey hair had diminished and cold blue eyes protruded from his round face. It gave him an unscrupulous appearance. I detected a tiny bit of insecurity in his eyes. It surprised me. Did I make him nervous? Why?

He pointed towards the house next door. "Let's go in there," he said as he pulled the front door of the one he just had come out of shut. I looked at him, confused. He noticed my astonished gaze and quickly expounded, "That's mine too." He motioned to follow and I stumbled precariously behind him.

The house we were heading to was in a light green colour. It was the same size, but without a garage. I caught some barking from the interior.

"I hope you are not afraid of big dogs."

I shook my head, but started to feel queasy with a shudder rushing through my body. Somehow this man made my skin crawl and discomfiture took the better half of me. Perhaps it wasn't such a good idea to come here?

Boll unlocked the door. When he pushed it open, two big dogs darted towards us and began to gnarl at me with clenched teeth. I flinched and my vision became blurry. Memories of the past when I was around twelve years old entered my mind. I was delivering magazines to private houses. One of my customers had these two big German shepherds.

Each time I walked up the path to post the journals through the letterbox, the dogs began to bark angrily from inside the locked house. One warm summer day the owners had forgotten to close the door. As I drew closer, the dogs lunged out from behind and growled aggressively at me. At this point I feared an attack. I legged it and they chased after me. I saw myself already bitten to death, when the owner came to rescue me. He shouted out for his dogs and ordered them back to the house.

Since then I was wary of big dogs. Particularly when the owner gave me the shivers, such as my dad's former captain. Being struck with awe, I was not far off spinning on my heels. Perhaps I was too frivolous and shouldn't trust this man. I had been warned by several people. But what could he do to me? Did I actually tell anybody where I was? I had informed Sally, yet I couldn't remember if I had mentioned that it was today. *Stop panicking and pull yourself together,* I reminded myself. I straightened up and lifted my chin. No way would I expose my fear.

Boll managed to quieten the dogs and he gestured to step in. Compared to the well maintained exterior of the house, the interior looked filthy with dust all over the place. Not what I had visualised. It was barely furnished and I wondered if he kept his victims in here. My mind was playing tricks with me as I imagined Boll as a serial killer. I jerked with obnoxiousness and instantly discarded the absurd idea.

Boll glanced at me and as if reading my face he swiftly explained, "We live in the other house. This one is used as an office and for the dogs."

I nodded in order to show that I understood. It made sense. In contrast to the other day over the phone, he appeared to be unperturbed. Still, some incertitude was reflecting in his eyes. I didn't have to wait long to find out why. Not even one minute in the house and he shot away, "Listen, I need to rectify here some of what I said the other day." We stared at each other and I waited for more to come.

"It wasn't me who found your father dead in the flat. It was the landlady!"

Bewildered, I stopped. *Hang on a minute*, I almost said aloud, but managed to suppress it. Instead I uttered, "I don't understand. Didn't you say you found him?"

He waved his hand in denial. "No, you completely misunderstood what I said. The next day I was made aware that your dad had failed to turn up for duty. So I went to his flat. It was part of my duty as a captain, to look out for the welfare of my soldiers. But by then it was too late. He had been found by his landlady with a shot to his face."

Bullshit, crossed my mind. I didn't buy his story at all. Why all of a sudden the change? And what nonsense was he talking about? Him looking out for the welfare of his soldiers…! Ha, very funny. Boll certainly didn't care about my dad. No doubt about that.

I subdued the feeling to challenge him and sat down in one of the chairs he offered. The ground floor of the house consisted of one big room with a kitchenette and spiral stairs leading up to the top floor. I also spotted a door to a basement. The sink was full of dirty coffee cups. A pile of magazines and newspapers smothered the only table in the room. A huge bookcase full of files and various books filled the rest of the room. I pictured the top floor in a worse state.

Boll flopped into the chair across from me. We started with some small talk. He queried about my family. I didn't make a secret of the difficulties we faced after my father's death with the purpose to arouse a guilty conscience in him. He didn't let on if I was succeeding and we soon changed the subject to why I was here. I sensed that the answers to my questions could be found in this house. Still, I wasn't dense. It was clear from the outset. Boll would only disclose information that didn't incriminate him.

"Well, let's get to the point then. The reason you are here. Shall we?" he cheered and his hand slid to one of the paper files resting on the table. I presumed it was the one he had referred to on the phone. The one he had scrounged from the barracks.

"I was not supposed to take this with me. But the fact that your dad and his colleagues were treated like criminals from higher up," he rolled his eyes, "I thought it would be wise to keep hold of it. Just in case, as I like to think." He began to caress the front cover with his open palm. "Oh, apologies, how rude of me!" He leaned back in his seat and pointed towards a bottle of lemonade on the kitchen surface. "I forgot to ask, would you like something to drink? Some cold lemonade?"

"Yes, I'd love some." I regretted my words immediately when I noticed that the bottle was open already. Perhaps it was poisoned. I told myself to stop being foolish.

Boll rose from his chair, grabbed the bottle and two glasses from the cupboard and returned to his seat. He filled up our glasses and passed one to me. "Did you know that your dad installed a sauna for us? Right here in the basement." He pointed his sausage finger to the floor. "He was incredibly talented, your dad."

I was aware of my dad's gift as he had constructed so many things at home. However, I had not known about the sauna.

"We clicked, your dad and me."

I looked up, irritated. What was he talking about? According to my mum they didn't get along at all. My dad had distrusted Boll after the incident, so why was he claiming such a thing? Anybody I had spoken to, confirmed that my dad had been disliked by his superiors, especially by his captain Max Boll. And my dad's folder showed that he was bullied, again mainly by Boll. So why was he lying through his teeth?

I twisted the glass of lemonade through my fingers. I began to understand. It was just a game for him. The invitation to the house, pretending to be the concerned former captain and, and, and…! I opted for playing along and asked, "Was my dad a good soldier?" Conscious that he would tell me what the bereaved liked to hear after losing a beloved one, I added, "I know he liked the women, you said so over the phone and my family said so too. Just tell me the truth, please."

Boll waved aside, most likely part of his game. "Ah, it wasn't just your dad's fault. Women were crazy for him. It was hard for your dad to resist. But of course, your dad was a very good pilot and soldier. The major and I tried our best to get him out of his misery. We tried everything to save your dad."

"What's his name?" I shifted in my chair.

"Who?" Boll looked confused.

"The major, what's his name?"

"Oh, the major, Benjamin Kraft. We are also very good friends, always have been and always will be," he said proudly and raised his chin.

I knew it. Benjamin Kraft, my dad's former major was the one who gave my dad this ridiculous character reference shortly after the incident. I was tempted to run to my car to show Boll what his so-called best friend said about my father. I managed to stop myself in time. I had to slow down. At least for now! The folder was probably the only thing I had against him. And under no circumstances would I reveal it to him. Not now, it was far too early. *Just play along*, I reminded myself.

CHAPTER 31

Boll was clinging to the paper file in front of him. His head was slightly tilted. Was he afraid I would take it off him? Dithering in my seat I asked patiently, "Can I have a look now?"

First Boll hesitated. With twitchy cheeks he eventually opened it. "What exactly is it you want to know?" His grip was tight around the margin of the file. Indubitably he didn't want me to get hold of it. His silent message was clear.

"Well, obviously I'd like to know about that day. What happened that afternoon in February?"

Boll cleared his throat and slowly began to talk. He touched on the fact that all three pilots didn't stick to the correct flight altitude and subsequently failed to report the incident. "If they would have reported it straight away it could have saved them a lot of trouble, believe me. Any pilot occasionally doesn't stick to orders. It's not a big thing. However, in this case it went wrong. Still, none of them had thought that their decision on that afternoon would have such an impact on their future."

At one swallow Boll finished his glass of lemonade. "I felt bad for them. I was their captain and it was my responsibility to support them as best I could. Therefore I decided to change the flight mission. The pilots were supposed to fly a minimum of 400 metres by good weather. But as they had flown below that I altered the altitude to 150 metres. I know I shouldn't have done this, however it was the only way out."

Boll looked at me with great visual acuity. "But don't you think you can do anything about that now. It's too late."

His tone had changed. He looked at me spitefully. Was he threatening me? Was he all of a sudden showing me his real character? I haven't even said anything. I adjusted in my position.

"Who was in charge?" I demanded. I knew from my dad's folder that nobody had been in charge. However, my dad had mentioned in his appeal letter that if he had been told that day, that he was in charge of the operation, he would have never allowed Andrew Mann to continue flying.

"Your dad, of course. He was the one with the most flight experience." Boll browsed through the file. "Here, it says." He paused and jiggled his chair closer to the table. He turned the page upside down and began keenly pointing at a paragraph.

I scanned the words briefly. And in fact, it stated that my dad had been in charge of the operation. I was 100% sure it was written after the incident, the same as with the flight mission. I was vexed. It was all a big lie and there was nothing I could do. Musing over whether I would find any more lies, I dropped my hands on the file and launched into turning the pages.

Abruptly I was stopped by Boll. He yanked it off me and looked daggers at me. "Your dad was interviewed in a tape recorded interview," Boll continued. "But it's too late for you to check it out. The tapes don't exist anymore." A small smirk appeared on his face.

What a cheeky person he was! He knew exactly why I was here. He understood I was blaming the army. "Did Andrew Mann fly into something in the past? I mean before this one?" I asked directly. Boll glared at me in bewilderment. No doubt he was faking it. He most likely wondered how I knew about it.

"No, it was the first time. Why would you think that?"

I replied with a shrug. It became like a game between us. I challenged and he lied. My eyes dashed to the file in his hands. I had this burning desire to snatch it off him and run out. I knew my chances would be nil, probably he would set the dogs on me. "Why did you not want me to speak to Lech?" I pressured.

"I don't trust him. He is usually up to no good." Much to my regret I had to agree with Boll on this one. Or perhaps Lech's intention hadn't been bad at all. Maybe, out of solicitude, it was his way of telling me to let bygones be bygones. Who knew? Still, I believed that Lech had something up his sleeves. He had been acting too weird.

I was getting fed up of this game and decided to throw down the gauntlet. "Didn't you mention something on the phone that my dad had left a suicide note for you?"

The question threw Boll off balance. He began rubbing his forehead in an attempt to remove the sweat drops that covered the best part of it. I was disgusted by it and lowered my head to evade the sight. "The one where he had blamed you for his misery?"

Boll empurpled. No doubt, he had hoped I had forgotten about it all. And he was not a person who liked to be challenged, particularly not by Hunt's daughter, I could sense it.

"I reckon it is with his death record. The suicide notes were seized by the police." He grumbled and skimmed quietly through the rest of his file.

Clearly I wasn't allowed to see the whole thing. Yet I remained defiant. "Can I have look for myself?" I leaned forward with an open palm. In turn I was assailed with a hostile gaze.

"That's all you need to see," he grumbled abrasively.

His face began to soften, as if he had sensed how he made himself suspicious with his abrupt behaviour. "I am sorry. But I can't show you more. It contains information about the others, too."

I knew it was just a lame excuse. Boll was worried I would unearth something I wasn't supposed to see. The atmosphere was tense. Thus, I went off on a tangent before it escalated.

"Do you have any children?"

Boll looked relieved by me changing the topic. He started talking about his three children and their success in life. The oldest one was from his first marriage and the other two from his current one. He blasphemed about his ex-wife, even calling her a hussy. When I asked about the time of their divorce, he said to my surprise, "Not long after your father's suicide."

Unmistakably he detested his ex and I began to wonder if it had anything to do with my dad. Had my mum not mentioned something about an affair with the wife of a comrade? My dad got into trouble big time and he was relocated down south. Perhaps it had something to do with Boll's ex-wife? Potentially they met when my dad installed the sauna? Giving Boll a reason to punish my dad? Boll's eyes bored into mine as if he was trying to read me.

I averted his gaze and picked up some fluff on my dress. "Did you know my dad's new partner Lucy?" I looked up again, settled back and crossed my arms.

"No. I've heard of her, but we never met in person." He seemed relaxed again.

"I thought she was working at the same barracks?" That first Lech and now his former captain claimed they had never met Lucy, really bothered me.

"Perhaps she worked in a different building!" Boll replied without turning a hair. Unsure if he was lying or really didn't know her, I settled on a plan of action to find out Lucy's whereabouts.

The sudden bark from one of the dogs, who had long since moved to the patio, brought me back to reality. He was dashing into the room and growled in a guttural fashion. It didn't take me long to find out the reason. A cat was balancing along the balustrade. She was quickly chased away by the other dog. I revolved in my seat and focused on my host. The most important question was not out yet. It had been spooking in my head since I arrived. And although I had the answer in my dad's folder, I needed to hear it from his former captain. It was a one-time opportunity to yell at Boll that sixteen months' flight prohibition, for something my dad hadn't even caused, was ridiculous.

I signalled to the file and with stiff expression I asked, "Could you show me how long my dad had been banned from flying, please?" I dropped my hands and clasped the arm rests. My heart was in my mouth and I stopped breathing.

"Of course I can. It's here." Boll turned one of the pages and a satisfied look encased his face. Again he flipped over the file and slid it towards me with one finger stuck to the page.

I leaned forward and began to read. *What the hell…?*

I nearly gasped and clapped my hand over my mouth. In an instant I was utterly in shock. I read it again and again to assure myself it wasn't a hallucination. Without a warning my whole life began to fall apart.

I was reading seven months! My dad had been banned from flying for seven months! Why on earth did my dad's folder show sixteen months?

I moved my eyes to the next line and perused the banning times for Alex Feld and Andrew Mann. It was inconsistent to my dad's folder too. Andrew Mann had been punished for twelve months, not sixteen, and Alex Feld only for four and not six months as my dad's folder stated. I was absolutely stunned. Although I had known all the way along that some things weren't right, this was not one of them. In a trice everything made sense. The way Boll was so protective around his file. Lech's strange behaviour. The contents of my dad's folder. My dad's documents were forged. My dad had been forced to believe that he would never fly again. He was bullied into his death!

CHAPTER 32

After Zoe had left, Max Boll picked up the phone and rang Benjamin Kraft, the former major of their unit and his long-time friend. They had known each other from secondary school and both joined the armed forces at the same time. At some point they went their separate ways, and years later they met again at the barracks in Bueckenau. Both of them with a helicopter licence under their belt and in a superior position. Still Kraft, the brighter one, had managed to climb the ladder faster. He was one rank above Boll and in charge of the unit. Boll's thoughts were all over the place. He had hoped this would be the end after the visit of Hunt's daughter. His sixth sense told him otherwise. She had kept something from him. David Hunt had been dead for more than twenty-five years. Why now after all these years did she want to know all this?

Perhaps the time had come and now he was to be punished for his sins, for what he had done to Hunt. Maybe Hunt was watching him from heaven and it was his revenge to send his daughter. Boll slapped his hand on his forehead. He felt like a fool. Hunt was dead, for God's sake. He'd never been a very religious man and no way did he believe in angels or ghosts. After twenty-five years most of the evidence was gone. Boll was positive that the documents in his house were the only ones that still existed. Yet he had a bad hunch. Perhaps someone had talked? Nonetheless, why now after all these years? Or the daughter had found something? But what? He remembered his wife had said something about a folder the girl had brought along to Hunt's former neighbour. Still, it could have been any folder. The girl might have put something together for herself.

When he heard the familiar voice on the other end, Boll breathed heavily into the phone. "She was here. I only showed her what you told me to. Still, I think she kept something from me. I think she knows more." Boll waited for a reaction. He was greeted by silence. For at least thirty seconds Benjamin Kraft didn't say anything. It could only mean one thing. His friend had an idea and needed time to ponder. Boll's sweaty hand was adhered to the phone. "What is it?" he badgered.

Kraft, the one who saw things more logically, groaned. "Do you remember the day when we followed Hunt?" Boll stopped short. This time it was his turn to keep mute, only for a different reason though. He had no clue what his friend was talking about.

"His missus was also following him, remember to the lake?" Kraft said.

Boll tried to recall the day. He had followed Hunt plenty of times. He had been watching every step of

Hunt. He marched to the window and glanced at the blue sky as if to find the answer up there. The heat of the sun warmed up his face. "Come on, you must remember the day. It was the day his boat capsized. Does it not ring any bells?" Kraft stressed. He was running out of patience.

"Of course, yes. I do remember now!" Boll clapped his hands together. How could he forget? That was fun, watching David Hunt nearly drowning in the lake along with his precious folder in tow. And he nearly took another life with him, his new lover at the time. Boll had felt gratification, to finally see the back of the folder.

He had been so sure that was the end of it. Yet constantly Boll had surmised that there was something else out there. He had searched for any other clues, even after Hunt's death. Nothing else was ever found. That specific afternoon when they spied on Hunt and spotted the folder under his arm, he had known the contents. Just days before that Hunt accidentally left his folder in the changing room. Boll had found it just in time. As he leafed through it and saw the evidence that could be used against them, he knew the only way out of it was to destroy the folder. Unfortunately he never came to it. Hunt returned almost immediately and Boll had no other choice than to let it go.

Several days later he and Kraft followed Hunt to the lake. When they witnessed the drowning of the boat, Boll had been confident the folder drowned too. After Hunt and his lover were rescued by the coastguard, they had watched the couple returning to their car empty handed and soaking wet. Undeniably they had been mistaken. Boll was putting one and one together. He ground his teeth and swore under his breath. The folder his wife had talked about was the one which should be on the bottom of the lake.

"I know now what you mean. It's the folder, isn't it? It never reached the bottom of the lake. And the daughter must have found it. What a mess!"

CHAPTER 33

In the wake of discovering that my dad in truth had been grounded for only seven months and not sixteen as he had believed, I left promptly. I was concerned I would lose control if I stayed another minute under one roof with my dad's former captain. I kept quiet about the sixteen months, at least for now. Without proof that my dad's documents were indeed forged I wasn't getting anywhere. As I sat behind my wheel I caught my breath and raised my hand to my chest to control the abnormal beating of my heart. I felt completely overwhelmed with the news. The thought, that my dad would potentially be still alive if he had known the truth, flashed through my mind. I glanced towards the house I just stepped out of and spotted Max Boll behind the window. I quickly turned away and brought my car to life.

My tires screeched as I revved up the engine a tiny bit too much. A look in the rear-view mirror displayed a cloud of smoke I had left behind. Nothing made sense anymore. You couldn't even put it down to a spelling mistake. Seven and sixteen months was a huge difference. And even if it was only a misunderstanding, Boll and even Benjamin Kraft, the major, had had plenty of opportunities to correct it when they replied to my dad's solicitor. No, it wasn't some typing error. It had been done on purpose. My dad's document was forged. But why? And then the letter in which my dad blamed Boll? And all the other suicide notes? Why had I never heard of all this before? All these thoughts were going through my head as I headed home. My tummy began to rumble, reminding me that I hadn't eaten anything.

It was early afternoon and the sun was going still strong. I had to put my sun visors down to free my eyes from the dazzle. It was about time to get in touch with Lucy. Possibly she would be able to fill some gaps. I couldn't help it, but suddenly doubted the way my dad had died. I recollected the death of my granddad, the father of my dad. What a horrible death he had. And we still don't know if it had been suicide or just bad luck. My mum often wondered if it was in the family, committing suicide, first my dad and then his own father. And I recalled I'd once heard that somebody else in my dad's family had killed himself. It gave Mum cause to always worry about my brother, fortunately as yet without reason. As was usually the case, when I thought of the death of my granddad I smelled fire.

The day my granddad died I was twelve. Living alone and unable to overcome the separation from my grandmother, he was in need of help. During this time my mum began to reach out for him. Still living in the big house in which he raised his family, he was incapable of keeping up with the payments. And sadly it resulted in his eviction. And then the day before he was supposed to move to his new accommodation, he lost the plot. The next day when the police called to inform us that my granddad was in hospital with severe burns after he had set the house on fire, we headed to his place or let's say what was left of it. The scene was horrendous. What once had been a beautiful house was completely wrecked. The smell of fire in the air was still very strong.

The neighbour, who had raised the alarm, was utterly in shock. Woken up not only by the noise and smell of fire, but mostly by the horrific screams out of my granddad's mouth, traumatised him, probably for the rest of his life. My granddad had set himself alight. He came running like a burning Christmas tree out from the blazing house, screaming in agony. The neighbour tried to help him, still it was too late. My granddad passed away the same day. The investigations afterwards confirmed that it had been arson, committed by my granddad. However, speaking for us, his family, we never came to know if he purposely set himself on fire or if he just got caught in it. The remembrance sent cold shivers up and down my spine.

Half an hour later I arrived home. I got my hands on my laptop and woke up Google. I began a desperate search over the net for the whereabouts of Lucy. I even dismissed the growing noise of my stomach. I was well aware it would be arduous to locate Lucy without knowing her current name. My grandma had once mentioned that Lucy had married not long after my father's death. I only knew her maiden name and that she was from Hanwau. I typed into the search box of the Google phone book her maiden name Raube and the area of Hanwau. I then pressed enter. I hoped to locate some relatives who could help me further.

Lucy's maiden name wasn't very common. So I was more surprised when I couldn't find her name at all. Surely there must be somebody left in the family with this name. I decided to call the town hall. These days people often had private numbers to avoid cold callers. Perhaps it was the case with Lucy's family and they could help. A young female voice answered the phone. She was very forthcoming and I had the perfect story on the tip of my tongue. I pretended to be on the hunt for a schoolmate of my mum's to surprise her for her 50th birthday. I must have sounded quite believable. The woman came up with two phone numbers. Only two citizens in the voters' list were registered with this surname. I recorded the numbers and hung up.

After taking several deep breaths I picked up the handset and opted for the first one. The Christian name belonged to a woman. It somehow raised my hopes. I wasn't kept long. The other line came to life with the voice of an elderly female. I was gasping for air and a queasy feeling spread around my tummy. Without hesitation and before I could change my mind I asked for Lucy. I didn't even query if she was indeed the mum, I just assumed it. Luck was on my side and the elderly lady turned out to be the right person. I chose to be honest and went with the truth. I regretted it instantly. When the woman heard the name of my father, her attitude changed. Sounding cold and repellent, she answered, "I don't know where my daughter is. I haven't heard from her for years and I don't have any contact with her. Please don't call ever again." She ended the call. Perplexed by her reaction, I let the cradle drop.

CHAPTER 34

Entering the old building I swivelled on my heel and began absorbing the historical artwork disseminated on the walls. The foyer was massive and made distinct by a huge chandelier dangling from the middle of a high ceiling. The paintings showed the structure in different decades. It started as a new build in the late 1700s and presented the fine architecture which over the years had been regularly remodelled and reconstructed. A flight of winding stairs lay in front of me. To my left I noticed a small reception area occupied by a young lady in a light blue suit dress. It was my first time in a courthouse and I was anxious to finally confront the death of my father. Since my visit to Boll I had spent my days delving into locating any friends, family and former colleagues. Yet it had been all in vain. Not that I had imagined it to be easy after twenty-five years. But come on, somebody out there in the world must know more.

I approached the desk and explained I had an appointment. The receptionist was brusque. She picked up the internal phone to announce my arrival. Within minutes a middle-aged slim woman with a hint of grey roots in her blonde hair climbed down the stairs. She was dressed in a white blouse and dark grey suit pants. "Are you Miss Hunt?" she asked.

Nodding my head, I brushed down my T-shirt in an attempt to flatten it. In my simple red T-shirt and blue jeans I felt vaguely out of place. "Yes I am."

She gave me a reassuring smile and motioned to follow. We mounted the stairs and the clack of her stilettos echoed in the lobby. We attained the first floor and the woman, I assumed it was a secretary, opened a gigantic old oak door. She signalled me to enter and walked away. As I set foot inside, a man in his early sixties met me halfway. He extended his hand to shake mine.

"I am Judge Jones." I shyly looked up and took his hand.

"Thank you for seeing me, Sir."

"No worries. It's a pleasure. Your father's file is ready for you to view. Please follow me." I tottered behind him and we reached a wooden table with two armchairs in the corner of the room. A binder filled with a variety of reports sat on the surface. "You have to understand. It might be cumbrous for you to view the file."

Cumbrous? I never saw it from this angle.

With an altering voice he continued. "There is a picture of the scene. If you don't want to see it please let me know and I will remove it, before you start."

I could feel my stomach twitching. "I will be fine,"

I reassured him.

"OK, I will give you a few minutes on your own. If you need anything you can find me next door." He pointed to a small door on the other side of the room.

I thanked him and lowered myself into one of the chairs. Judge Jones pivoted and left the room. Compared to the enormous establishment I perceived this room to be tiny. It presented a sinister atmosphere with its dark wooden walls. Apart from the table and desk, the only other furniture was a bookshelf. With mixed feelings I devoted myself to the task in front of me, my dad's death file. I opened it and the first sheet was the report from the crime investigation department of the local police in Bueckenau. It was a synopsis of the discovery of my dad's suicide. It outlined how the landlady had found my dad in his bed, his face covered in blood and his shotgun next to him. Now I understood why Boll had been so desperate to explain himself. He must have known that it was in the police report and realised that I might go and view it. The ambulance had already been at scene when the police arrived. They confirmed that a male had killed himself with one single shot.

I knew from my mum that no post-mortem took place. Also none of my family had ever seen my dad's body. Apparently Boll had urged my mum not to because of deformation of his body. It was in my mum's hand and she followed his advice. He was even the one who had identified my dad. I was astounded by how much my dad's former captain had his say in my father's death. The next few pages were some witness statements of the landlady, my mum and Lucy. The one from the landlady didn't say much, only how she had found him. The next one was from my mother. It must have been the day, when the police came to our house and Thomas and I were sent away. I recalled that day very well, probably one of the rare moments I actually remembered from my early childhood. The statement confirmed that my mum had been separated from my dad for more than a year and that he had moved in with another woman called Lucy. It also divulged his infidelity, their financial problems and that once in the past he had made a remark to end it all.

Lucy's statement relinquished how they met and the beginning of their relationship. It briefly outlined the helicopter incident and the financial issues caused by the loss of my dad's flight allowance. It also mentioned another woman my dad was seeing right before his death. It was the main reason she had left him. That piqued my curiosity. I scratched behind my ears, a habit when I was ruminating. It was new to me that my dad had cheated on Lucy too. I carried on reading and paused on the next line. Ten days before his death, he divulged another suicide threat to Lucy? I shook my head in sadness. I had to stop repudiating the truth. My dad wanted to end his life. It was a matter of fact that my dad had suicidal thoughts beforehand. Still, I strongly believed there was more to his death than met the eye. My gaze budged from the statements to the photograph that lay beneath them.

I set them aside and stared at the picture. A torso with a face beyond recognition glanced back at me. The photograph of my deceased father and the scene of the suicide slid into my hand. My hands began to tremble. It was the first time in my life that I was confronted face to face with the death of my father. With fuzzy eyes I had to blink a dozen times to see straight. I swayed the photograph from one hand to the other.

Focus, I told myself. I tried my best to recognize any familiar features. The blood from the shot wound smudged all over his face made it difficult. I dropped the picture, rubbed off my clammy hands on my jeans and set my elbows on the table to support my head with my palms. I stared down at the picture once again. My dad's body was in the nude and only visible from his waist upwards. Apart from his bare chest and his brown hair, only blood and parts of his brain was on display. Therefore I found it virtually impossible to see my dad in that picture.

CHAPTER 35

Still rattled by the photograph of my dead father, I proceeded to the next pile. I gripped my dad's suicide notes. After all these years I was finally holding them in my hands. Until recently I didn't even know that any of them existed. One of them was addressed to his parents. The other one was for Lucy. I grubbed through the whole pile trying to ferret out some more.

Come on, there must be one for my mum at least! I dug into the pile, again and again. I clearly wasted my time. I dropped my gaze and a single tear landed on the paper. Although at the time of his death Thomas and I were very young, he still could have dropped us a line. I angrily dried off my face with a tissue I'd managed to find in my pocket. I felt let down. Yet I had always known it. My mum would have brought it up otherwise. I found it selfish. And wouldn't you say committing suicide was an act of selfishness anyway? Abandoning two young children, just to end the pain instead of fighting it? I focused on the letters and began with the one to Lucy.

Dear Lucy,

You've decided to break up with me. Before I go, I'd like to write to you. It is not that easy to lose you. I love you too much to ever let go. No other person ever meant more to me than you. I admit, I made loads of mistakes and you had to put up with many things. I appreciated that. But I had to take a loss, too. It wasn't easy for me to be without my children. You meant to me as much as my children. Please forgive me for all the agony I caused. I wanted you to be my wife. I wanted to have children with you. I am sure you would have been a great mum. We would have somehow coped, others can do it too. I would have given up everything for it. But now you've decided to leave me. I was hoping I could deal with it, but I just can't… The time with you was the best and happiest in my entire life. I never want to be unhappy again. When you read this letter, I will be dead. This is the last pain I am going to put you through. There is no way out, please forgive me. It is not your fault. Thank you very much for everything you did for me. I wish you all the best for the future, most of all a partner who is faithful and you can trust. I will love you forever.

David.

P.S. Please forgive me for what happened with Sharon.

My hand dropped to the side with the letter between my fingers. Further tears stung my eyes. It was the first time I caught sight of my dad's handwriting. I had seen bits and pieces on some film tapes. My dad used to film us a lot when we were kids. He had labelled the tapes with the description, name and year, but I never saw a proper letter from him.

Not until today!

I raised my hand and glanced one more time at the letter. 'Please forgive me for what happened with Sharon', I once more read. Who was Sharon? Was this the woman he started seeing before his death? The one Lucy had mentioned in her witness testimony? The only person who was able to answer this question was Lucy. I really needed to find her. The whirring of a fly circling the room captured my gaze. The hum began to distract me. Unsure how long I was allowed to spend time with the death file of my dad, I glanced at my wristwatch. Nearly half an hour had passed. Not wanting to lose any more time, I regained my focus and resumed to the last letter.

Dear parents,

Lucy has left me. She loves me, but she is unable to stay with me. We have too many problems. I am in too much debt. I was trying to sell some of my stuff, but without luck. I am not able to cope on my own anymore. And to go back to Emily doesn't make sense. If at least one of you came to visit us, Lucy would have loved that. But the whole family excluded us since I left Emily. The only ones who loved to visit were Thomas and Zoii.

Zoii? I paused. I scratched my forehead in confusion. What an odd way to spell my name. Surely my dad must have known how to spell my name! I had never seen anyone writing my name with two 'I's at the end. I shrugged my shoulders and my eyes wandered back to the page.

They loved to come, especially Zoii. If I didn't take her to us, she cried. Still, it wasn't enough. I love Lucy and cannot live without her. And now she is gone. This is the reason why I did it. It's difficult to understand. But she is not able to carry on like this. It's not Lucy's fault. She is the best woman I've ever met. Please don't blame her. But the situation is no out of control and I have no other choice.

Please forgive me. Goodbye.

David.

I dropped the letter on my lap and wiped the wetness off my face. I was deluged with pure sadness. It was almost like I felt my dad's black despair. What must have been going through my dad's mind to give up life that easily? Taking into consideration that his whole life was still in front of him? And being a father of two young children? Surely it couldn't have been just because of the break-up and his financial problems? I'd learnt from my mum about the financial problems we had. Apparently my dad used to live like a lord. With two boats, at some point even a sports car and many other gadgets the liabilities increased constantly. No wonder he was in huge debts. When my dad passed away, my mum received a lump sum from his pension. It enabled her to amortise the outstanding debts.

With all this going through my mind, I remembered the letter in which he blamed the army, mainly his captain, for his death. The one Max Boll had alluded to. It was definitely not in the death file. I quickly rummaged one more time through the pile, to reassure myself I had not missed anything. When my eyes found the letter to my grandparents, I again stared at the strange spelling of my name. The last letter of my name was spelled with an 'E', so why on earth did my father spell it with a double 'I' at the end? The labelled film tapes came to my mind. I was positive that my name was recorded on some of them. Suddenly I couldn't wait to get home to check how he had spelled my name. After I had sought permission from Judge Jones to copy the suicide notes and police reports for my own records, I promptly hurried away.

Less than thirty minutes later I stormed into the house like a lunatic. I quickly descended to the communal basement and disappeared into our cellar room. The tapes were hidden in some cardboard boxes. I got down to work right away. And as usually is the case, I unearthed the tapes in the last of the heap. I fetched one by one out of the box and examined them carefully. Almost every tape displayed either mine or Thomas' name. And not even one single one was misspelled. As anticipated, my dad had spelled my name correctly.

So why on earth was it showing differently in the last letter to his parents? Was he trying to say something inconspicuously?

CHAPTER 36

Nervously he pounded against the window. The office was situated in a tall glass building overlooking the best part of Nassau. It was the capital of the Bahamas and a bright blue sky loitered above the city's head. As a very successful architect, working alongside five partners, he was a very busy person. It had been tough to get where he was. And not only a tiny bit was he proud of himself. He stretched his arms and yawned. He hadn't slept much. The call he had received just yesterday had spooked all night in his head. It was only midday, yet he was already on his fifth cup of coffee to make it through the day. He had reacted promptly when he heard the code. He contacted Lech right away. Lech on the other hand had promised everything was under control. Be that as it may the situation was jeopardised, an incontrovertible fact. He understood it was his entire fault. No one else was to blame for it.

He pressed the intercom and directed his personal assistant to order some flowers. They were to be for his wife, with an apology card explaining that he wasn't able to meet her for lunch. Today was Wednesday and every Wednesday he had lunch with his wife at their favourite Italian restaurant 'La Rosa'. Today, however, he was in no mood at all. Running his hands through his thick brown hair, he racked his brains – why suddenly now, twenty-five years later? Something must have triggered it. He had to do something about it. Too many lives were at stake if the truth ever surfaced. Although the air conditioner was on and exposed the room to a gentle breeze, he suffered with a sudden fieriness. Perspiration poured out of all different parts of his body.

With a profound sigh, he flopped into his office chair. He leaned back and dragged his fingers across the keyboard. The computer came to life and he swiftly typed in 'Zoe Hunt'. He pressed enter and waited. Several pages appeared on his screen, some with photographs, and some without. He scrolled down the page, unsure where to start. At first glance he didn't recognise anyone in the picture. He moved his cursor to 'Images' and pressed enter once again. The third on the second row looked familiar. He clicked on it and the picture enlarged on his monitor. He froze. Beyond doubt this was the person he was looking for. It was a Facebook profile picture. A photograph taken in some other part of the world, he assumed a holiday picture. It showed her in a short dress with her long blonde hair whirling around her pale face.

Unfortunately he was not a member of Facebook. He didn't know how to use it either. He was beyond the age for all this social networking websites. It was enough that he had to view his face occasionally on the company website. He wasn't keen on photographs of himself. It just showed you how fast humans aged. He moved his mouse to the Facebook link and clicked once more to see if any further photographs or other information popped up. A message came up and said 'if you want to connect to this person, sign up today'. He clenched his teeth and swivelled in his chair. Was there no other way to view a person's profile on Facebook? Perhaps he should ask his teenage son. He was an active member of it.

He glanced remorsefully at the framed photograph of his wife on the desk. The picture was taken ten years ago. She hardly had changed and still possessed a stunning face. He felt bad for letting her down today, however he was not in a mood for a chatty lunch. He took a second gander at the photograph on his screen. He began fiddling about with his thumb on the edge of the keyboard. For a split second he imagined the face of his wife if she ever found out. The thought frightened him. Unequivocally it would be the end of their happy family life. No doubt about that! No way could he let this happen. Even if it meant he had to involve himself. He would do anything to prevent the truth being revealed.

CHAPTER 37

"And then this letter arrived from your father. It was the day after his death." I felt a clump in my throat. I sat across from my paternal grandmother in her tiny flat, with a spoon of homemade tomato soup half in my mouth. After pestering her with questions, I wasn't any wiser. For that reason, to learn something about a letter from my dad caught my attention.

"What did it say?" I blinked. Finally we were getting somewhere.

"It was an envelope with another one inside addressed to the armed forces. It was for the attention of one of his superiors. I can't remember the name. Your dad asked us to post it after his death. So I did."

With my hands jammed under my thighs I shuffled in my chair. "Does the name Max Boll ring any bells?" My grandma shrugged her shoulders.

"Honestly, I can't remember."

I wasn't yet to give up and asked, "Did you read the letter?"

"No, we never did. The letter was sealed. But now I wished I had."

Without revealing too much, I had given my grandma a brief explanation for my sudden visit and interrogation about the past. I assumed the letter she was talking about was the one Boll had referred to. I was pretty sure it didn't exist anymore. "Did you ever hear anything about Lucy again?" I placed my spoon aside. That was enough for me.

"We saw her sometimes after your father's death. After a few months the contact stopped. She married someone else within a year."

I nodded. She had touched on this many years ago. However, I hadn't known that Lucy had married in such a short time.

"I was surprised how quickly she got over David. I suspected she knew this man when your dad was still alive." My grandma shoved her chair backwards and cramped her fingers into a fist. Her soft features changed to a furious expression. I looked at her sympathetically. I knew what went through her head. If my grandma was right, the suicide of my dad may have suited Lucy. It was cruel to think like that, no question. But what if Lucy had played a part in all this?

An hour later I left my grandma's. It had been only yesterday when I went to court, however it felt like years ago. I had even managed to shut out the image of my dead father. I now sat on the edge of my bed with crossed legs. My laptop rested to one side, on the other lay my notebook. I went through my bullet points, ticking the ones that were done, highlighting the others that still needed attention. I grabbed the pencil from behind my ear, another strange habit, and twisted it around my fingers. I brought the pencil down to my notebook and added a new bullet point. After discovering the different spellings of my name I compared the copied suicide notes with the labelled tapes. I didn't spot any discrepancies. Still, it was something to look into, to eliminate foul play. I scrawled 'handwriting analyst' and underlined it twice.

Before spending a fortune on my investigation – after researching online I had ascertained that a handwriting analyst was costly – I planned to locate Lucy albeit without the help of her mum. I had already spent a fair amount of time on the net, combed through all different kinds of social networks to locate Lucy, but without knowing her current name it proved to be an impossible task. Hold on…! I stopped in my tracks. Didn't the lady from the town hall provide me with two phone numbers? I had all forgotten about it after Lucy's mum took the wind out of my sails. I flipped through my notebook and found it on the last page. I leaped to my feet and lunged at my mobile that sat on my dresser. Ten seconds later I was on the phone with a distant cousin of Lucy.

A big smile widened my face. Not only was I lucky that the number belonged to a relative of Lucy, she also appeared to be the opposite of Lucy's mum. She was happy to supply me with her cousin's new contact details. Lucy's married name was Mohr. I was told that together with her husband she had her own business, an electric shop right in the city centre of Hanwau. Instead of calling Lucy I settled for an email. I found it easier to express words in writing. I became quite edgy when speaking about my dad to strangers over the phone. It made me forget things I wanted to ask. And wasn't it so much better to send an email than talking face to face with someone you might not like?

It gave you also the option to edit, delete or write it all over again. I brought my laptop back to life and Googled for the name of Lucy's shop. At first go, a website for the shop came into my sight. I clicked on 'Contacts' and an email address cropped up. Clicking on the link it redirected me to Microsoft Outlook. I aimed for a short text, just in case as I wasn't sure who would view it first. I introduced myself and outlined a quick explanation with the reasons for my intrusion into her life. Reading it a dozen times, I finally plucked up my courage and shifted the cursor to the 'Send' button.

CHAPTER 38

Lucy was wrestling with the copier. Again she was left high and dry by this stupid thing. She kicked her foot against the bottom in frustration. It was time to get a new one. She ripped the invoice from the surface and inserted it into the slot of the fax machine. Luckily she was able to make her copies in there. Still, it was not a long-term solution. Today she was able to catch up with all the admin work that had accumulated over the last week. As proud owners of an electric store in the city centre of Hanwau, boredom became a foreign word to Lucy and her husband. The business kept them well occupied, even at weekends. It was a small store with only a few appliances on display. Most of them were ordered online. Their main trade lay in the service of their products. Lucy was responsible for all the administration side. Her husband mainly dealt with sales and customer service.

Today was one of the rare mornings where it seemed to be peaceful. Ultimately Lucy had time to check her emails. She made herself a cup of coffee and sat down in her small office in the rear of the store. Whilst uploading the computer, she took a sip. The inbox popped up with many unread emails. Lucy cursorily scanned through the senders. It was the usual enquiries about prices, maintenance issues or complaints. Some of them came from regular customers, others were from potentially new customers. All at once Lucy went rigid. She gawked at her screen. Out of a million of emails, she would have recognised this one instantly. She turned around to peep through the half-open door to ascertain that she was still alone in the shop. Her husband was with a customer. Satisfied that he had not returned yet, she consecrated herself to the email.

A feeling of unease crept over her. She tried to keep cool and collected. It was presumably just a new enquiry about their products. The email was somewhere among all the other ones. Normally she would open them by date. Howbeit Lucy's nosiness took precedence and inevitably the surname brought back memories. It wasn't so much for the surname as it was quite a common one. It was more the first name that perplexed Lucy. David's daughter was called Zoe. Still, it could be just coincidence. But when reading the subject line, Lucy knew it wasn't any random person. It said in bold 'David Hunt'. A shiver shot down her body. Slack-jawed, she gaped at her monitor. Instead of opening it, Lucy found herself enwrapped in the past, back in July 1983.

Even the abrupt tinkle of the phone didn't bring Lucy back to reality. It stayed untouched. She had lingered at her mum's when the call came in. Miss Sturm, her former landlady had somehow managed to find out her mum's phone number. The day she rang to inform her about David's suicide, had been the worst day of her life. First Lucy had blamed herself. It came as a big shock. David. her first big love, had killed himself? She had struggled to comprehend this fact. Although she was the one who had ended the relationship, she had truly loved David. And she had to admit she still did, if you can love a dead person? She never overcame his death. And now at this moment in time twenty-five years had gone past and she was staring at an email from his daughter. Unbelievable!

How had Zoe found out about her? Surely it must have been strenuous. After all, her last name had changed and she had never passed it on to David's family. A few months after his death she had stopped all contact with his family. Lucy tilted her head with narrowed eyes. Why now after all these years? And what did Zoe want? Unsure if she should open the email or pretend she had never seen it, Lucy writhed. One way or another she would eventually open it. No doubt about that. She would ignore the heartache that would automatically follow. Still she underwent a ten-minute debate with herself about the pros and cons, before ultimately clicking on it. Fully aware that she had just reopened an old wound, she bent forward and began to read. Zoe had finally found her. Lucy was having doubts, whether to feel pleased or frightened.

CHAPTER 39

Two days had gone by since Lucy had opened the email. She was no longer the same. The email threw her off course. Even her husband had noticed. She had not made up her mind yet, if she should reply. It still hurt, even after all these years. She thought about her own daughter. If her daughter had lost her dad in such a tragedy, she probably would have many questions too. Memories from the past appeared in flashbacks. Lucy was asking herself if she could have prevented it. If she had not left him, perhaps David would be still alive. She knew it wasn't her fault. At the end of the day everybody is responsible for their own life. Nobody knew what was going on in somebody else's mind, even if it was your own partner. Yet did she not see any signs of suicide beforehand?

Lucy stood up from her sofa and poured herself a glass of wine. The rain was splashing against the window. The clatter from a loose pipe, caused by the strong wind, banged against some metal next door.

The television flickered in the background with no sound. It was set on mute. Half a dozen candles glimmered on the window ledge, exuding a romantic atmosphere. It was Saturday evening and Lucy was all alone in her cosy lounge. Her husband was out watching the football and her two teenage children were staying at friends' for a sleepover. It didn't bother her. In fact she appreciated having some time for herself. It gave her time to mull over it. She chose to answer Zoe. Back on her sofa with curled up legs, she began typing on her laptop.

Dear Zoe,

I received your email, thank you. I was a bit confused, but also pleased. Over the years I often wondered how you and Thomas were doing. I guess you are now in your late twenties. By the way, my mum never mentioned your call. I can just imagine that you have plenty of questions about your dad. Even after all this time I still think of him with love. My time with your dad was the happiest in my life, but also a very sad one. Believe me, I often asked myself if I could have prevented his suicide. I was probably just too young, only 20 years of age, to see the signs. The first half-year of our relationship was wonderful. Your dad was full of beans. He always had new ideas and we had lots of fun.

Lucy came to a halt. Her body suddenly twitched and she began rocking back and forth, tears spilling down her cheeks unchecked. The memory was just too painful. With a vigorous gesture she polished off her tears and returned to her keyboard.

You and your brother's welfare were very important to your dad. Sometimes he was allowed to take you both to us. I was always pleased to see you both. I guess you won't remember, you were just too young. Your dad loved his job. To be a pilot meant everything to him. He put his heart and soul into it. He never told me much about the incident. It changed him completely. He started going out alone and became very petulant. When I discovered that he cheated on me, it broke my heart. This is what I meant by not having enough life experience. Perhaps even with the indignity, I should have stood by his side.

Lucy paused, put her glass to her lips and took a sip.

When I challenged him and he admitted to his infidelity I decided to leave him. I told him I would move out. But please don't think badly about your dad. I think he was always on the lookout for something, which neither I nor your mum could give him. Potentially no one could. I don't know. Your dad was not himself after the incident, he was much disoriented. Something didn't feel right. I don't understand why David never told me more about that day. Perhaps he couldn't. Did you not say something about a folder you discovered? I would love to know more about it. I hope that is OK with you. Your dad was a very important part of my life. Therefore I would love to know more to come to terms with the past. I hope to hear from you soon.

Love Lucy

Before Lucy had the chance to change her mind, the email vanished from her screen.

CHAPTER 40

It was Monday morning and I was on my way to the local paper *Sommer Daily* in Bueckenau. Exploring the internet for any newspaper article about the incident in 1983 had been in vain. Not one single word came up. I reckoned it was because at the time no internet existed. Hopefully I would be more successful walking into the branch and asking directly. Surely they must have an archive. The email from Lucy popped up in my head. She seemed to be a nice person. I considered trusting this woman. I was now at ease that she most likely had nothing to do with all this and was as innocent as I. Perhaps she was able to help me in finding out the truth. And even if she was somehow at fault I had nothing to lose by meeting her. Lucy had suggested getting together and we agreed to meet the following weekend in a local restaurant in Bueckenau.

The constant whirring of my wipers slightly vexed me. It was summer and indeed we had been lucky the last few days. But now the rain had returned and there was no sign of improvement. Many things I had stumbled on in recent days didn't make sense at all. Nothing seemed to be as it had looked over the years. If I hadn't unearthed the folder I would have accepted the fact that my father had killed himself. Perhaps the folder was meant to fall into my hands. Fact was, the deeper I dug, the more discrepancies I discovered which raised more questions. I was fortunate. I found a parking spot right outside the branch. I turned off the engine and lifted my eyes to a big black sign above the glass window of the entrance. It read 'Sommer Daily local newspaper of Bueckenau'.

I dashed from my vehicle and swept off some raindrops which had splashed near my eyes. I could feel my mascara running down my cheeks and made a mental note for next time to buy a waterproof one. I scudded quickly inside the branch. With a tissue from my handbag and a small pocket mirror I dabbed off the smudge. The branch was a middle-sized room with four desks equally lined up on either side with monitors. At the far end was a corridor with doors on either side. I assumed this to be some offices. I approached the first desk and a young slender man with some beard stubble smiled at me. "How can I help you?"

"Do you have any newspaper articles from the beginning of the eighties?" I asked and returned his smile.

He pointed to a computer resting on a corner table right beside the window. "This one is for our customers. You will be able to find any news story with the last fifty years."

Wow! I was amazed by what technology could do these days. He quickly explained how to use it. I placed myself behind the screen in a comfortable position. In a swift movement I drove the mouse to the search box and entered '20th February 1983'. More than thirty pages bobbed up. Unsure if there had been a story at all or what the headline had said, I launched into browsing all pages. Luckily I didn't have to go that far. Page eleven appeared on the screen. The headline boasted, 'The near miss of a military helicopter in the valley'.

I studied the article, which was kept very brief and factual. It elucidated the near crash of a military helicopter in the Buchesener Tal, after flying into a power supply line. It mentioned the power breakdown of a nearby village and that the cause of the mishap was not known yet. As I further read along the lines, my ire grew. The report referred to the flight mission, an altitude of 150 feet. What a lie! I was disgusted when I finished reading. Just the thought of it infuriated me. I slammed my right fist against the edge of the desk, triggering a few heads to turn my direction. I promptly glanced down, avoiding any eye contact. Like my dad had indicated in his folder, the flight order had been modified. I wished I was able to prove it.

Still the main part that troubled me was the discrepancy about my dad's flight prohibition. My dad's folder alone was not proof enough. I needed to find something on paper that my dad had his licence withdrawn only for seven and not sixteen months. If I just could get hold of Boll's file my problem would be solved. There were still a few people out there I intended to speak to. This included the other two pilots but also Major Kraft. To my disadvantage it had been so long ago, it was complex to track down the ones involved. I had contemplated contacting the army directly. Perhaps they kept something in their archive? I sifted through the search box in the chase for further stories. It took me a while until I came across another one. Interesting! I pursed my lips. This one was published in October, three months after my father's suicide.

I remembered the court warning I had discovered in my dad's folder. The last one had been for October. My dad never made it to this one. He was long dead before that. I started reading. 'Helicopter pilot exonerated'. My face dropped. I was totally appalled. The pilot acquitted of any wrongdoing? As I read along the lines, my hand covered my mouth over and over again. The mishap was explained with the simple explanation that the power supply line was a new one, and it wasn't sketched in the pilot's flight map.

"My arse," I mumbled under my breath. I was cocksure, Max Boll had fabricated this lie. Just a further one that added to the humbug! All this hassle for nothing. Andrew Mann, the pilot who had caused all this shit, got away with it, but my dad who hadn't done anything wrong had to pay with his life. "What a joke," I spat out quietly or so I thought. The harrumph from someone within the branch told me otherwise. I was fuming inexorably. With an apologetic smile I stood up, thanked them, and left.

CHAPTER 41

Max Boll vacated the town hall in Bueckenau, an old historical building from the 1900 century and one of the main sightseeing attractions beside the famous castle in this city. He had just renewed his passport. He loped to his vehicle that was parked across the street, on one of the main roads along the *Sommer Daily* newspaper branch. For some reason, Lech was spooking in his head. The days leading up to David Hunt's death, Lech had loitered too often outside his office. What if he knew about the forged documents? After Hunt's death, Boll had tried to speak to him to work out what he knew. It was to no avail, Lech had avoided him. That was one of the reasons he didn't want Hunt's daughter to speak to him. There was something about him, Boll just didn't like.

Boll approached the pavement. As he trudged along with the best effort to avoid all the puddles that blocked his way, he abruptly stopped. Across the street, emerging from the *Sommer Daily* newspaper branch was David Hunt's daughter. What was she doing here? Didn't she live in Brielen? He concentrated with his eyes, and drew his face closer to the entrance of the branch to determine that she wasn't some doppelgänger. Boll rapidly took cover behind a van, when the woman glanced in his direction. He didn't think she saw him. Boll, however, was confident, it was Zoe Hunt. His lips formed a slight frown as he bristled with anger. The downpour had altered to a drizzle, still raindrops were tickling his skin. Boll brushed them off his face and took a step back to find some shelter under the roof of a butcher's shop.

He kicked his heels until Zoe retreated to the inside of her vehicle and roared off. When she had gone, he bolted across the street and swung open the door of the newspaper branch. Scant of breath, he walked straight up to the same desk Zoe had done minutes earlier. The man was very young, most likely an apprentice, and Boll used this to his leverage. Pulling up his best innocent face, he asked with a friendly smile, "I was wondering if you could help me. I am looking for my niece. I was supposed to meet her here." Boll hesitated just for a second. To avoid any attraction he wanted to get this right. He raised his chin in a musing position and began describing Zoe Hunt as best he could.

"Did she come in?" He folded his hand in front of him and glanced around the room in an attempt to spot her in the building. None of the other staff paid attention. He was glad and preferred to keep a low profile. Confident that he sounded quite convincing, he put on a disappointed expression. The young man's face expanded to a smile.

"Oh, I know who you are talking about. She literally just left. She asked about some newspaper article from the eighties. I am pretty sure you will catch her if you hurry. I think she headed to the left towards the town hall." He pointed out the window.

"Damn," Boll cursed quietly. Being no fool, he knew exactly what newspaper articles Zoe had looked at. It was starting all over again.

CHAPTER 42

I was still trying to digest the terrible news I had been given by Lucy. She sat across from me in the beer garden of a popular restaurant situated on a hill overlooking the castle. A dozen round tables were covered with red tablecloths and decorated with yellow tulips in vases. It was midday and the garden was filled with pensioners and families enjoying a sunny warm weekend under white parasols. After getting to know each other by telling our life stories, Lucy revealed a secret about my mum which came like a bombshell. My mum was sexually abused as a child, by her own father? I found it difficult to believe. But why would my dad mention this to Lucy if it wasn't true? Nobody would make up such a thing. The only reason Lucy decided to disclose it was that I would be able to understand why my mum was drinking. My mum had once confided in my dad. And to explain the reason for my mum's alcoholism he had disclosed it to Lucy.

I felt quite upset by the news. I had loved my late

granddad and never saw him as anything else. Feeling somehow in shambles, I pushed off the shocking news and focused on the reason I was here. I switched the subject to my dad. After all, that was the reason Lucy and I sat across from each other. "I am surprised you never received any suicide note. The police must have seized it without showing to you." I straightened up.

"I am still dumbfounded. All these years I was wondering why he didn't drop me at least a few lines. And now, twenty-five years later, I am learning from you about a letter to me? Incredible!" Lucy swallowed.

I nodded sympathetically. I rummaged through my bag to locate the copy I had made for Lucy. I handed it to her. It was a two-page letter. She clung to it with watery eyes. Her bottom lip quivered as she dipped into it.

I picked at my chicken Caesar salad, failing to enjoy it. Not after what Lucy had told me about my mum. I probably needed a long time to come to terms with it. The love for my mum was very strong, and that she had suffered even more than I could have ever imagined depressed me. I glanced up at Lucy, who was still reading the letter. She was obviously in her own world right now. It was understandable. I pushed my plate aside, excused myself and arose. I headed to the ladies' to refresh myself. I wanted to give Lucy some space. It must have come as a big surprise hearing after all these years about a suicide note.

Five minutes later I loafed back to the table. I had to admit that Lucy, now being in her fifties, was still a good-looking woman. She was of a slender figure and had curly brown hair which she kept in a short fashionable style. Her checked T-shirt and blue jeans gave her a youthful appearance. I detected that the tears in Lucy's eyes had become bigger. They steadily trickled along her cheeks. I glanced around, yet nobody paid attention to us. The other guests were too deeply absorbed in their own conversations. As I approached, not sure if I should give her some more time, Lucy clapped both her hands over her mouth.

She stared at me, incredulous, and cried out, "Oh Zoe, if I had known about this before." She lifted up the letter. "All these years I felt to some extent betrayed."

I waited to give her time to gather her thoughts. Lucy dried her cheeks and lit up a cigarette. Her hand was trembling. She inhaled a deep drag. "So tell me, Zoe, tell me about this folder."

I had asked her in my email if she had any knowledge about my dad's folder. She didn't. So I began. I told her the contents of the folder and also about my encounters I had with Max Boll and the others.

The sun dazzled my view. I cocked my head and jerked backwards to hide behind our parasol. "When I mentioned you, they said they'd heard about you, but didn't know you. Is that true?"

"I never came across your dad's superiors. I worked in the office on the other side of the barracks. I had nothing to do with the light aircraft group." I nodded. That made sense. At least I didn't have to worry any longer about whether Lucy was somehow involved. I didn't think so and began to trust her. I contemplated if I should show her the folder I had left in the car. Perhaps it was a good idea, to hear her opinion.

"I still can't get it, why David's correspondence is different to his captain's. And why is he keeping it at home? Is he allowed to do so?" Lucy dragged on her cigarette, the smoke swirling around her puffy eyes.

"I don't think so," Lucy mumbled, answering her own question.

I shrugged my shoulders. "No idea why he has it at home." I leaned back in my chair. "Did my dad never tell you how long he was banned from flying?"

Lucy shook her head. "I am afraid, Zoe, he didn't. He changed a lot after the incident. He wasn't himself anymore. We rarely talked. I couldn't cope with his sudden moods and infidelity. Any conversation we had ended up in a quarrel. He kept the details to himself and I never asked. I believe he didn't want to involve me. Apparently it was a tense atmosphere after the incident. But seven months and sixteen is a huge difference. I can't get my head around it yet. I am certain David would have been OK with seven months. But sixteen?" Again she shook her head, her curls twirling from one side to the other. "That is really odd. And you are saying it was signed by a colonel?"

I nodded.

"Would you mind if I have a look at your dad's folder?"

I tugged some hair behind my ears. "Not at all. Hang on, I have to get it from the car." I rose to my feet, grabbed the keys that I had dumped on the chair next to me and disappeared through the inside of the restaurant to the car park. Two minutes later, the folder on the table, I carried on with my interrogation. "Do you know of any friends he may have entrusted himself?"

"No, not that I know of."

"He must have confided in someone?" I wondered. "I can't imagine that he kept this all to himself."

Lucy stubbed out her cigarette in the ashtray. "After your dad split up from your mum, he stopped contact with their mutual friends. He wanted your mum to have contact with them. Your dad secluded himself, especially after the incident."

"What about colleagues?" I settled back.

"I don't know, Zoe. He never referred to any. I doubt he trusted anyone, not after what had happened."

The affair my dad had been involved in pierced my head. With prying eyes Lucy peeked at the folder. Still, I wasn't ready to unveil it just yet and fired further questions at her. "Lucy, did my dad ever disclose to you a fling with another soldier's wife? Before he met you, of course!" I quickly clarified. "And as a punishment he was moved down south?"

"Yes, he mentioned something, but not much. Why are you asking?" Lucy asked sceptically.

"Well, when I went to see his former captain, Boll talked about his divorce from his first wife. It was right after my father's death. And he wasn't speaking very nicely about his first wife. Perhaps that's the lady in question?" I was only speculating here, most likely she had nothing to do with it. But who knew?

"Apparently my dad installed Boll's sauna. Maybe this is how they met?"

"Honestly Zoe, I don't know. He never revealed any names. Perhaps it would be worth speaking to her."

I agreed and added it to the list in my head. I shoved the folder towards Lucy. "Have a look and tell me what you make of it."

Lucy winked at me. She leaned forward and consecrated herself to the task in front of her. I kept mum and began inspecting the emails on my phone. I observed from the corner of my eyes, how Lucy flipped through the folder and every once in a while paused to get granular on certain pages.

"Can I get you something else?" The sudden voice from the waitress made both of us wince. I ordered another apple juice; so did Lucy. Her eyes shifted back to the page, on which she had swayed back and forth for the last five minutes.

"What is it?" Intrigued, I leaned over the table.

Lucy gasped for air and uttered, "Look at this." She pointed flutteringly to the document that showed the lengths of the flight prohibition. It was a two-page-long document.

She leaped up from her seat, moved beside me and pressed her right index finger on the signature of the next page. Lucy must have noticed my clueless gaze. She gave me a nudge and indicated to the first page. "Can you not see? It was signed by the colonel on the second page. However, the length of the prohibition is displayed only on the first one which doesn't have any signatures. I think it might be a fake!" Lucy panted.

I paused. That's what I had missed the whole time. Lucy was right – how easily could this document have been altered? Without even forging a signature! You only had to modify the numbers on the first page. From seven to sixteen months! Clearly I had no proof if it was indeed forged. Yet it was a plausible explanation as to why Boll's document presented seven months. And if this had ever come to light, nobody could have been accused of forging a signature. In fact, it could have been explained simply as a typing error. Tremendous!

CHAPTER 43

Now in front of a cup of coffee and still dumbfounded by Lucy's unearthing, we talked about the other contents of the folder. We both came to the conclusion that my dad was stitched up. Lucy also pointed out to the re-adjourned court date in October, suggesting that it had been done on purpose, so my dad had no chance to rectify the situation. When I told her that Andrew Mann, the pilot who had caused it all, was acquitted in court of any wrongdoing, Lucy slammed her fist on the table, attracting the other guests' attention. I successfully managed to disseminate an apologising glance around the beer garden.

"I am a hundred percent convinced your father would be still alive, if he had known that he was grounded only for seven and not sixteen months," Lucy snorted. I chimed with her view. She lit up a further cigarette and after dragging at it crazily, she gradually composed herself and prompted, "What else would you like to know?"

"Tell me about the last few weeks before his suicide. Did he make any indication about taking his own life?"

Lucy pushed the folder aside and once again grasped for the suicide note. Rotating it in her hand, she answered, "It has been quite a while, Zoe. So excuse me if I don't get it all right. Your dad was cheating on me, the reason why I left him. But also financially we struggled, more than ever after he'd lost his flight allowance. I told him approximately two weeks before his suicide, that I wasn't willing to continue like this and I would move back home. No question he was disappointed but as far as I remember he accepted my decision. I then spent my time mainly at my mum's hunting for a new job. I only returned a couple of times and your dad, who was present, appeared to be OK. I gave notice to our landlady and began to move out."

I interrupted, "In your witness statement to the police, you mentioned something about my dad threatening to kill himself two weeks before his death. Is that true?"

"Yes Zoe, he did. But I didn't take it seriously. Your father didn't strike me as a suicidal person." She looked sheepishly at her plate of spaghetti. Lucy hadn't touched her food much. Her cigarette was dangling between her fingers and the ash elongated.

"It's not your fault," I reassured Lucy. "When was the last time you saw my dad alive?"

"I can't tell you the exact day. I think it was about three days before his death. I came to the flat to collect the rest of my belongings. My mum came with me.

When we left your dad was alright or so I thought. Otherwise I wouldn't have left him on his own…"

Her voice trailed off. I sensed she remembered something and leaned forward. I nodded to her to let it out. "I recall that day very well now, actually. Your father wasn't at home first. I let myself in and my mum and I found a suicide note in the bedroom. It was different to this one. Much shorter and he also mentioned Sharon, his lover at the time. I can't remember the contents. I felt very upset in that moment. A short time later your dad returned from a jog, can you believe that?" She scoffed and shook her head. "He seemed absolutely fine. He apologised for the suicide note and threw it into the bin." She pressed out her cigarette and glanced wistfully at a young couple beside us, immersed in their own world, chuckling away.

"Your dad hated smokers." She grinned. Wetness still reflected in her deep green eyes. "Most times I smoked secretly behind his back." She gasped. "A few days later, I recall this day very well. My mum and I sat in the kitchen when the phone rang. It was our landlady." Her gaze wandered back to me. "She informed me of your dad's suicide. I was very shocked. Although I was the one who broke up with him, I had hoped for another chance. Someone from my family, I even can't remember who, drove me to Bueckenau. I recall both of your grandfathers there, trying to sort out your dad's belongings." With a sniffling sound, Lucy buried her face in her hands. She swallowed down a sob. "I never went to his funeral because of your mum. I didn't want to make it worse."

My mum's words came into my head. She once

told me she had seen a woman, she believed to be Lucy, stood behind a tree on my dad's funeral. I kept quiet. If Lucy wished to tell, I was sure she would. Perhaps she preferred to keep this for herself. Or my mum got it wrong.

"Have you ever spoken to the other two pilots?"

"No, not yet, it's on my list though. It's not easy to locate all these people after so many years. Some moved away, some are not listed anywhere. It involves quite a bit of digging," I sighed.

"I can imagine. But you found me. I guess it wasn't easy, especially without a surname. And my mum refusing to help didn't make it easier, I guess. I still don't understand why. Probably she just wanted to protect me. Someday I will tell her though. In spite of everything, we still managed to meet. I am grateful for that." Her lips unfolded into a smile.

All of a sudden Lucy became silent. "What is it?" I asked, stirring in my chair.

"I just recalled something very odd actually," she exclaimed. She waved away. "Most likely it's nothing."

"Go on, Lucy. Every detail, even the slightest, can be important." The laughter from the next table became louder.

"I sometimes followed your dad. First I only suspected that he was unfaithful to me. I had no proof. So I began spying on him. Don't get me wrong. I wasn't this kind of person. But I was hurt and wasn't blind. I needed to know."

"You don't have to apologise. I would have been the same." I relinquished a knowing smile.

"I remember this day very well, just a month before his suicide. Not because of where he went, it was the state he came home that night. Your dad pretended to be on standby. He left with the excuse he had been called for duty. My gut told me he was lying. I followed him. It turned out, I was right. He was heading out of town."

She paused and took a sip of her coffee, before continuing, "I was driving a fair distance behind him. He never spotted me. After about thirty kilometres we arrived in Schossen. He turned into a residential area and stopped right in front of a family house. I watched him emerging from his car. I remember it very well now. He was holding a folder under his arm. I had no idea what it comprised."

Could it have been this one? I wondered. She glanced at my dad's folder, possibly thinking the same.

"Well, anyway, he buzzed and someone let him in. At this point I was unable to see the person in question. I waited for an hour and finally he reappeared with a young woman, ambling arm in arm to his vehicle. Although I had known all along, his adultery came as a big jolt. I was deeply upset and left abruptly. They never saw me. I was crying the whole way back home. Still to this day, it is beyond me how I made it back home safely."

I gaped at Lucy, not knowing how to react. After all, she was talking about my dad. Even though it wasn't my fault, I felt somehow culpable. I felt the urge to apologise for my dad's behaviour. "I am sorry to hear all this. I was aware my dad had been unfaithful to my mum. Not just with one, but with several women." I recalled the day when my brother showed me several love letters from various different women to my dad, hidden in my mum's desk. She had kept them for all these years and they still existed. "But not until I saw your statement to the police, did I know he had done the same to you."

Lucy forced a smile. "It's OK, Zoe. It's not your fault. That day I decided to leave your dad. I had enough of it." She exhaled. Her eyes darted to a passing plane in the sky. Her gaze sank back to me.

"I am telling you all this for a different reason though. There was something very odd about that day, or shall we say night. When your dad came home, it was about two in the morning and I wasn't expecting him anymore. I had long assumed he would stay at his lover's house. Just thinking of it now, feels like it happened yesterday. I was still awake that night. I wasn't able to drift off. Too many things were playing on my mind. I had been waiting for your dad, ready to tell him to his face what kind of a liar and cheater he was, but then I wasn't sure if he was coming home at all. He did eventually, but you should have seen in what state." Lucy paused, shaking her head. Her hands moved towards her pack of cigarettes. Right before it, she stopped in her tracks. Instead of taking another one out, she began pulling off some paper.

"Just the thought of it makes me wonder what actually occurred that night. David's clothes were soaking wet. I was baffled. When I challenged him, he admitted he had spent the day with his lover. She was called Sharon. He took her on a boat trip at the Schossener Lake, the place where your dad kept his boat. Then something happened. The boat crashed into a rock and overturned. As a result it cracked the hull and sank. According to your dad both of them nearly drowned. But the strange thing about it was that, as claimed by your dad, he was carrying all his documents on him. I still don't know what exactly he meant. I didn't ask. I was too upset. But now I am asking myself, what was he trying to tell me? And why was he carrying a folder with him that day? Why would you even carry all this stuff on a boat trip?"

Lucy looked up without another word. I sensed what she meant. I was thinking the same; still, we never spoke it out aloud.

CHAPTER 44

Andrew Mann gawked at his phone. The handset still in his hand, he felt unable to move. What was that all about? It was still early morning and he had been fast asleep when the phone rang. Usually he was an early riser. However, it had been a long night the day before. The gathering with his former comrades from the light aircraft had ended up jolly, it usually did. He had consumed a fair amount of alcohol. Andrew had left the army decades ago. Still, after all these years they tried to keep in touch and met once a year in the summer for a barbecue. They took it in turns and this year it took place at his place. They were a nice little bunch together, back from their days in the squadron, including their former Captain Max Boll and Major Benjamin Kraft.

He was now the proud owner of a small hotel at the Schossener Lake, which he managed together with his wife. It was going very well. He never regretted leaving the army, too much pressure and all that. He didn't last long there. After the second incident with the helicopter, he decided to leave the army once and for all. Although he was acquitted in court, he wasn't able to retrieve his pilot licence and was glad to leave the past behind. And now the phone call brought it all back. First when he answered and caught the sound of an unfamiliar female voice, he presumed it was a cold call. However, when the woman introduced herself as the daughter of David Hunt a cold shiver ran through his spine. It wasn't without reason. After all these years he still felt somehow accountable.

Not that he was at fault. Well, actually in one way he was, they all were, including Hunt. They purposefully lied about the incident, about the altitude. They all had known, it had been changed in his favour to spare him. But he was also aware that there had been more to it. There were rumours going around that the captain used the incident to destroy Hunt's career. Andrew didn't know any details. At the end of the day it was just gossip. And then Hunt all of a sudden dead, it just didn't add up. They all had been aphasic when they heard the tragic news of Hunt's suicide. Some days he puzzled over whether he could have impeded it. Yet he had chosen not to get involved and had stayed out of it.

Even when he was approached by Hunt – Andrew had been thrown off his guard – telling him something completely different about the lengths of their prohibition, Andrew kept reticent. When Hunt ended up dead, he was tempted to come forward to raise his suspicions. But he didn't. Conscious of the actuality that it was for the best not to mess around with the captain, he remained silent. There was not much he could have said anyway. A sound caught his ear. He glanced out the window and watched his wife clashing with empty beer bottles around the garden. She was tidying up the mess from the night before. He smirked. What a good wife she was. He went to the bathroom to relieve himself.

Why was Hunt's daughter calling out of the blue? After so many years! Funnily enough, the day after his annual get-together with his former comrades! Andrew shrugged his shoulders. He wasn't sure what to make of it? Why was she asking all these questions?

When Zoe first asked how long he had been prohibited from flying, he happily provided her with the answer. Twelve months he had been banned from flying. He had also explained that his licence automatically ceased to exist after twelve months and that he never bothered to do it again and left the army shortly after. Andrew was still happy to provide her with the answer when she asked about her father's prohibition and also that of his colleague Alex Feld. As far as he remembered it had been seven months for her father and four months for Alex Feld. Out of them, David had been the most experienced pilot. Therefore, he was held accountable for their actions and received three months more than Alex.

But when Zoe told him otherwise, that it was indeed sixteen months for her dad, he was taken aback. He had tried to drag out some more information, querying if someone in her family had told her so. Zoe on the other hand became abruptly reluctant. She began asking about documents, if he had kept any. Yes, he had. Nevertheless, finding it peculiar that she was asking now, decades later, he lied and told her otherwise. He also didn't want to stir up the past. He flushed the toilet, hurled a bathrobe over his shoulders and descended to the kitchen. Still thinking about it, he switched on the coffee machine and poured himself a glass of tap water. Perhaps he should have listened to David, when he was approached by him. Didn't he allude to sixteen months, too? He recalled the day when Hunt talked to him in the changing room.

Yet he struggled to summon up the conversation. Well, no surprise, it was more than twenty-five years ago. And it was too late now anyway. And if David's daughter wasn't obliging any particulars, why should he? In any case it was better to have a hands-off approach. Most likely it was just some misunderstanding. He was wide awake now. He filled his cup with coffee, grabbed the morning paper from the counter and ensconced himself on the kitchen chair. At least it was Monday. Mondays were the closing day of their restaurant. The few hotel guests they had were managed by his wife. It gave Andrew time to recover from his hangover. He tried to focus on his paper under his nose. It was in vain. His conscience was gnawing at him, it wouldn't go away. Anew he wondered, if he'd come forward all these years ago, maybe, just maybe Hunt would still be alive?

CHAPTER 45

The soldier sat behind the desk. He was currently on office duty, responsible for any incoming phone calls and the admin site at the barracks in Hanwau. It was only 10am, still a long day to go. Since he was bound to a chair, he kept a close eye at his watch. In his opinion a soldier should not be behind a desk, unless you were high up the ranks, which he was not. His own fault it was, stupid injury. Playing football with his son and as a result spraining his ankle could only occur to him. However, being on the mend, he felt optimistic that in the near future he would be able to return to his usual duties. Flinching at the fulminating sound of the phone, he rubbed his nose and grabbed the receiver. A young woman, he reckoned in her mid-twenties, was on the other line. She was asking for a file from 1983.

The barracks in Hanwau retained old files of any air traffic incidents or accidents within the last fifty years. It was the main archive for the North of Germany. Whilst he took the lady's details and the necessary facts, he was already having a whinge to himself that it would take forever having to go so far back. Twenty-five years seemed a long time. In order to root it out, he would have to rummage through the whole year. He promised to call back before midday and went to work. Speculating the reasons of the request, he climbed down to the basement which was once a bunker used for protection and weapons facilities. Nowadays it was used mainly as an archive. It was a large room with dozens of shelves containing files from every year. It wasn't common that people rang to ask for files from more than twenty years ago. Yet it wasn't his business, so he didn't ask why.

His ankle was still sore, and his limp became stronger as he reached the bottom of the stairs. Two doors down the corridor, he reached his destination. He didn't hesitate and went straight down to work. It was sorted by year. He began scrutinising the row comprising the occurrences from 1983. After sifting through the whole year without any findings, he repeated the process a couple of times. He eventually gave up. He raised his eyebrows. It was out of the ordinary. Regardless of the fact that many years had elapsed since the incident, the file should be right here in this room. Perhaps he had written down the wrong year? Or someone had misplaced the file? Scratching his left earlobe, he aimed for the rows containing the years close to 1983. Again he didn't find anything. Ultimately he ceded his endless search and headed back to his office.

Following his unsuccessful quest, he conducted some calls to local barracks in an aspiration to locate it somewhere else. All the trouble was for nothing. He was slowly developing doubts over the trueness of the story. Possibly it was a hoax? He immediately abandoned the thought. He was pretty sure it wasn't some kind of joke. The girl had sounded genuine. With blowing cheeks, he rang back and gave her the bad news. The crestfallen tone in her voice was enough proof to him that the incident had taken place. On that account he was unable to explain himself what had happened to the whereabouts of this particular file. Finding it inscrutable, the conversation stayed with him all day and he kept puzzling about it.

CHAPTER 46

I slumped down at the kitchen table. I felt frustrated. So far all my efforts had been for nothing. After being turned down by Andrew Mann and then the bad news that there was no trace of any file in the archive – I assumed Boll had taken everything – I contacted Alex Feld, the other pilot. With the help of Facebook ferreting out the other two pilots proved to be easier than expected. Feld gave me the same information that Mann had. Sadly neither of them had kept any documents. Scrolling through my dad's folder, I spotted that every single correspondence either from my dad or his solicitor reached first Boll or Major Kraft, before being remitted to the relevant department. Perhaps it was procedure within the armed forces.

And there was something else that bothered me. I replayed the conversation with Lucy in my head. Didn't she mention the court date in October? I turned the pages until I found the court warnings. My dad had been warned to court to appear as a witness against the person responsible, Andrew Mann, for the end of July. He received this notification four weeks prior to the court date. But then two weeks before the trial he received a new one, an adjournment of the trial for October. That was strange. Usually court dates only get adjourned if one party, either the crown prosecution service or the defence, applies for additional time. In most cases it was done to finding some further evidence or just to gain some more time. Potentially it had something to do with my dad's complaint to the commissioner?

Thinking of the complaint commissioner, I brought to mind to check if I had any reply yet. The other day I had sent an email to determine if they had anything left from my dad's complaint. Bringing up my emails, I saw an unread message sitting in my inbox. It was in fact a response from them. With a modicum of hope I perused the email. Sadly I wasted my time. I was notified that they kept files only up to ten years. Therefore any documents related to my dad's complaint, if it ever reached them, had ceased to exist. When scanning through the last paragraph, I halted.

"What on earth…?" I shouted out loudly. I didn't finish the sentence, as I didn't want to wake up my mum, who was asleep next door. I straightened up, stunned by what I saw.

They had managed to retrieve one document that was sent to the military department for cases of death in Mitzen. It was sent on 29th of July 1983, the same day my dad was found shot in his flat. It was an alphabetic telegraph from the Light Aircraft Group, in which my dad was described as withdrawn, reserved, isolated and inconspicuous. His suicide was explained on the grounds of private and financial problems. Again, due to the time lapse, they were unable to establish how the armed forces came to this conclusion. Fuming at the sight of the last paragraph, my veins began to throb. I found it very questionable that the same day my dad was discovered dead in his flat, a message was sent to the parliamentary commissioner, constituting the reasons for his suicide as only private.

Not even one word was mentioned about the problems he had after the helicopter incident. Someone clearly had reacted hotfoot to notify the responsible authority. Didn't it usually take some sort of investigation? Only one person came to my mind. And that was my dad's former captain, Max Boll! Most likely he had feared some kind of investigation into the death of my father. And therefore decided to take the matter into his hands by explaining the suicide was caused by private problems. I began to marvel about the letter my grandma had sent on behalf of my dad. The one in which he blamed him. I assumed it ended up in the wrong hands, possibly never reached its destination. There was actually one more person I was desperate to speak to. Benjamin Kraft, my dad's former major and Boll's former superior and best friend according to Boll.

Yet I had low expectations of learning anything new. I was certain that by now he was fully aware of me snooping in the past. I opened my notebook, sifting through my notes. Hold on… I stopped at the bullet point, Boll's ex-wife. Of course, I had totally forgotten about her. For all I knew, she could be the key to everything. I began browsing online for a contact number. I didn't want to miss the chance that she could bring some light to the end of the tunnel. I was convinced that they crossed paths when my dad installed the sauna for them. It didn't take me long to dig up a phone number for her. She still went by her married name and lived in Mitzen. Five minutes later with the phone pressed against my ear, I peevishly moved my bottom from one side to the other. "May I speak to Mrs Boll, please?" I asked.

"Speaking, how can I help?" A cold female voice answered.

I gasped for air. I revealed my name and queried if she was indeed the ex-wife of Max Boll.

Her contemptuous affirmation, stayed with me for hours. Although she sounded very sceptical, I felt positive to solve a piece of my jigsaw. "Well, you might be surprised by my call. Your ex-husband was the captain of my father, David Hunt. He passed away in 1983. I was wondering if you know anything about that. According to my knowledge, my dad installed the sauna in your house. Therefore I thought you might have met him at some point. I understand you may wonder why I am ringing. It's difficult to explain, but..." I stuttered when I was suddenly interrupted.

"I have no contact with my ex-husband at all. He can rot in hell. And I've never heard of a man called David Hunt. Don't call again."

The sound of a click and she hung up. Just like that! As I was at my wit's end after such an awful conversation, out of the blue a crazy idea popped up in my head. The press! I felt all of a sudden very excited. I would go to the paper. I was pretty sure they would be interested in my folder.

CHAPTER 47

Diane Boll put her mobile phone down. The call had been redirected from her home phone to her mobile. Sat in front of some figures at her place of work — she was an adviser for a large insurance company in Mitzen — she felt thrown off the track. Of course she had known David Hunt. She remembered him very well. He had been the reason for their nasty divorce. Not that it had been his fault, not at all. Just the thought of her ex-husband made her feel sick. She despised him. David had been a very interesting, handsome man. But she also recalled his reputation as a womaniser. One of the reasons she didn't bite, when he started flirting with her. Her husband had told her that he was known to be a bit of a philanderer. Or should she say, warned her? Not that she had ever given her husband a reason to be jealous.

However, it didn't escape her husband that she felt attracted to David. And somehow she had this inevitable feeling that her husband had been envious of David. Not so much to her surprise. Compared to

David her husband was pug-ugly. Crinkling her nose, she asked herself more often these days how on earth she had once found him attractive. The time when David fitted the sauna in their house returned to her mind. He had started flirting with her, she felt flattered. But that was all. She had never begun an affair with him. Yet her husband had accused her of it. At the end they got divorced. That wasn't the only reason though, it just added to a nastier one. After ten years of marriage, filled with bitterness and the only reason it lasted so long being for the sake of their daughter, she at last managed to ditch him.

Her husband's delicate businesses played a major factor too. In her eyes her ex was a dodgy man, not trustworthy at all. She knew he was doing things he shouldn't do. When she decided that she did not want to spend the rest of her life with this man, he had accused her of leaving him for another man. With a hint he had referred to David. She had asserted that this was not the case. At some point she just gave up and they stopped talking to each other. When she heard a few months later that David had killed himself, she wasn't sure what to think of it. She had heard about the helicopter incident that occurred months before David's death and that he was somehow involved in it. She had also read something in the local paper.

The time that followed after the helicopter incident, her ex-husband, at this time still husband, had acted very strangely. And then she had overheard the comment, 'We need to sort him out.' Her husband had made this remark to his best friend Benjamin Kraft. At this time she had not known what he was referring to. Afterwards Diane had asked herself if it had anything to do with David as his name was mentioned throughout the conversation. Yet she had no idea what they were talking about. Still, her gut told her something was wrong. Not long after David's death they got divorced. She never remarried.

"Are you all right?" The sudden voice of her colleague from across the room, made her jump. She must have looked like a ghost when she answered her call.

"Yes, don't worry. Everything is fine. I just need some fresh air." Diane had no intention of revealing any details of her chat to her nosy colleague. She excused herself, stood up and headed outside. She walked to a bench in front of the glass building and settled on it. The scent of autumn lingered in the air. Her shoulder-length dark blonde hair whiffed into her face, as she was struck by a strong blow of the wind. First when she heard about David's death, she thought her husband had his fingers in the pie. Then when she learned that it was suicide, she discarded the preposterous notion. Still, a nagging feeling stayed with her all along. However, she chose not to involve herself, in fear for her ex.

And it shouldn't be any different now. One of the reasons she had reacted the way she did, on the phone to David's daughter. When Zoe introduced herself, of course she had known who she was. She remembered Zoe as a little girl. David once brought her with him. She recalled Zoe as a cute little girl. However, it didn't change anything. The best she could do right now was to ignore Zoe, to deny any knowledge of her dad or anything else. In the past she didn't want to get involved and she still felt this way. She preferred not to have anything to do with her ex and hoped not to see him ever again. She commiserated with Zoe, yet she had to think of what was best for her. Diane sprang to her feet and returned to her figures.

CHAPTER 48

Max Boll was on his way home from a business meeting in Hanwau. It had been a long day and he hoped traffic wouldn't make it any longer. First the screen of his mobile phone began to flash. Then the sound of short interval rings. "What now?" he grumbled to himself and rolled his eyes. He suspected his wife, boring him either with the latest news of some gossip around the neighbourhood, or some groceries she had forgotten to buy. He picked up his phone from the passenger seat and glanced at the caller's ID. Instead of home, Benjamin Kraft's mobile number beamed on his screen. Boll didn't have a Bluetooth hands-free car kit. Despite the fact that he was a business man and constantly on the road, he was certainly not a fan of all this new technology. His friend had to wait now. Boll would call him the minute he arrived home. He discarded it in one of the storage compartments of his centre console.

"Idiot," he blustered, when another road user pulled suddenly out from a by-road placing the posterior of his vehicle right in front of Boll. He managed to brake just in time. The sound of his mobile phone came to life again. He peered at it, to catch sight of the same caller ID. Perhaps it was urgent? Curiosity took over. He wasn't keen to get caught red handed with a phone behind the wheel. Boll manoeuvred his car to a parking bay, placed the gear in neutral and pulled his handbrake. He proceeded to take hold of his phone, when it rang again. He pressed the green button and was swamped by his friend's firm voice.

"You won't believe it!" he snarled. "She went to the press. A newspaper article came out this morning. Fortunately only in the local paper, but it's still too much. It's one of my worst days ever, Max, and your entire fault." Kraft was breathing heavily.

"Hang on a second! What are you talking about?" Boll interrupted.

"The girl, David Hunt's daughter! What is she called again? Well, it doesn't matter. It's a disaster."

"Calm down, Benjamin. It can't be that bad," Boll reasoned, but was he fooling himself?

"You with your sloppiness!" Kraft scolded. "You have to stop her right now with this bullshit."

"For God's sake, calm down, Benjamin!" Boll, now yelling too, was fuming inside. Droplets of sweat were building up on his forehead. *Fucking bitch*, he thought. "I'll get it sorted. What does it say?" Boll asked, exasperated.

"'In search for the truth', the title says…" Kraft scoffed. "The story says something about a folder she came across that once belonged to her father, and the discrepancies she had discovered after speaking to former colleagues, meaning you, you jerk." Another agitated sound escaped from Kraft's lips.

"It also refers to the alteration to the altitude made after the incident. It raises the question if it was the fault of the army or personal reasons that pushed David Hunt into his death. Best you read it yourself. Where are you now?" Kraft demanded. "I think we should meet up sooner rather than later. We'll have to get this sorted before it escalates."

Kraft had simmered down again. Boll was glad for it. He didn't blame Kraft for being mad. It was clearly his fault. He wished he could turn back the time. Why did he really believe the folder drowned in the lake? He should have searched better. Consistently he had sensed that there was still something out there, which could jeopardise their existence. He should have known it after Zoe's phone call.

"I am on my way home. Give me an hour. I call you as soon as I get in." Boll ended the conversation. Seething with rage, he began to hit the steering wheel with his bare hand again and again. He stopped when the pain became unbearable. He began shaking his hand to ease the pain. She was like her dad. This girl needed sorting out. He hit the road and slammed his foot on the accelerator, ignoring any speed limits. He was now in a real rush to get home.

Contemporaneously he considered his options. He had to be careful. Certainly he couldn't risk raising suspicion. After all, he had no idea who was in the know. And worst of all it was in the paper. He may have to pay the local branch a further visit.

CHAPTER 49

Forty minutes later Boll arrived in Bueckenau. He stopped at the local newsagent and purchased the today's paper. Instead of going straight home, he headed for his favourite café. No way could he cope right now with his wife's babbling. She was a chatterbox and never stopped. Fortunately she hadn't seen the paper yet, otherwise he would have known about it. He entered the café, which went by the name 'Melan' and was situated around the corner from the newsagent. He settled for the alcove. The waitress approached his table and took his order. He opted for a black tea. He paused until the waitress returned with his tea. He paid for it and as the waitress vanished behind the counter, he slowly unrolled the newspaper.

Thank God the report wasn't on the front page. Instead it was on page eleven. With a gasp of relief, he strongly hoped that it wouldn't catch the attention of the whole region. A bunch of boisterous teenagers entered the café and ordered some ice creams. Boll gaped at them impatiently. He forced his eyes to concentrate on the story, but the chatter and giggle disconcerted him. He gave them some dirty looks. The youths on the other hand just shrugged it off. Eventually ten minutes later, each with an ice cream in their hands, they decamped from the café. Shifting in his chair and with twisted lips, he focused on the story.

In search for the truth,

Twenty-five years have gone by and Zoe has no memories of her late father. She was still a young child, when her father committed suicide. But then not long ago, Zoe discovered a folder that once belonged to her father. The folder contains some correspondence of an incident within the armed forces. Since then, Zoe has been searching for the truth. It raises the question of whether private problems or the procedures within the armed forces pushed the soldier and helicopter pilot into his death. With the help of the folder, Zoe is trying to get closer to a dad she had never known.

Back in the early eighties, 20th of February 1983: Three helicopters, after a day of practice, on their way back to the base of Bueckenau. David Hunt, the most experienced one of all three, is leading. All three of them are flying below the flight mission. Then suddenly Hunt receives a transmission via airwave. It's one of his colleagues, informing him that he flew into a power supply line and has to commence an emergency landing. Hunt and the other pilot are landing next to him. Fortunately the helicopter sustained only minor damage and is still fully compatible to be flown again. And this is where it all began. The pilots make a fatal mistake. Instead of reporting the incident there and then, which is compulsory in the armed forces, all three of them fly back to the base.

The responsible pilot doesn't report it immediately. It was the second time for him; the first time he collided with a telegraph line, hence he feared the consequences. Hunt and the other pilot support his decision. Although it was not Hunt who caused the incident and neither was he in charge during the flight, still, because of misunderstood camaraderie and possibly put under pressure by his superiors, Hunt takes full responsibility. Furthermore, the senior air traffic officer that day is forthcoming. He changes the altitude in favour of the responsible pilot after the event. The instructions are changed from a minimum of 400 feet to a minimum of 150 feet.

Running his hands apprehensively through his hair, Boll grunted. He was well aware that they referred to him as the senior air traffic officer. His eyes darted back to the newspaper.

Hunt doesn't object. Not until he becomes suspicious. By then it is too late. He attempts to disclose the truth to his superiors, yet they ignore him. The pilot quickly realises that he is being bullied. He has been made responsible for the whole incident. And then the rules and regulations within the armed forces meet Hunt at full tilt. His pilot licence will be revoked for a period of sixteen months and they withdraw his flight allowance. Not only this, also his career within the armed forces comes to an end. His major confirms, Hunt is unable to fulfil the tasks that is expected of him and therefore recommends his dismissal from his career path as an officer.

After the incident the soldier faces tough times. He is plagued with personal problems too, the separation from his wife and a break-up with his current partner. The loss of his flight allowance causes him to take a further loan and his debts are increasing. And then on 29th of July 1983 Hunt is found dead with a gunshot wound to his head. In a suicide note he writes, 'I have no other choice. Please forgive me!' After 25 years the daughter is searching for answers. As children, when she or her brother asked, the family explained his suicide was provoked by the repercussions of the incident. His tragic death was rarely brought up within the family. The army declared Hunt's suicide caused by private and financial problems. Not one word was mentioned of his problems within the armed forces.

Zoe Hunt is convinced she still doesn't know all the answers. She is searching for more information, particularly the last few months before her father's death. The folder and information she has gathered from former colleagues are different and incomplete. One document shows even only seven months' flight prohibition. It raises the question, is there more to it than meets the eye? Zoe is certain that she doesn't know the whole truth. Hence, she is asking the public for help. If you have any information, please contact the newspaper.

Written by Ralph Stark.

Boll felt speechless. What on earth was Hunt's daughter doing here? When he saw her leaving the newspaper branch the other day, he sensed she was up to no good. He should have stopped her right away. Boll jumped up, raging. His chair squeaked as he arose and other guests turned their head. He couldn't care less. Patchy red blotches appeared on his cheeks. With a frowning face and the newspaper under his arm, he stamped off. He contemplated heading straight to the local branch. "Don't be stupid," he mumbled and stopped. He would make a fool of himself, probably even cause more suspicion. He needed to get a clear head before he challenged the paper. He fished his phone out of his pocket and dialled the familiar number. Benjamin Kraft picked up immediately. "I am back in Bueckenau. I just read it, it's shocking."

CHAPTER 50

Ralph Stark lingered in his office. He was engaged with a report for the new purification plant coming to town. Quite a boring task, he yawned. Not like the story he wrote the other day about the daughter, in search for the truth. In his late twenties and driven with ambition, he was still awaiting the jump in his career. It was a childhood dream to become a reporter. After he graduated from university and found a position at the local newspaper his wishes finally came true. First he was very pleased, then after a while it felt monotonous. He was consistently publishing the same things. Bueckenau and his region were quite a small area. Not much was happening here. Yet he wasn't ready to move to the big city. He was quite a family orientated person and his friend were from around here too.

So when Zoe Hunt walked in and outlined her story, he finally thought that would be the key for his future. However, today, for no reason he was in a bad mood. He wasn't sure if it was the miserable weather —

it had started raining again – or something else. The day when the girl came into his office, explaining her request and leaving a copy of the folder in his office including the suicide notes and death report, he thought it would be a brilliant story. Right now he began to doubt it. He was beset by a foreboding. His boss, who had acknowledged the report, had mentioned the possibility of sparking trouble with the armed forces. However, Stark was a journalist, it was part of his job, stirring things up. Yet he was possessed with the odd feeling that this one would go wrong.

He reviewed his emails once more. The report had been published last night. Three former colleagues had responded so far. He forwarded their contact details to the daughter. He still hoped for further replies. Perhaps for somebody to step forward to give him more to write. Unfortunately the area they covered was small, therefore the chances were low. After studying the folder and the other bits, he tried to put himself into the young soldier's shoes. He tried to visualise the thoughts the soldier must have had when he put the gun to his head, knowing that he would leave two young children behind. The soldier had been only twenty-eight with his whole life in front of him. Stark could only imagine in what kind of distress the soldier must have been in.

Suddenly his thoughts were interrupted by raised voices in the corridor. One of them belonged to his boss, the director for the paper. The disgruntled tone was impossible to miss. All at once the handle to Stark's door was pushed down and the director rushed into his office.

"I've never liked this guy," he bellowed. "Even

though I've never met him until today, now I understand why nobody likes him. What an awful person he is." A big wheeze escaped from the director's lips. He stood against the door jamb with his elbow leaning on it.

"About whom are you talking?" Stark looked up with narrowed eyes.

"Max Boll, respectful business man in the community, what a joke!" His boss sneered, entered the room and began to pace up and down with clenched fists. "It's about the pilot. He stormed into my office like a madman and threatened me. Can you believe that? He accused us of false allegations and warned that if we don't stop right now it would have serious consequences. Not just for the paper but also for me. He made direct threats towards me personally. Apparently he still has some influence within the armed forces."

He froze beside Stark, who was sat in his swivel chair. The director placed a hand on his shoulder and glanced down at Stark. He had regained his composure and sounded more relaxed. "I am sorry. I understand you have put lots of time into this and bonded with the girl and her fate and all. I am also aware of your expectations of this to become a big story and your hopes to write more. But unfortunately we can't pass any messages to the girl anymore. And please, no further stories about this!"

Stark's face dropped and he leaped to his feet. The director's hand fell off his shoulder. Stark took a step back and turned to face his boss. Crestfallen, he objected.

"You aren't serious. Are you? What's Boll going to do? He has long since left the army and he is somehow responsible for this soldier's death. I am sure of this." Stark stamped with his feet against the laminate floor. His boss now frowned at him.

"Listen, if you want to keep your job, just do as I say. I know for a fact, that it's better not to mess around with this man. And if he was telling the truth and indeed still has contacts within the armed forces then this could cause serious damage to the paper. Don't you think a man like him could easily destroy our reputation?"

Stark scowled at his boss. He didn't know what to say. He was boiling. He plunged back into his chair and sank his gaze to the report he had worked on without taking it in. Yes, he had a big story in mind. But he also wanted to help the girl, find answers to the death of her father. He began to sympathise with her and was hoping to find justice. Stark held onto the armrests in frustration. Perhaps he should move on and write for a different paper, for one he was allowed to write stories like this. He looked up to the director who had moved in front of his desk with his arms folded against his chest whilst displaying his thumbs.

"So what do you want me to say to Zoe Hunt?" Stark queried with a challenging undertone.

"Listen, I know you are disappointed. But we are not some cheap paper. We are a serious one. You know I hold you in high esteem. You are one of my best reporters. But you need to let this go!" His boss gave him an encouraging smile and moved towards the door. "You could tell Miss Hunt, there were no further replies. I am sure she will stop asking after a while. And if she intends to go to another paper, then that's not our problem. But we can't risk it. We are a serious distinguished paper. I am not losing my job because of whatever happened to that soldier all these years ago. Understood?" His boss, already halfway out of the door, waited for an acknowledgement.

Stark had no other choice as to give in. "Yes," he replied with a pout. His boss, satisfied that Stark was finally seeing reason, exited the room. Stark gritted his teeth and pressed his clenched fists against his cheeks. He was still furious. His anger was not towards his boss though. He was getting along with him. It wasn't the director's fault. And he had to admit, if he was in the position of his boss, he wouldn't have reacted any differently. At the end of the day, as a director of a serious paper, his boss had no other option. So he would do as he was told. There was no alternative if he didn't want to risk his job. Still, his enragement was towards the inequity of power.

CHAPTER 51

He stopped at the site for private airplanes. It was part of the Lynden Pindling International airport of the Bahamas, about 13km from Nassau. The weather forecast on the radio announced some upcoming thunderstorms in the afternoon. Angry clouds already swept over him, another reason to quickly knuckle down to work. Big plans for the weekend were lying ahead of him. He had arranged this short trip with his family to the Westside National Park many days ago. And right now he was on the way to prepare his private jet for tomorrow's departure. It was a surprise for his family. He intended to make up for his mood swings recently. The last few days had been very stressful. He currently was engaged in a big project overseas for an entertainment centre in the centre of Santa Monica, California.

Yet the reason for his mood swings lay somewhere else. It was the call he had received the other day that worried him. He hadn't received any further calls since then. Hopefully it was a good sign. The heat struck his face as he began to set up his plane. The hotness didn't bother him anymore. He had long since gotten used to it. First when he arrived all these years ago, he had struggled with the sultriness. However, like any other human body, he became resistant to it. The engine noise from the big planes next door droned in his ears. He covered his ears with his ear protector. An hour later he was glad to turn his back to it. On his ride home – he resided with his family in the suburban of Nassau – he admired a freshly painted house. It was a new addition to the artistry of the colourful houses that stretched along his way.

Fifteen minutes later he turned into his driveway, surprised to see his wife's car in front of their double garage. Wasn't she supposed to be at work? She had her own business, a clothing shop in the centre of Nassau. And although she had two employees, she almost never took any time off. He sometimes wondered if his wife didn't trust her staff. He positioned his vehicle behind her Beetle and scudded worryingly inside. Their house was a modern, medium-sized mansion with two floors protected by a cream-coloured stone gate and a black fence. The curvy glass ground floor walls blended in with the surrounding hills. A flat roof with a sun terrace on top completed the picture. The garden overlooked the ocean with a large swimming pool to one side. The complex was his design. He had done well over the years and it showed in his lifestyle.

He took off his shoes and put on his slippers. "Why are you home so early, sweetheart?" he called. His wife emerged from their modern kitchen.

"I took the afternoon off to sort out a few things. How was your day?"

He was taken aback by the hint of sarcasm clearly lying in her undertone. What had bitten her? He chose to ignore it. He trusted whatever it was that bugged his wife, his impending surprise would make up for it. "Good, the project is going well so far. The time I have spent on it is paying off. I've got a surprise for you guys tomorrow. So don't make any plans for the weekend." He winked and smirked at his wife. "I am not willing to tell you though, so don't ask. Just pack a few clothes for all of us. We will be leaving very early in the morning. I am sure the boy will love it."

With a big smile on his face, he turned towards the floating staircase. It was made out of wood in a long curvy style. The cold tone of his wife made him stop dead in his tracks. "Great," she hissed at him. He decided not to let it go this time. Something definitely was wrong. He had to know. Perhaps it had something to do with their son?

"What's the matter, honey?" he asked, concerned.

"Well," she jeered, "perhaps I should ask you if there is something wrong. Is there anything you might want to tell me?" She bored her gaze into her husband's eyes. He hated it when she looked at him like this. He knew she was trying to read his face. He didn't like that. He had no idea what she was talking about. He wasn't aware of any wrongdoing. He stared at their newly laid carpet in the hallway, playing with his toes against the smoothness of the surface. And then the truth dawned upon him.

He all of a sudden felt awkward. He looked at his wife, unassertive. The first thing that came to his mind was that someone had told her. But then he waved the thought away. How could she ever possibly know? No one knew, except for one person, or should he say two. Unless they wished to jeopardise their lives, they would never talk. Assuring himself that probably something else bothered her, he shook his head.

"Maybe you should take someone else on your trip instead of your own family?" His wife said sarcastically.

He yanked his head backwards. He had no idea what she was referring to. She looked at him like he was cheating on her. He wasn't. He wouldn't even dream of it.

"I don't know what you are on about. Just tell me!" he demanded with one foot on the step and a demanding tone in his voice.

His wife met his troubled gaze with a chilling stare. A dash of disappointment was visible on her face. She had never looked at him like this before. His eyes averted from her gaze down to her hand. He spotted an unsealed envelope.

"Just look for yourself!" She furiously squeezed the envelope against his chest. "I didn't mean to open it. It thought it was for me. Too late I realised it was addressed to you. Anyway, I am glad I opened it. Now I know what's going on? How could I be so blind?" Tears streamed down her cheeks and her lower lip began to tremble.

He was about to take his wife into his arms, to reassure her that everything was all right. But it would be wrong. He knew exactly nothing was OK.

Even without seeing the contents of the envelope, he realised their life was falling to pieces. Whatever it was, he assumed it had something to do with his past. After all these years it all of a sudden was haunting him. He grabbed the envelope from her hand. His face was unreadable. All the excitement about their trip was gone. His wife returned quietly and disenthralled to the kitchen. He went into his study and flopped onto his precious rocking chair. The neat writing displaying his name and address was unfamiliar to him. He felt deluged with uneasiness. He slowly removed the contents of the envelope. The first item that fell into his lap was a folded clip from a newspaper article. What was that? He lifted it up with raised eyebrows. He unfurled it and the face struck his face.

Taken aback and nearly falling off his chair, he recognised the girl instantly. The resemblance was clear. But seeing who the sender was, felt even worse.

CHAPTER 52

Mirco found the house straight away. He scanned the neighbourhood to familiarise himself with his surroundings. His employer had paid him more than adequately, a reason not to mess it up. He was still very young, only in his mid-twenties. Yet he was well acquainted with the business as he had been undertaking it for years. Taught by his old man, he learned to rejoice in it. Today should be an easy job. He had done far worse ones. Still, the area was too quiet for him. Apprehensive to draw attention to himself, he took cover behind a newspaper as he reclined in the driver's seat of his Mondeo. It was one of the nicer parts of Brielen. A nearby park was within walking distance and the estate mainly consisted of one-family dwellings.

The house he was supposed to watch was a block of flats. It stood out slightly between the one-family houses. Still, it looked pretentious compared to the one he resided at. It had the structure of a Bavarian home, painted all in white, with brown balconies, some of them shrouded by washing, others decorated with plants. Uninterested in the newspaper, he leered from behind the page at an attractive young woman with a miniskirt and stilettos balancing past his vehicle. He managed to suppress a wolf whistle, reminding himself to be careful. Under no circumstances could he afford to spoil it. Just the thought of his employer somehow gave him the shivers. He was quite a cunning individual, a man who wouldn't get his hands dirty.

His name was Max Boll and apparently he was some kind of well-known figure in the better world. But then all of his employers were in some way dodgy. In this kind of business you just had to be permanently on your guard. Boll was known to pay well, that was the only thing that mattered. Merely the money counted for Mirco. And if anybody was getting in his way, then perhaps this particular person had to suffer. Still, he had promised Boll to complete the job without calling too much attention. Not to mention avoid leaving any blood trail. He would certainly try his best. He couldn't promise that, of course, and his employer was aware of it. This kind of work was unpredictable. Occasionally you had to adjust to situations, if any unexpected surprises bobbed up.

To his advantage it started drizzling. Hopefully it kept pedestrians inside their houses and off the balconies. It would make it easier for Mirco to complete his assignment. His objective was the ground-floor flat on the right. Surveying it from a distance, his view to the flat was magnificent. He reached out for his binoculars resting on the passenger seat. A quick glance around and he swiftly placed them on his eyes to catch a glimpse from the interior. As he had anticipated, a figure close to the front window confirmed that the occupant was at home. It was a waiting game for Mirco now. He wasn't in a rush, yet he wasn't a very patient person. Fortunately he was squeezed in between some vehicles half on the kerb. It allowed him to keep a low profile and to remain undetected by any residents.

Mirco's patience was stretched nearly to the uttermost, when finally after more than an hour the sound of a front door was audible. A woman in her fifties emerged from the targeted flat. Mirco sighed with relief. He licked his lips and adrenaline shot through his blood. He excitedly eyed his prey when she made an appearance. The woman, who was quite small and petite, walked past his vehicle without even glancing at him. He noticed a sad expression on her face. Mirco began studying once more the photograph he had pinned against the steering wheel, to verify she was the right one. He looked up. The lady in question was now roughly ten feet away from his vehicle, her back turned to him. Still, he had seen enough. He was indeed satisfied with his findings. She was definitely the right woman, Emily Hunt, his target for today.

CHAPTER 53

Mirco observed Emily Hunt from his rear-view mirror. She was rushing to the bus stop that was approximately 100 yards from her flat. The bus was already approaching. When the driver spotted Emily, he halted. Within seconds Emily disappeared from the scene. Mirco surmised Emily was on her way to work to commence her evening shift at the hotel, which was on the other side of Brielen. It would chime with her daily routine. His employer had briefed him in details. According to Max Boll, Emily used to live alone, however, her daughter Zoe had recently moved in. He took a hurried look around, to check the daughter's car was not in the vicinity. The sound of his mobile phone made him cringe. He squinted at the screen, which prompted him to roll his eyes. It was Boll, most likely desperate for an update. He answered the call and after less than a minute he managed to put his employer's mind at rest that he was about to set to work.

It was mid-August and still daylight. Because of

the neighbours he decided to wait a bit longer. Just minutes ago he had noticed an elderly woman from the same building stood behind the blinds, watching his target leaving her flat. Mirco assumed they all knew each other in one way or the other. He wasn't an amateur. He had done this many times before. He even considered himself a pro when it came to breaking into premises. Usually he preyed on big houses and villas, the dwellings of rich people. He had never been caught, touch wood. Anticipating that it would take another hour before the twilight set in, he turned his key in the ignition and the engine began to roar. To kill time, he set his car in motion to take it for a drive.

Two hours later Mirco navigated his Mondeo back to the estate. Before turning into Emily's road he came to a halt. To be on the safe side, he parked his vehicle at the top of the street across from the bus stop. Half of his face concealed with a baseball cap, he ambled towards the Bavarian house. It was still raining. It had long since changed from a drizzle to something far heavier, keeping people off the street. He had established beforehand that there was no CCTV in the area. And with no pedestrians in his immediate vicinity, he called it a lucky day. He stepped in front of the building and moved his finger towards the buzzer displaying 'Hunt'. Although all the lights were off and the daughter's car was still nowhere to be seen, Mirco had to be sure that no one was home. His prayers were answered and he began to move fast.

The flat was on the ground floor. He sneaked to the back of the house and advanced to the rear window. The top part of the window was left ajar. It made his job so much easier. He assumed the crime rate in this area was very low, one of the reasons people became careless. For anybody else it may have been difficult to open the window, but not for Mirco. He had a very easy technique. He dug out a wire from one of his pockets and swiftly shaped it into a hook. He scooped the length through the gap of the window and connected with the handle. He twisted the hook at the right angle and budged the handle down by pulling at the wire towards his body. The handle moved to a horizontal position.

Still to unbolt the window, Mirco had to fiddle a bit more to get it into a vertical position. He pulled at it once more without any reaction. He flashed his torch towards the inside of the window to face his problem. The wire was entangled with a loose screw. A curse escaped him and he held his breath as he tried once more. This time the handle gave in and the silence was interrupted by the sound of a snap. Mirco squeezed against the glass and the window stretched to the inside. His pupils darted once more around him. Except for some light in one of the top-floor windows on the house next door with nobody in view, the estate appeared to be extinct. With a quick move he vanished to the inside.

As he found himself stood in Emily's bedroom, he nearly tripped over the bed whilst his eyes adjusted to the dark. Conscious of the possibility that some nosy neighbour may have seen him, Mirco was on high alert to move fast. He kept the lights turned off, to avoid any unnecessary attention. Only with the beam of his torch, he began his hunt. A cursory search of the whole flat gave him a rough idea of the layout.

The flat was quite compact with a large and a smaller bedroom and a combined dining and living room. The kitchen was not much bigger than a box room. Even with only the beam of his torch, Mirco had to admit that the woman had taste. The flat was furnished with some antique reproduction furniture that presented a warm atmosphere.

He first started off in the combined room. As he flashed across the room for any drawers and cupboards, Mirco caught sight of a 100-euro note abandoned on the dining table. His hand reached out only to be stopped by his other one. He remembered the words of his employer. Boll had inculcated to him several times, that whatever he found, he was meant to focus only on the folder. His break-in was also supposed to be some kind of warning for the daughter, to stop her from messing around with his employer. And taking the money would make it look like an ordinary burglary and all the warning would be out of the window. In another situation he wouldn't care. But in this case, he didn't want to disappoint his employer. He knew there was the possibility Boll would find out.

Mirco ignored the money and focused on his task ahead of him. He had no idea why his employer was so mad for this folder. Boll had characterised the folder to him as a bunch of documents from 1983, mainly from the armed forces. And if Mirco rooted up some loose pages from that year, he was expected to bring them along. But with no sign of any folder or any other documentation, the search in the living room turned out to be for nothing. After a quick rummage through the kitchen that could only be reached through the dining area, Mirco proceeded to the hallway. His attention was immediately drawn to an antique desk. Pulling out the drawers consecutively, his quest in there was also in vain. He returned to the bedrooms and after turning them upside down, he finally gave in.

Convinced that he had not missed anything, Mirco was cocksure the folder was kept somewhere else. He glanced at his wristwatch. Nearly two hours had gone by since he broke into the flat. Time to disappear before Emily or the daughter returned home. By now the flat was in a state of chaos, as desired by his employer. All at once he felt the urgent need to take a leak before making his exit. As he emptied his bladder in the toilet and pondered how to deliver the bad news to his employer, the sudden jingle of a key from outside made him jump. He shook his head in disbelief.

Pretty sure they were heading his way, he rapidly felt for his gun in his pocket. Within seconds somebody inserted the key into the lock and opened the door.

CHAPTER 54

After a long day out and about I was on my way back home. Having spent part of my day with a graphologist comparing the suicide letters with some other handwritten letters from my dad, I was anxious for the outcome. Since I saw the incorrect spelling of my name, I was sceptical that my dad was the person who wrote them. Sally was the one who came up with the idea. The fun had cost me 300 euros and I was told to come back in two days. I was certain it was worth the effort.

As I turned into my road, it had gone past ten at night; I saw a police car parked up in front of the house. At first I didn't think much of it. I assumed it had come for one of our neighbours. Not that the police turned up here on a regular basis. No, not at all! It was a quiet area with rarely any issues.

I drove into my usual spot and found myself staring at the illumination inside of our flat. Every single light was switched on. My mum wasn't supposed to be home yet. And I was certain my mum had turned them off before leaving for work. She always did. I felt slightly irritated. Perhaps my mum had an early dart after a quiet night at the hotel? I alighted from my Golf and locked it. As I was proceeding towards the house, the sudden flash of blue lights filling up the street made me jerk to a halt. I looked back to spot an ambulance heading towards me. It stopped within spitting distance of my vehicle. Two paramedics jumped out and scurried towards me. I gaped at them dubiously.

"We are here for a Mrs Hunt. Does she live here?" The chubbier one asked.

My heart began to drop and I was deluged with terror. In a split second I was picturing the worst scenarios in my head. I managed to get some words together and stuttered, "It's my mum, what happened?"

"Dunno." The slimmer one shrugged with his shoulders. "We just got a call from the police to rush. I think your mum was attacked."

My vision became blurry and my head was throbbing with pain. It was one of the moments when you see the world in front of you collapse. I just looked at the paramedic blankly, like someone who was slow off the mark. Within seconds I was back down to earth and ran towards the house like a lunatic. I grazed my arms on some thorns from the bushes as I stumbled along the path leading to the entrance. I heard the paramedics close on my heels and assumed them to be shaking their heads by now. I couldn't care less. In this moment the only thing that mattered was my mum. Bad thoughts were rushing through my mind. Was she still alive? Was she hurt?

What happened?

I reached the front of the house to find the communal entrance wide open. The door to my mum's ground-floor flat to the right was ajar. I pushed open the door and stormed into the flat when a policeman in the hallway blocked my way. "Who are you?" he asked. I stopped short of breath. I was on the edge of hysteria.

"I live here with my mum. Don't tell me something has happened to her. Where is she?" I fidgeted with my hands wildly in the air and hopped on my feet to cast a glance over his shoulders.

"Are you Zoe?" He still didn't move.

"Yes I am. Where is my mum? Is she OK?" I wailed as I was running out of patience. I felt tears welling up in my eyes.

"She is fine, just a bit shaken up. A burglary has occurred at your flat. We ordered an ambulance as precaution." He pointed behind me, indicating to the two paramedics who now stood behind me.

I began to relax when I recognised my mum's voice from her bedroom door. It took a load off my mind. She was gabbing away and as I looked past the police officer I caught sight of a police woman in the bedroom. "Can I go in?" I asked him, pointing towards them.

"Yes, but make sure you don't touch anything. We are still waiting for the crime scene investigators." My mouth dropped wide open as I let my gaze wander across the hallway. Drawers from my mum's antique desk were pulled out and various papers such as bills, insurance documents and other bits lay scattered everywhere on the floor. I advanced to the lounge to find the same in there. I assumed the whole flat to be in a jumble.

I made my way to the bedroom. My mum sat on the edge of her bed with a pale expression. Her small torso was trembling. A quick glance through my mum's room confirmed my presumption. Not even one drawer or cupboard was left alone. Bundles of clothes were strewn on the carpet. The blanket was torn apart. Furniture had been moved around. And, and, and…! Whoever had broken into the flat took his time. Not even one piece seemed to be untouched. I guessed it was the same in my room. A cold breeze struck my face and my gaze progressed towards the window. It was wide open. My mum's favourite plant that once sat on the window sill was slumped to the floor. I bent down in front of my mum. My knees touched the ground and I placed her hands in mine.

"What happened?"

"Zoe, I am so glad you are here." She sighed, her eyebrows slightly pushed together. "I came home from work and when I walked in I noticed the desk drawers in the hallway were wide open. First I thought it was you, who had left them open. But then I heard a man's sneeze from the bedroom. I panicked, ran out and knocked at next door. The neighbours called the police. I stayed there, until they arrived."

"The best thing you could do." I bit my lower lip. Just the thought of what could have happened raised my blood pressure. The police lady nodded her head and spoke for the first time since I entered the bedroom.

"You see, your daughter has the same opinion." She turned her attention to me and explained. "Your mum felt a bit upset that she couldn't describe the person to us, as she never saw him. But as I explained to your mum, she shouldn't worry too much. Your mum is safe and that's the main thing."

"Oh, I totally agree. You shouldn't worry about this. The police might be able to get some prints." I encouraged my mum. I wasn't stupid. Most likely gloves had been worn, but still there was a possibility to catch the intruder. "What has been stolen?"

My mum shook her head. "I don't think anything has been taken. It's just a mess, that's all."

With my head tilted to the side I glanced at the police lady and asked, "How did whoever it was manage to get in?"

"Through the bedroom window, your mum left the top part ajar. Not difficult for someone with experience!"

"I know you told me many times to keep it shut when not at home. But I forgot. And it's too warm anyway," my mum interrupted, her voice slightly defensive. At this very moment my mum looked so vulnerable. I endowed her with a big hug to provide her with some comfort.

"Don't worry. It doesn't matter. Are you feeling a bit better now?" I rubbed my mum's shoulders in an affectionate gesture.

"Yes, a bit. But don't you think that's odd? I have lived here for so many years and was never burgled before. Well, I know what you want to say. Anytime could be the first. The police lady said the same. Still, isn't it odd that nothing was stolen?" I raised my eyebrows. My mum was right. We had a few valuable items in here. So why break into a flat if you don't intend to steal?

"Are you sure nothing is gone?"

"Nothing! I even had a 100-euro note on the dining table along with my bank cards. It's still all here. Look for yourself." I nodded. "My jewellery is still here too." She pointed to a jewellery box in the top drawer of her bedside table, which now stuck out. Strange! Perhaps the person got spooked off. But as quick as the thought came to my mind, I discarded it.

Whoever broke into our flat had enough time to go through all the drawers and cupboards but not enough time to steal anything? It didn't make sense. "Do you often have cases like this?" I asked the police lady with a further glance combing through the room.

"I have to admit, it is rare that somebody leaves empty handed, especially if something is right in front of you." A sceptical looked appeared on her face. "We already asked your mum, if whoever broke in may have looked for something in particular. Perhaps you have an idea?"

I shrugged with my shoulders. "No idea," I replied, perhaps too quickly. A bad thought suddenly crept into my mind. What if…? I managed to suppress the sudden urge to expose my thought. No way could I say it aloud, especially not in front of my mum. And the police would probably think I was crazy.

"Can the paramedics have a quick look at your mum now?"

My thoughts were disrupted by the policeman

entering the bedroom. I threw a look at my mum, who nodded. "Yes, of course." I arose and stepped away.

An hour later the police and paramedics departed. The crime scene investigators that arrived half an hour later were not able to retrieve any prints. Later as I lay in bed, I struggled to fall asleep. Weird thoughts crept into my mind. Who could have done this? I didn't think it was just an ordinary burglary. Trying to think like a burglar, I came to the conclusion I would rather target a big house instead of a two-bedroom flat. Certainly we weren't loaded. The more I pondered, the more I was convinced that Max Boll played a part in it. The state of the flat spoke volumes. Whoever was in our flat tonight, had taken his time and searched for something specific. A burglar wouldn't risk that. He would take whatever he could and leave. I suspected Boll was after the folder. I was glad that I had taken the folder with me, stored in a safe place at Sally's house.

CHAPTER 55

Right before the door was pushed open Mirco was able to escape without being noticed. He used the same route he had come in through. By a hair's breadth he had not been caught. Back in his car he left the area immediately. He didn't stop until he'd put a fair distance behind him. A police car with blue lights even hurtled past him. No doubt about their destination. He then rang his employer to deliver him the news. Although it wasn't good news, he still had managed to leave a mess with the intention to get a warning across. Boll of course wasn't delighted. But it wasn't Mirco's fault. Beyond question the folder was retained somewhere else. Still, Boll had remunerated him as arranged. Nothing else mattered. It was time for Mirco to move on to his next job. Thankfully his new employer seemed to be less gruesome.

*

Max Boll on the other hand wasn't happy at all. Two hours ago he had been confident he would finally get a grip on this goddamn folder. He had imagined himself dancing on it, then ripping it to pieces and eventually tossing it into the fire. But it wasn't meant to be. He didn't hold Mirco at fault. The folder was probably hidden somewhere else. Hunt's daughter, however, was a different story. She'd turned out to be a right pain in the arse. Now and then he toyed with the idea of getting rid of her. It would solve all his problems. Of course, it was only a notion. Too many people knew about it. And now it was even public. Boll grasped for his car keys, his coat and scudded from the house. Ten minutes later he pulled up outside his friend's house. He knew he should have called before, but at this moment he didn't care.

Fortunately Kraft opened the door and not his annoying wife. Boll shook his head, simultaneously shrugged his shoulders and said sheepishly, "Nothing."

Kraft looked at him enigmatically. "What nothing?"

"The folder! I can't find it! I sent somebody around, but it's gone. Most likely hidden somewhere else!"

Kraft frowned. "You must be joking. Did you not say you had it all under control? What is it with you, Max? This girl can seriously damage our reputation. Perhaps even more!"

Boll glanced at him apologetically. With a flushed face and flared nostrils he motioned his friend to come in. They vanished into the kitchen.

"Don't worry, she is not at home." Kraft explained, referring to his wife. His friend and wife abhorred each other. They once had fallen out during a get-together and since steered clear of each other.

Boll breathed a sigh of relief. He watched his

friend remove two cans of beer from the fridge. They proceeded to the conservatory. It was Kraft's favourite place. It was fairly new, built only a few months ago and the only place in the house where he let himself go. Furnished with no more than a black leather couch, a low wooden table and numerous growing green plants, it relinquished a relaxing atmosphere. Kraft passed one beer to his friend. He snapped open his and poured half of it down his throat, before moving his gaze expectantly at Boll.

"I promise. I'll get this sorted, trust me." Boll leaned over to reach his can. Kraft put his beer on the table and crossed his arms. He was still having reservations.

"More than twenty-five years ago, you told me exactly the same. And then it nearly got out of hand. Thankfully Hunt committed suicide. I know I shouldn't say this. I don't wish anyone's death, even not my dearest enemy. But otherwise…!" His tone trailed off as he shook his head.

Boll drew away in abashment. His friend didn't know everything. And it should stay this way. Boll dissembled his thoughts and looked up. "Believe me. I've got it under control. I spoke to the director of the paper. We don't have to worry about them anymore."

A sneer escaped Kraft's lips. He knew it didn't mean much. The girl could do far worse damage. "She sent me an email."

Boll looked up in astonishment. "Pardon me. She did what?"

"She sent an email, asking about her father," Kraft repeated.

"Did you reply to it?"

Kraft leaned back. "Yeah, just the usual bit, to get her off my back!"

Boll had expected it. He wasn't worried about Kraft. There was no threat coming from him, that was for sure. His friend was involved nearly as much as he was. He wasn't concerned about the other two pilots either. Alex Feld didn't know anything. And with Andrew Mann he had spoken the other day. He first feared Mann would potentially become leery. All these years ago after the helicopter incident Mann had approached him. He asked if the lengths of the prohibition had not been made clear to Hunt. When Boll wondered about his question, Mann explained that Hunt came up to him and questioned the lengths of their prohibition. Boll had managed to sweet talk around it. When he spoke to him the other day, Mann admitted that Hunt's daughter had contacted him.

Nevertheless, Mann reassured him that he hadn't been of any help. After all, he really didn't know anything. And Boll reminded him so often anyway, that the trouble began with Mann's failure to fly a helicopter. The lies and deception had accrued to save his sorry arse! Mann was fully aware of it.

The only thing Boll fretted about was the existence of the folder in conjunction with the story in the paper. What else would Hunt's daughter be capable of? Hopefully she got the message after the break-in and finally gave up. That was the objective all along. Of course with the folder still out in the world, Boll had to be on high alert. Nevertheless, after a long-winded talk with his friend, they came up with the idea to keep a low profile for now.

If, however, she didn't stop, Boll had no other choice than to silence her tongue. Then under no circumstances could the truth ever be revealed.

CHAPTER 56

Standing again in front of the huge modern glass building beleaguered with different companies, I straightened up in front of the glass door. I glanced at my reflection when I was buzzed in. I walked straight through the door. The graphologist's office was on the fourth floor. Feeling too lazy to climb up the stairs, I aimed for the lift. I pressed number four. The lift came into motion and I was elevated in the air. When the lift came to an abrupt stop as we reached my chosen floor, I nearly lost balance and had to prop up myself against the wall. The door opened and I loped for the graphologist's office, who was also a forensic document examiner conducting work for local police forces. The small reception area to the right was occupied by the same young lady who had been there two days ago. With her long brunette hair and immaculate figure she would suit being on the front cover of a fashion magazine more than behind a desk.

She recognised me instantly and pressed the intercom to announce my arrival to the graphologist.

Once more I admired the wall of the lobby which was covered by several awards, one of them from a police force addressing the graphologist's excellent work. She indeed had a very good reputation. I suddenly experienced a strange emotion, unsure what I would find out today. The graphologist, an attractive woman in her mid-forties appeared from the door next to the reception area. The edges of her face were covered with blonde curly hair and she was wearing a decent amount of make-up. Dressed in an elegant black outfit she looked very smart. "Miss Hunt. It's a pleasure seeing you again. Please follow me." I trudged behind her feeling slightly uncomfortable. We stepped into her office with the sun gleaming through the window.

The graphologist strolled towards her desk. It was right in front of the window, facing the door. At the same time she gestured towards her cream-coloured leather couch on the other side of the room. "Please sit down. Just let me fetch your report. Can I offer you a cup of tea or coffee?"

"Coffee, please."

I went round the glass table, decorated with a jug of water and two glasses, to reach the couch and plopped down. The graphologist ordered some coffee and with some paper in her hand she ambled towards the couch and lowered herself next to me. Before I left home, I had attempted to reach Lucy, to tell her about the burglary and also to keep her up to date with my findings. Funnily enough I was told she had gone on holiday to the Bahamas. I was confused by the news and still tried to figure out why she didn't mention anything.

Back to reality, I stared at the graphologist anxiously. I felt like I was sitting an exam. Full of anticipation I sat up with my bottom shifting on the couch and asked, "Have you found anything unusual?"

"Well," she started. She glanced down at her notes and slowly raised her head, looking over the top of her spectacles, straight at me. "I have completed the work and written a full report of my analysis. And I have to say, I have done this for years and I have discovered many strange things in this field of work. But this one…?" She shook her head with raised eyebrows. "It took me really by surprise. Your dad's suicide notes are written by more than one person," she said bluntly.

I swallowed and glanced at her in bewilderment. "I don't understand?" I held my head back and froze. What was she trying to tell me?

The graphologist swiftly nodded her head. "Yes, I know. It's peculiar. Even I am not sure what to make of it."

She leaned forward and kept strong eye contact with me. "Basically, one shows your dad's handwriting, the one to Lucy. I have compared it with the letter I was provided with, and can confirm that it is indeed the same handwriting. However, the other letter, the one to his parents, which almost looks identical, has been written by somebody else."

I gawked at her. I felt so perplexed I wasn't even able to think straight. I had no words and just stared at her blankly.

"At least we know now that it wasn't your dad who

spelled your name wrong." She went on. "It just astonishes me that your dad is the author of the one to Lucy. I guess we just expected both to be from your dad or none."

I steadily shook my head and leaned back. "It doesn't make sense at all." I scratched my forehead incredulously. "I am sorry. I just don't know what to say," I said apologetically.

"Perhaps you should speak to the police. But I doubt they can help. Too many years have passed!"

I agreed with her. It would be just a waste of time. Without any hard evidence that something didn't add up, I had no chance. It shouldn't come as a shock. Not after what I had found out so far! One thing was for sure. The more I dug into my dad's past the more questions I had. Perhaps it had been a big mistake to poke in the past. I took the report, thanked her and left. Back in my car I opened the report and began to scrutinise the contents. It corroborated what the graphologist had told me. I was at my wit's end. I just didn't know what to think anymore.

I doubted more and more that my dad had killed himself, but then on the other hand too many things suggested he did. And one suicide note was in fact written by him. But who drafted the other one? If you intend to kill yourself would you really ask another person to write a last note for you? Of course, you wouldn't. And even if you did, I struggled to imagine that anybody would support it. A reasonable person would ring the police straight away or at least alert a friend or a family member. I shook my head once again.

The sound of my mobile phone interrupted my thoughts and I cringed. I glared at the screen. Withheld number? I hesitated. I detested cold callers and withheld numbers, out of ten, nine of them usually were. But if this one was number ten? It could be some kind of emergency and someone urgently needed to get in contact with me. The police or hospitals usually don't show their caller IDs.

I reluctantly pushed the button and answered with a halting hello. I never said my name. It gave me the option to feign someone else if indeed it was some cold call or scam. A deep man's voice on the other line asked if I was Zoe. Although I didn't recognise the voice, somehow it sounded familiar. It gave me a queasy feeling. I pushed away the nagging feeling that something bad had happened and asked who was calling.

It wasn't relevant, the man said. I frowned. I didn't like his answer and was just about to protest, but I refrained from it when I heard his next words. He warned me, and demanded to stop what I was doing and to let my father rest in peace. Otherwise he wouldn't be able to help me anymore. I stared at the phone utterly in shock. What the hell was that?

And then he only said five words and my whole world collapsed right in front of me.

PART 3

THEN

CHAPTER 57

The night David ran off changed his life forever. He had known that he was followed earlier on. After his altercation with Lucy, he decided to leave. He knew his captain was on to him. He had recognised the car, belonging to Max Boll's wife. With Boll himself behind the steering wheel and Kraft, the major on the passenger seat. It was waiting for him around the corner. Strangely he hadn't noticed Lucy who had been on his tail too. David's gut told him it was about the folder. When he had accidently left it the other day in the changing room and just in time returned to get it, he had seen the folder slipping out of Boll's hand. He couldn't figure out why Boll was after it. The documents shouldn't be any different to the ones the army possessed. The folder, which until up to today his constant companion, was quickly swapped with an empty one at Sharon's house. The real one had been in the boot the whole time and now was hidden very well in Emily's cupboard.

On the boat he easily spotted Boll and Kraft observing him. He had long since decided to cause the accident on purpose. They must have seen him taking the folder on the boat. And David hoped that they now thought the folder was on the bottom of the lake, when indeed it was an empty one. He still felt sorry for Sharon. She must have been scared to death. But he had no other choice. Misleading them was the only way to get rid of them, or he hoped so. So he ran the boat onto a rock and caused a hole in it. He was a good swimmer and he knew so was Sharon. The boat sank, and with it the empty folder. He wasn't bothered about the boat. That was one of the reasons he took the wooden one out. They both managed to swim to the shore, just before the coastguard finally noticed what had happened and arrived.

When they went back to his car, drenched, the vehicle that had followed them was gone. David dropped Sharon off at home and headed straight to Emily. He hid the folder and went back to his flat where Lucy was waiting for him full in anger. So he grabbed the gun and left. He drove around for hours until finally in the early hours of the morning he went to the barracks to hit the hay. There was always space for soldiers. And every so often he took advantage of it.

Daylight surged through the half-open blinds in the dormitory. Stretching his limbs, David sneered at the thought of the previous night. With another day off, he chose to spend it with his children. However, beforehand he needed to check his mail as he had no reply yet with regards to his complaint.

In three days he was supposed to give evidence in court. He was actually looking forward to it. Finally his chance would come to expose the truth. Everything was prepared for this day. David had outlined a nice summary of the true events and was looking forward to disclosing it to the court. He grabbed a quick shower and dressed casually. The mailbox for soldiers was situated in the building where the captains had their offices. As he ambled past Boll's office, he abruptly stopped. Had he not just heard his name? David approached the door, which was left ajar.

"At least the goddamn folder is gone." The voice belonged to Kraft.

Great, David thought. At least they had bought it. Still, David couldn't make out why the captains were so desperate to get hold of his documents. If they were after the stuff from his solicitor, they should have a copy of it anyway. Or was it about his complaint to the commissioner? Still, what would it change?

There must be something else they were after. David's head moved hastily from one side to the other to ascertain he was still the only one in the corridor.

"Have you had any luck with the court yet?"

David's eyes widened and he drew nearer to the opening.

"You know we are in huge trouble if it goes ahead in three days. We can't let it happen that Hunt gives evidence." Kraft's voice sounded slightly agitated.

"I should hear today from Andrew Mann's solicitor. I told him we had more evidence but wouldn't be able to present it just yet. Don't worry, I am sure it will get sorted today. I will get on to it right now," Boll reassured him.

David's face contorted in in outrage and his lips began to quiver. He couldn't believe what he'd just heard. The upcoming court date had meant so much to him, and now Boll was trying to get it re-adjourned? Why? But hadn't he just said it, to stop him from giving evidence?

"If someone finds out we forged the documents it will be the end for us. You know that. It's in your hands, you started it. Get it sorted before it's too late," Kraft hissed.

Forged document? David declined with puckered brows. He had no idea what they were talking about. Clearly something was going on, something big, and it was all about him. He realised that now. Suddenly he heard a door slam. It was further up the corridor close to the administration office.

David cringed. Whoever was up there would usually take the route past the captain's office as this was the only way out from the building. He straightened up and quickly vanished around the corner. He stopped and hid against the wall that led to the changing rooms. He leaned forwards and his eyes dashed to the direction he had come from. Shit, it was Lech, one of the other pilots but in a different unit, marching towards Boll's office.

David wasn't sure if Lech had seen him. He prayed

not. He had lost faith in anybody within that building. Even in Lech, who he once trusted. He took a step backwards and swiftly vanished inside the changing rooms. He plumped onto the bench in front of the lockers and rested his head in his hands. Confusion was going right through his mind. He knew he had been stitched up, but nothing made sense. They systematically wanted to destroy him.

Forged documents, change of court date? David shook his head. Nothing made sense. A conversation he once had with Andrew Mann popped up in his head. They talked about the flight prohibition. When David mentioned sixteen months, Mann had looked dumbfounded and quickly walked away. He knew that they both had received the same punishment. Still, Mann had seemed surprised and had avoided any conversation since then. Not just Mann, it seemed like everybody had turned their back on him. David had no idea why. It felt like a curse hovering over him.

After spending several minutes in the locker room chewing on the conversation he'd overheard, he eventually leaped up and made his way to the admin office. Once in the room his heart began throbbing with hope. His pupils took a on vast shape. But when he found the tray empty, his heart sank into his boots. He felt utterly gutted. He'd never been a friend of patience. Slamming his right fist against the wall, a curse escaped his lips. He span on his heels and dauntingly exited the building. Before heading towards his car, he hurriedly looked once more at the building. Something caught his eye. He glanced again and spotted a shadow. With a slit-eyed glance caused by the brightness of the day, he flinched when Lech met his eye. Lech, with a cigarette dangling from his mouth, watched him leaving.

CHAPTER 58

Lech had spotted David Hunt outside the captain's office. Had he been eavesdropping? Lech was actually quite surprised seeing David at the barracks. Was he not supposed to be off duty today? Lech wasn't everybody's cup of tea, some comrades even called him strange. He considered himself an ordinary guy, who approached others carefully before opening up. Inquisitiveness took over. He purposely walked past Max Boll's office to see what caught Hunt's attention. As he approached, he recognised not only Boll's voice but also Kraft's. He paused.

"Don't worry. I've got everything under control. Nothing will leak out. I've got an idea how to silence Hunt." It was Boll speaking.

Lech furrowed his eyebrow. What did he mean, he had 'an idea how to silence Hunt'? He was familiar with the finical situation in which Hunt currently stood. His pilot licence was revoked and rumours said the captain had it in for Hunt. Lech didn't know any details, only that it was related to the incident.

He stepped closer, leaning forward with his left ear close to the doorframe. Footsteps from behind the door advanced his direction. Lech stepped aside to walk off when Boll's face surfaced. "Are you looking for someone, Officer Lech?" The captain's voice echoed in his ears.

"No, just on my way to collect the mail. How are you today, Captain?"

"Fine, fine," Boll grunted. A slight trail of worry escaped from his lips. He paused. Lech assumed he wanted to say something more.

Boll decided otherwise, swivelled on his heel and wandered off. Kraft, the major who had followed Boll swept past Lech, without acknowledging him. The door was slammed behind him. What was that all about? Lech shrugged and watched both of them exiting the building. Perhaps a bit of snooping around wouldn't do any harm? To be always one step ahead was his motto. It wouldn't be the first time that he was playing detective. It was always good to have something in your hand just in case it was needed at some later point.

After nipping out for a cigarette and watching Hunt roaring off, he returned to his duties longing for the day to end. He hated early duty and today he was only on the ground. Finally it had just gone after five; the captain and major departed from the building. Lech observed Boll and Kraft from the canteen window. When they were gone, he took his chance. Research in the past had proved to be handy. He knew exactly where to find the key for Boll's office. He entered the administration office and quickly grabbed the keys hidden in one of the drawers.

Almost everybody had left the building by now. Only the troops on late duties were lingering somewhere around the premises. He made one full length up and down the corridor, just to be on the safe side. Soldiers laughing echoed from the yard. That didn't bother him. No way would they come this way and in any case he always could hide.

He eyeballed the corridor one more time up and down, before inserting the key into the lock and pushing the door open. As Lech entered, a big sigh rushed through his mouth. The office was a jumble. The surface of the desk was hidden under a heap of papers scattered around. Even the office chair wasn't spared. A pile of loose pages completely covered the surface. How was his captain getting away with this? After all, the captain was a soldier and like everybody else had been taught to be well organised. Unsure where to begin, Lech aimed for the desk. Luckily the office was quite compact. With only a desk, some chairs and a filing cabinet it shouldn't take Lech too long. Poking around amongst flight missions and other irrelevant documents, none of them in any particular order, Lech progressed to the drawers. He pulled at the first one only to find it locked.

It was the same for the other drawers. He tried the cabinet without effect and slouched his shoulders. He couldn't believe his bad luck and was gutted. Still, he wasn't one who would quit easily. *Think outside the box,* he told himself. With his hands in his pockets he glanced around the room. A lone cactus on the window ledge caught his eye. It implied something. Scratching his forehead in a thinking mode, a concept entered his mind. His grandma used to hide her keys under a plant. He knew of others, too.

Suddenly frozen in terror by the unexpected voices in the corridor, Lech began to panic. The voices belonged to Boll and Kraft. Lech's heart embarked on a rampage. Like a timid fawn his eyes began to dart around to search for sanctuary. Confident they were heading his way, Lech felt sweat erupting from his entire body.

Praying with his hands towards the ceiling, short gaps of breath escaped his mouth. With no place to hide, not even under the desk, he launched with his mind into different scenarios for a reason to be in here. He could play the innocent person, claiming he was watering the cactus, or delivering the mail. He slapped his hand against his forehead over his own stupidity. No way would anyone buy such nonsense. Nobody was allowed access to the captain's office without permission, except his superiors or the cleaning lady of course. He narrowed his eyes to a slit and gritted his teeth.

The footsteps now right in front of the closed door, Lech was getting ready for one of the worst moments in his life. He took one big sniff and embedded his mouth into his open palms.

CHAPTER 59

As quickly they had approached, the voices along with the footsteps departed. First Lech felt confused. He tried to refocus. He gathered himself and exhaled the air he had been adhered to. Never feeling more relieved in his life than right now, he tiptoed from the room. Not one second longer would he stay in here with his superiors in the building! They were probably heading for Kraft's office opposite the admin office. Still, they might return. As he emerged he checked to his left, then to his right. It was clear. He didn't even bother to lock the door. He quickly disappeared around the corner and went straight into the changing room. His racing heart began to slow down.

After twenty minutes he ventured to establish if the captains had vacated. If they saw him in the barracks at this time, they might question his intentions. Lech hoped they hadn't seen his vehicle. A quick glimpse to the parking lot and in fact the cars of Boll and Kraft were gone. Finally! Lech hastily returned to the captain's office. He converged to the window sill. His face widened to a vast smirk, as he lifted up the cactus. A small silver-coloured key smiled at him. Rubbing his palms together in excitement, he snatched the key from its hiding place and proceeded to the drawers. He inserted it into the lock. It matched perfectly and Lech pulled on it. Greeted by a pile of papers, he briefly nuzzled through them. Satisfied that he had not missed anything, Lech moved on to the next drawer. This one was stuffed with several files.

Whilst going through them, he stumbled upon an envelope. It was addressed to the service complaint commissioner for the armed forces and unsealed. He raised his eyebrows, wondering what it was doing in Lech's desk. He grabbed it to his chest and removed the contents. Steadily he lowered himself onto the swivel chair, oblivious to the bunch of papers underneath his buttocks. He wrinkled his nose and began to read.

It was a complaint to the commissioner, and the sender was none other than David Hunt. Lech's heart throb started up again, this time with exhilaration. Had he finally found something? Instantly he distinguished that it was about the helicopter incident. It was a complaint against the flight prohibition, discovered in the drawer where it certainly didn't belong.

It was a brief description of Hunt's version of events. Turning to the second page, Lech gasped. He recapped on it several times and still the number didn't alter. Incredulous, he stared at the letters. Sixteen months' flight prohibition? Hunt was grounded for sixteen months? What the heck was Hunt talking about?

Deluged with discomposure, Lech discovered that Hunt also alleged the same for Mann. Feld, the third pilot, got away with six months. Lech felt confused. Not much did he know about the incident, but one thing was for sure. He'd heard that Hunt was grounded only for seven months. And it wasn't that long for Mann or Feld either. That the flight mission had been changed in hindsight was known among themselves. Not officially of course. Gossip also said that Hunt by virtue of him being the most experienced one of all three of them, was mainly blamed for their actions that followed.

Lech leaned back. His eyes fell on a photograph on the desk displaying Boll with his stunning wife and young daughter. Like everybody else Lech was amazed that the captain had caught such a beautiful wife. The couple reminded him of the beauty and the beast. His gaze returned to the letter. Now, after the unexpected discovery Lech began to empathise with David Hunt. After twelve months a pilot licence ceased to exist; frankly speaking the pilot would have to commence the entire training again. Provided they would be given the opportunity, and in most cases there was no second chance. No wonder Hunt felt upset. What was happening? Had Hunt been set up? Why? And why was the letter with the captain's stuff? Shouldn't it be in the hands of the complaint commissioner?

Perhaps he had gotten it all wrong and the punishments had been harder than first anticipated. Maybe it was indeed sixteen months for Hunt and the seven months he'd heard about had only been a proposal. Lech put the letter down. Now feeling fully inspired, he hoped to unearth more. He rummaged a bit further through the drawers to no avail. He was on the verge of ceasing his search when he touched on a file on the bottom of the drawer.

Saucer-eyed he sneaked a peek of the headline. Goddamn it, he almost had missed this one. 'Accident case number 789 MANN/HUNT/FELD' unveiled the headline. With tons of adrenaline rushing through his limbs, he grasped it from beneath and lunged at the contents. What would he find now?

The first page was a summary of the incident, followed by the flight mission, the stipulated altitude. Lech assumed it was the altered one. The next few pages were a compendium of rules and instructions for military air traffic. Skimming through the pages, he eventually excavated the one he was on the manhunt for. He found it on the bottom of the file. The official document of the flight prohibition concerning all pilots involved. With a lowered chin and his mouth wide open, Lech gaped at the paper. He brushed along his eyes, unable to trust them.

As a matter of fact it was seven months for Hunt, one year for Mann and only four months for Feld. For all three of them a lot less than Hunt was assuming. So what was Hunt referring to? And why was Hunt's complaint to the commissioner in Boll's drawer?

CHAPTER 60

Andrew Mann lopped his scrawny torso towards Max Boll's office. His undesired gawky side surfaced more often than he wished for. Today it caused him nearly to trip over some bucket, left out by the cleaning lady, as he was rushing to the door. Boll needed to see him desperately. Why could it not wait until tomorrow? It was his day off duty, but his captain had urged him to come in. Mann felt slightly at unease. In a few days his trial at court would come up. Perhaps that was the reason he had called him in. To give him some advice what to say if he agreed to take the witness stand as a defendant. Or it was about Hunt? Mann was aware that the bosses had made Hunt responsible for their actions when they failed to follow procedures. Maybe Boll feared he would talk and reveal the change of the flight mission. But of course he wouldn't, why should he risk his position? He definitely didn't fancy walking out of court with a conviction.

At the time when all three of them had been interviewed, Hunt voluntarily agreed to lie, nobody had coerced him into it. Or perhaps somebody did? Actually, Mann wasn't so sure anymore. He had noticed the change in Hunt. He was introverted since that day. Especially the conversation the other day stuck in his head. Hunt had approached him, wanting to know his thoughts about the lengths of their prohibition. Hunt had seemed really distressed, complaining it was a joke being grounded for sixteen months because of something like that. Andrew had felt aphasic. With no idea what Hunt had been referring to, he had felt at a loss for words. He himself, who had caused the damage, was grounded for a year. Hunt and Feld as far as he was aware had received less than that. With an uncomfortable feeling he just walked away. Assuming that the captain had his fingers in the pie, he preferred to sit on the fence.

Now knocking at Boll's door, he was hit by uncertainty. "Come in."

As he did so, leaving the door slightly ajar without even noticing it, he found his captain smartly dressed in a white shirt, a tie and black suit pants, sat behind his desk. Why was he dressed like an office person? Andrew felt slightly irritated. "Captain, you wanted to see me. Is everything OK?" he asked politely.

Boll chuckled. "Of course everything is OK. It couldn't be better. I went to the court today. That's why I am dressed like this. It's about the trial." Boll chuckled as he looked down at his outfit. Usually known to be mercurial, he was in a good mood today. That surprised Andrew. His captain had been very grumpy lately especially since the incident. Perhaps he got laid again. Gossip was going around that the captain's marriage went downhill.

"What about?" He tilted his head and folded his hands in a slightly defending gesture. "I know what to say. Don't worry, I will be fine. We have discussed this now so often. I promise I won't cock up."

Boll placed his right index finger on his mouth to quieten Mann. "It's not about that. I know you will do fine. I asked you to come in to inform you the date has been re-adjourned. The trial will be in October. The new court warning should be in your mail box by tomorrow. It gives you time to prepare yourself." Boll grinned.

Tongue-tied, Mann rolled his eyes. He had actually hoped to finally get it out of his way. He certainly didn't need more time.

"Why is that?" Andrew stepped forward.

"I have spoken to your solicitor. We might be able to gather more evidence to work towards an acquittal. However, we do need more time!"

"What is it we need?" Andrew sighed and glanced at his captain dubiously.

"Oh, don't you worry about it. I will sort it. You just go back to your duties and in the meantime don't cause any mishaps." Boll smirked.

Boll gestured with a wave of his hands. It clearly meant he was dismissed. Mann turned his back to his captain to exit. With a hand on the door handle Boll suddenly stopped him. "One more thing."

Mann, spinning around to face his captain once more, asked. "Yes?"

"I know I've said it before but I strongly advise you to avoid David Hunt. Don't get engaged in any conversation with him. He will most likely protest against the rescheduled trial. He is causing huge problems for us. And I don't think you'd like to get involved, do you? Not that you could afford it right now." With pursed lips, Boll stretched his neck. His commanding tone was unmistakable.

"No I won't, Captain," Mann replied and left in bewilderment.

CHAPTER 61

Lech had sensed something wasn't right. Still, he had not expected it to be that bad. Maybe he shouldn't get involved? After his discovery, Lech had considered pretending he never saw it. Yet it was too late. He wanted to know the truth. No way would he just ignore it. He wasn't stupid. You didn't need to be a geek to comprehend what was going on here. Hunt was clearly bamboozled. They led him to believe that he had lost his licence forever; implying Hunt must have received forged documents. It seemed their intention was to get rid of him for whatever reason. Before leaving the office, Lech had made a copy of each document.

Now the following day he once again eavesdropped at Max Boll's office door, this time a chat between Andrew Mann and the captain. When he heard that the court date had been adjourned, Lech settled on a plan of action.

Several hours later the end of the day was approaching. Not long after that Lech found himself following Boll in his vehicle outside town to a nearby forest. Boll turned into a car park of a keep fit trail. It was filled with people stretching their limbs to keep healthy and the usual strollers either on their own or with their quadrupeds. Lech parked on the other side of the parking, well hidden from Boll's view. He emerged from his vehicle and spotted an ideal position behind an oak tree to watch his captain. Boll remained in his vehicle. Despite the windscreen, Lech had a direct view of him. The ground was beleaguered with gleaming leaves caused by the earlier drizzle. It made the surface slippery and he carefully weaselled on it.

First he puzzled over whether Boll was having an affair and they had chosen this to be their meeting point. But when he watched a young lad with tanned skinned approaching Boll's vehicle, he was assured this was not the case. The young man stepped into the car. He didn't look older than twenty-five. He was of medium height, proportionate build with short dark hair. Lech stopped short. He brushed along his moustache and inclined his head. Somehow the lad resembled David Hunt. Lech had no idea who he was. For a split second he imagined Boll had turned gay.

Not even five minutes had gone by when the young lad emerged from the vehicle with an A4 envelope under his arm. A closer inspection also showed a bulged smaller one in the other hand. Lech was pretty sure some business transaction with a large amount of money had taken place. He considered his next move, when the sudden noise of some leaves rustling behind his back, made Lech leap forward.

Shit, he thought as the young lad's attention was

abruptly drawn to him. Lech bounced aside out of view and turned his head towards the sound. An elderly female, with a small dog on a leash, frowned at him. "What are you doing?" she hissed at him. Her look spoke volumes. She stared him out in a manner as if he was some kind of pervert. The accusation in her tone was unambiguous.

Lech was known for his quick reactions in difficult situations. He tossed the camera, he had just used underneath his shirt and instantly replied, "Just hiding from my little lad over there." He pointed towards a small boy with a woman alongside him. The elderly female followed his gaze. Satisfied with Lech's explanation, she dashed away without any further hassle. To avoid raising any more attention, Lech promptly hurried away. He waited until Boll sped away and boarded his own vehicle. Resting his chin on his hand, he observed the young lad dissolving in a BMW and went after him.

CHAPTER 62

"I can't wait anymore. I feel like the whole world is against me." David, who sat in front of his solicitor sounded desperate. Since Lucy had moved out – she had given her notice and went back to her mum's – his life felt empty. Yesterday he had returned to his flat and discovered that most of her belongings had gone. Still, he hoped things were turning around for the better. But after finding the letter in his mailbox this morning, the modicum of hope slowly faded. First he didn't trust his eyes. Although he'd overheard the conversation between his captains about the upcoming court date, the rescheduling of the date was still like a blow to his face. October was a long wait for him. He had anticipated finally getting a chance to reveal the truth. When he read the bad news, he arranged to see his solicitor. Sadly his solicitor wasn't able to resolve the issue. David's whole world seemed to fall apart.

Full of rage, he drove like a lunatic to the barracks and stormed into the building where Max Boll's office was situated. The laughter of his captain met him halfway. Exasperated, David burst into the room and slumped on his captain's desk. With both hands leaning on the surface, he frowned at Boll. Boll, who sat behind the desk with the phone pressed against his ear, mumbled into it, "I'll call you back in a minute."

He hung up and his face went from pale to a blazing red. "Sergeant Hunt. What about knocking at your captain's door before entering? I know you don't respect your superiors lately. But I have to tell you, you are making it worse!" He frowned at him and lifted his chin annoyingly. He usually dishonoured such behaviour. David disregarded him.

"Why has the trial been adjourned?"

"What are you talking about?" Boll simulated.

"Oh, please, you know exactly what I am talking about. I bet you mastered it. You are afraid the truth will come out."

Boll turned livid. He started up from the chair with such an impact that the chair underneath his bottom tipped over. "Listen, David Hunt, and please listen carefully." He stretched his neck and turned red with wrath. "I won't tolerate your attitude towards your seniors lately. I want you to apologise right now!"

David burst into an ironic laughter. "Are you serious? How am I able to respect you when you are doing everything to destroy my career?" He gasped for air. "What have I done to you? Tell me, what is it? Why are you doing this to me?"

The captain, right in David's face now, barked. "Why? You are asking me why! Think, Hunt, and think hard. How many families have you destroyed for not keeping your dick in your pants?"

"What are you talking about?" David asked, clearly puzzled by the question. "It was three years ago, when I slipped. Yes, I admit it was out of order. But I was punished for it. Be serious; you are not seeking revenge for that now? It had nothing to do with you!"

"I am not talking about this," Boll grunted contemptuously and turned away.

David had no idea what his captain was talking about. With clenched fists David straightened up and snapped. "I honestly don't know what you are referring to. I have not upset anybody. The girls I am hanging around with have nothing to do with the army. Therefore it's none of your business."

Boll swivelled to face him again. He encompassed his desk and entered David's space. Right in David's face, Boll browbeat him, "I am warning you! You've made lots of enemies lately. On top of that you had the nerve to complain behind my back to the parliamentary of the commissioner. But believe me! Nothing goes out here, without us knowing."

David shook his head, distraught. He dumpishly asked, "What have I done to you, that you hate me so much? I was good enough to install your sauna. But now you are treating me like shit." With slumped shoulders David marched to the door. There was nothing left to say.

"Just think, Hunt. You couldn't even keep your hands off my wife." Boll exclaimed out of the blue.

David stopped dead in his tracks. Totally dumbfounded, he stared at the floor. He hadn't expected that. Somehow he had sensed that he had displeased his captain. He hadn't known why. Suddenly everything made sense. He remembered that day. He was in Boll's house installing the sauna. Boll's wife came downstairs to offer some coffee. She was flirting with him, so was David, it had been mutual. But that was all. Nothing happened. As they stood in the cellar, Boll's wife drew closer and gave him a kiss on his cheek. It was to say thank you for fitting the sauna. She had made an obscene comment but in a joking way. At this point her husband entered the room. Both of them started laughing and his wife quickly explained why she had kissed David on his cheek.

Boll never mentioned anything about this day again, surely not to him. Now he woke up to the fact that Boll had misinterpreted the situation. He had heard that the captain's marriage wasn't going well. But it never crossed his mind that he might be at fault. Now he wondered if he was somehow responsible for it.

"I never touched your wife," David hissed and slammed shut the door as he vacated the room. Any second longer in there and he would have strangled his captain. The cracking noise of the office door, followed by Boll's yelling hounded him down the corridor.

"That's my last warning, Hunt! Leave it alone and accept your fate!" David didn't bother turning around, he just kept on walking.

CHAPTER 63

Lech beat the devil's tattoo on his steering wheel. His patience was wearing thin. He had followed the young man for about twenty kilometres to Wagenhausen, a small town on the outskirts of Mitzen. The young man had turned into a housing estate. It was one of the impoverished quarters of Wagenhausen, mainly occupied by foreigners or families with low income. Lech had watched the young man vanish into one of the tall buildings that contained several flats.

He glanced at the time on the dash panel. Nearly an hour had passed. Assuming that the lad resided in one of the flats, the chances of his recurrence any time soon was slim. At least Lech knew where he lived. He could spy on him tomorrow. He had been tempted to confront the lad when he came to a halt at the estate. To find out about the business he was embroiled in with Boll. But then Lech saw reason and stayed in his vehicle. He had to think this through before taking any action.

His gaze averted to the romping of nearby

children. They cavorted among each other in the playground. All of different age groups with individual parents strolling around. Lech pulled the shades down to beat the sun and placed his gearbox in reverse. As he manoeuvred out of the layby, he captured from the corner of his eye the same young man emerging from the building.

Lech stopped his movements. He waited until the lad was behind his wheel and pulled away leaving a trail of smoke behind. Lech promptly set his vehicle into motion and followed him to Bueckenau. It didn't take long for Lech to work out the young man's destination. They were on their way to David Hunt. Lech's perception had been right from the start. Whatever had taken place in Boll's car involved Hunt.

He licked his dry lips and puzzled. What had he been paid for? Lech was suddenly apprehensive. What if…? He discarded his absurd thoughts and kept his eyes on the road.

They eventually reached the street of David's flat. It was a dead end. To avoid unwanted attention, Lech pulled into a side road and chose the footpath leading up to Hunt's flat. At the top of the track he stepped behind an adjacent building that was part of a community centre. He gained a clear view to the entrance of Hunt's flat which broadened up to the road. Lech located the old BMW parked up across from Hunt's flat. A shadow hovering over the dashboard of the vehicle suggested the lad had not moved yet. Surveying his vicinity, Lech located Hunt's vehicle right in front of the house. Hunt lived with his girlfriend in the ground-floor flat. He once before had been there, when Hunt invited him for a beer after a day shift.

It was close to 9pm and still daylight, a typical summer day in July. The sudden flash emanating from the inside of the BMW caught Lech's vision. It was the flare of a camera. The driver's window was wound down and the lad was dangling half out of his car, taking photographs of Hunt's flat. Lech froze, his blood ran cold. His suspicion proved to be right. The captain had hired this young man to set him on Hunt. And right now he was undoubtedly engaged in some preparation. Lech would have loved to know what it was. He only could imagine and his gut told him it was bad. Without any doubt David Hunt was a big problem for Boll. Still, Lech presumed that Hunt didn't know the truth. But how long would it take him to find out?

And if everything was about to come out, his captain's career would be over; not just his, others too. And most likely Boll would be found guilty of fraud too. His whole life would be destroyed. So what other choice did his captain have than…?

Lech's thoughts were interrupted by the bang of a door. He glanced towards the flat and watched Hunt shuffling along the front lawn. With cavernous cheeks Hunt presented a crestfallen impression to the outside world. Lech found cover behind the wall. Under no circumstances did he want to be seen. He observed Hunt getting into his car and roaring off. Lech surmised Hunt was on his way to start his night duty. The young lad was still taking pictures, this time of his target. Hunt was oblivious to it.

Five minutes later the lad alighted from his car. He approached the entrance to Lech's flat and knocked.

When nobody answered he reached into the pocket of his jeans and moved some implement towards the door. Lech, with no chance to identify the object, almost couldn't trust his eyes. Within a split second the young lad managed to gain entry through a locked door. He dissolved into thin air.

Lech crept towards the house. Straining himself to get a glance through one of the windows, he ducked to evade discovery. After several attempts he managed to gain one through the kitchen with his camera in his hand. What was this lad doing in there? Was he checking out the place? All these questions ran through Lech's mind, when all of a sudden a figure towered over him. Lech was startled; at the same time a silent cry escaped his mouth.

CHAPTER 64

Benjamin Kraft in general was a very controlled person, not someone who would throw in the towel in a difficult situation. He was in his mid-thirties. As a career-focused person he was determined to climb high up in rank. The helicopter incident in February, however, put his career on hold. Not that it was his fault. Still, it had an impact on his professional life. He was still quite new to the squadron and in charge of this unit. He joined three months before the incident occurred. He came from a base down south, but asked for a move back up north to be closer to his family. He had known Max Boll before that. They had been friends for years. They met in their basic training at the armed forces in Hanwau. They both had chosen to become pilots. Over the years they went separate ways, yet kept in touch. It was coincidence that they were now based at the same barracks. That Kraft ended up being Boll's superior, didn't change the fact that they were still friends. He respected Boll's views and wishes.

When Boll first changed the flight mission in favour of Andrew Mann, Kraft had supported the decision. In the armed forces it was normal to support your soldiers as best as you could, albeit it was the soldier's fault. It didn't apply to everybody. You had your favourites within a squadron. David Hunt was not one of them. It was obvious that Boll had a grudge against him. Even he had to admit that Hunt was sometimes a pain in the arse. First, he hadn't realised that his friend would use this opportunity to seek revenge against Hunt. Revenge for something which didn't make much sense to Kraft! Although they were both close, Boll actually never divulged to him the details of why he loathed Hunt. And then it was too late. There was no come back now. He recollected the evening. He was still at the barracks when Boll dropped in, booming, 'That's my opportunity. Finally I have something to teach Hunt a lesson.'

Boll let him in on his plan and then it was done. He was as guilty as his friend. He had supported Boll's decision to forge Hunt's flight prohibition from seven months to sixteen. Their intention was to push Hunt into leaving the armed forces voluntarily. However, at this point neither of them had realised that Hunt was not willing to give up so easily. He was a fighter. Now thinking of it, both of them had underestimated Hunt. And now his position was running into mischief. He had asked Boll to get it sorted before it escalated. Anyhow, Kraft didn't like the way it was going. He knew it was bizarre but sometimes he feared his long-time friend. Boll could be ruthless and capricious. It was part of his faults. He had asked him to get it under control. Kraft himself had no intention to get his hands dirty. He did not want to have any part of it whatever Boll was planning.

Kraft loped through the swinging door of the main building. It had just gone past ten in the evening. Only the droning of the boiler from the cellar interrupted the quietness of the premises. Hunt was on night duties. As part of his punishment, Hunt was currently placed on security duties. Kraft was conscious that Hunt abhorred his new tasks. He slightly empathised with Hunt. It must be hard for him. After all, Hunt was a pilot. He should be up in the sky but instead he was guarding the premises. Kraft followed the din that came from the kitchen. Light was irradiating through the open gap. He weaselled into the kitchen with Hunt's back facing him. Only two metres apart, Kraft cleared his throat to announce his presence.

Hunt revolved in a cringing position. "Shit, you scared me to death, Sir. Are you here to see me?" David hadn't expected anybody in the middle of the night, especially not his major.

Kraft nodded. "Yes, I came to speak to you. I believe you know why I am here?"

With his thumbs in his waistcoat, Kraft with a height of nearly 190cm and a weight of 100kg occupied most of the room left in the small kitchen. It was clear that he was showing off his authority. Hunt, not being dense was fully aware that he had to be careful around his superiors lately. He had alienated most of them with his appeal. Not to mention the complaint to the commissioner. Even so, he couldn't care less. It was inequitable, what they did to him.

"I am all ears," Hunt retorted.

A frown crossed Kraft's face. "First of all, I don't like your tone. Lately you have not been showing any respect towards any of your superiors. I strongly advise you to change your attitude." His tone didn't accept any protest.

Hunt shrugged his shoulders apathetically. Esteem towards his superiors had long since disappeared. Kraft, taller than David, moved right into his space and glowered at him.

"Sergeant Hunt, my patience is wearing thin. So I only ask you once to pay attention to what I have to say. It's a piece of advice, and if you don't follow it then God help you." He stretched his neck, the tone of his voice flannelly and tough. "The whole situation is getting beyond control. Too many things have happened and your input made it worse, as you know. It was very unwise to complain to the commissioner! I am sure Captain Boll rebuked you with regard to this matter. The only advice I can give you now is to resign immediately. Withdraw your complaint and appeal and resign. If you don't, then things may happen that are out of my hands. Do you understand what I am saying?"

Hunt glared at the major blankly. For him it didn't sound like a piece of advice. "Sir, are you threatening me?" he asked scornfully.

"Take it however you like. I won't ask again. Remember, it's out of my hands now. I am not here to protect you if something goes wrong," Kraft emphasised. Nothing else to say, he turned around and vanished into the pitch-black corridor.

Meanwhile David was still rooted to the spot long after the major had made an exit. He was trying to comprehend the context of Kraft's advice. David had sensed for a while that they aspired to get rid of him. But this one, in his opinion, was a proper threat. What did Kraft mean with 'it's out of my hands now'? Did he have to fear for his life? But what could they do to him?

Don't be stupid, he thought. David stretched his limbs and suppressed a yawn. He moved back to the kitchen appliance to finish off his sandwich. Still not sure how to take it, he recalled an incident with one of his comrades who had killed himself two years ago. The lad had been stitched up and the only way out of his misery was to hang himself. He remembered the case very well. He was appalled when he heard about his suicide. The soldier who had been in his early thirties had left four kids and a wife behind. However, David was a very obstinate person, by no means would he resign. He would fight until it was all over. Still, he didn't like the way the major had delivered the message.

CHAPTER 65

The next morning, after he was relieved by the morning shift, David met Lech in the car park. "Good morning," Lech said. "Finished your night shift?"

"Yes I have, straight off to bed. I am knackered," David yawned.

Lech, still amused by the events of the previous night at Hunt's flat, grinned. He was silently laughing his head off at the mere thought of it. Frightened to death because of a cat, how ridiculous! The shadow appearing out of nowhere came from a cat sneaking down the branches of a tree. Not long after that, the young lad AKA the intruder left and Lech called it a day. "How are you anyway? Are you not supposed to be flying again soon?" Lech asked purely for the purpose of obtaining some information.

David looked at him with a sad smile. "Still grounded, I appealed but have to wait for the outcome."

David dropped his gaze and gawped at his boots.

He hadn't polished them for weeks, another sign of his recent reluctance towards his duties. "Sixteen months is a long time. And as you know I have to do the whole shit again." He looked up and sneered. "Most likely I won't get another chance anyway."

Lech knit his brows. *So it's true.* Lech concealed his knowledge and feigned his surprise. "Sixteen months? That's a long time if you ask me. I always thought it was less. Seven months I've heard at some point."

David, now the one who looked astonished, shook his head. "No, it was never seven months. Always sixteen for something I didn't do." With a daunted expression, Hunt fidgeted with his hands in his pockets. The camouflage pants sagged on him, a sign of inadvertent weight loss.

"Cheer up! Better times are on the way." Lech endowed him with a vitalising smile and gave him a friendly pat on the back.

"I am trying. But right now I am going through a shitty time." David swallowed.

"I understand. It must be tough. It's not fair. Have you tried to contact the complaint commissioner?" Lech quizzed.

"Yes I have. Again, I have to play the waiting game, the same as with the appeal. My solicitor is handling most of the appeal. I have been advised to wait first for the outcome of the appeal."

"So when is the court hearing? Was it not supposed to be any time soon?" Lech glanced over David's shoulders.

"It was supposed to be in two days. And now it

has been adjourned for October." David shrugged his shoulders, sorrowful. His sunken eyes dashed to the morning troop parading on.

"Shit. that's not fair. Why?"

"No frigging clue. They won't tell me anything." David rubbed his eyes. He was overwhelmed by a sudden tiredness. It had been a long night and he was aching for his bed.

"They are probably pissed at you with your appeal and complaint. But mate, you've done the right thing." Lech gave him another pat on the shoulder. "I would have done the same. Sixteen months and it wasn't even you who caused it, that's ridiculous if you ask me." Lech glanced at his watch. It was time for him to parade on. Punctuality was important within the army. "If I can do anything at all, let me know. Don't give up mate, OK?" He put his thumb up and turned on his heels.

Lech ceased in his movements when David placed a hand on his bicep and uttered, "Listen Lech, can I tell you something in confidence?" Lech paused. David felt a big lump in his mouth. Still, he managed to pull himself together.

His eyes swiftly glanced from the parking lot back to the buildings. Satisfied that no one was within hearing range, David murmured, "Better someone knows, just in case."

"Yes of course, go on," Lech emboldened him. David's quaver didn't escape him.

"I have been put under pressure to resign." Lech knit his brows. "Not just this. They also want me to withdraw my complaint and the appeal."

It didn't surprise Lech as much as he had expected. Not after his discovery in the captain's office. What other choice did Boll have in order to keep the secret?

"I was threatened too. If I don't do as they wish, I will face some repercussions. Dunno what it means. But I'd prefer someone to know."

Lech looked at him thoughtfully. "Who threatened you?"

David shook his head. "Listen, it doesn't matter who said it. I only mentioned it, so you know."

Lech nodded. He respected David's wish. They said goodbye and David headed home.

In his own four walls, the emptiness of David's flat hit him instantly. Since Lucy was gone a dull ambience had been present. His whole life was gloomy. The situation at the barracks was escalating, which somewhat didn't come as a surprise. After all, David had made more enemies within a few months than he had made friends in his entire life. He kicked off his shoes and immersed himself into the warmth of the quilt. Still fully dressed, he shut his eyes and waited for sleep to come. Unfortunately his mind had other plans. He was pestered by woolly thoughts, unable to let them go. The chat he'd overheard the other day about forged documents popped into his head again. He still wasn't any wiser about what his captain had referred to. Perhaps he had meant the flight mission? Or was it something else?

And now the threat to force him to resign! Shadowed by dark thoughts, he repeatedly had to remind himself not to give up on life. Let alone for the sake of his children. They needed their dad. Still, the dark thoughts gained more and more control of his life. And sometimes he asked himself if the children were not better off without him. Was he really a good father? What could he really give them? With him gone Emily would at least get a lump sum and a widow's pension. Financially they would be sorted. With him alive they would never be able to pay off his debts. Not now when he was about to lose his job. Frustrated, he grabbed a pen and paper from the bedside table and started writing.

Dear Lucy...

CHAPTER 66

Lech gazed at his watch. It was close to 6pm. He lingered outside the block of flats on the lookout for the young lad. The lad's vehicle was parked up half on the kerb, half on the road, a sign that he was at home. Lech had no idea of his name or what flat he was living at. He could only wait and see. If nothing happened then he had to come back tomorrow. Precarious about his next move, if he should confront or carry on watching him, he lit up a cigarette and dragged on it as if it was his last one. Watching the trail of smoke dissolving into thin air, he went back and forth impatiently. An elderly man strolling past frowned at him when the smoke struck to his face. To avoid any clash, Lech stubbed out his cigarette and stormed rapidly off. Back behind his wheel he allowed himself another glance at the entrance. The door was pushed open and a group of giggling children stepped out of the building.

Lech was about to droop when the young lad surfaced and shuffled his way out through the crowd.

At last! Lech excitedly rubbed his hands together and started the engine. The young lad vanished behind his wheel and hurtled off. He was dressed in grey jogging bottoms and a blue T-shirt. Lech went after him. He again steered towards Bueckenau. Lech shadowed him for approximately twenty minutes when he was suddenly forced to brake. The country road, environed mainly with forest, had narrowed on both sides. The car ahead had come to an unexpected stop, blocking Lech's way. The traffic was usually very light on this road. Today with no vehicle in the immediate vicinity, Lech's warning bells switched on. "Shit!" He slammed his open palm against the control knob. Clearly he had been caught flat-footed. He glanced over his shoulder, mulling over whether to turn around, but his options were limited by the tight road.

He chose to drive past. However, by the time he closed in, the young man had emerged from his vehicle and placed himself in the middle of the road. *Holy shit! Is this guy crazy?* Lech swore aloud and struck the steering wheel in rage. He considered swerving to the right. He abandoned the idea. It was too risky. Embankments on both sides of the road would make it impossible to get away without causing damage to his beloved Mercedes or even an accident. Lech was left with no alternative. He stepped hard on his brakes to avoid a collision. Lech was in general not an anxious person. This time, however, was a different matter. He felt intimidated. He didn't know this lad. Nevertheless, being involved in some business with Max Boll and breaking into Hunt's flat could only mean one thing. This lad was potentially dangerous! He managed to come to a halt directly in front of him.

With a gesture, 'What are you doing mate?' he stared at him whilst remaining in his car. Deluged with uneasiness, Lech's gaze peered around in a spark of hope to catch sight of another human soul. It was in vain. The street was deserted, so were the nearby fields. Not even an agriculturist was hovering about. Lech's heart pounded rapidly. All at once he began to feel the heat emanating from his body. As part of his job, he had been taught to deal with difficult situations. This time, however, felt different. The lad made straight a beeline for Lech.

Lech gasped for air, stepped out of his vehicle and hollered, "Are you completely out of your mind? You could have gotten yourself killed." He stayed close to his Mercedes.

The lad scowled at him. Lech noted his deep blue, cold eyes and a shiver ran through his spine.

"I know you are following me. You watched my flat. What do you want? Who are you?"

Lech distinguished the foreign accent instantly. Still, he wasn't very good at placing accents and assumed it was either South European or Middle East. Lech contemplated feigning ignorance, but then decided otherwise. The moment had come. He cleared the lump in his throat and his voice deepened.

"I know you have been paid a lot to sort out David Hunt, the soldier," he said bluntly, keeping his words simple.

At the end of the day he didn't know what Max Boll had asked him to do. At this stage he only suspected. It surely had something to do with Hunt otherwise he wouldn't have broken into his flat. By all means he might have planted a bomb in there or some secret cameras. Lech knew it was a long shot and he doubted it; still, he must have been in the flat for a reason. He didn't believe it was an ordinary burglary. Supressing his jumpiness by wiggling his toes inside his boots, Lech stayed calm on the outside. He was still wearing his battle-dress.

"David Hunt?" the lad replied, feigning confusion.

Lech wasn't easily fooled. Fortunately he had taken some pictures too while he watched the lad with the captain. He had managed to do it just before he was approached by the old lady, and then again at Hunt's flat through the window. He reached into his vehicle and fished out two envelopes. Lifting up one of them, he gibed, "I've got proof, pictures of you, showing you with Boll involved in dodgy business."

The lad shrugged in an uninterested manner. "And? That doesn't mean anything."

Lech crossed his arms and, with a challenging gaze, remained silent.

"What's your problem? Boll is a friend of mine. Is it a crime nowadays to meet up with an old friend?"

Lech, who had anticipated such an answer, waved with the envelope. "Yes, you are right. That's not a crime. But breaking into a flat is a crime." He emphasised the last sentence.

The lad was caught off guard. He rubbed his nose and retorted, "What are you talking about? And anyway are you a cop or what?"

Lech shook his head. "No, I am not a cop. But there are some photographs showing you breaking into Hunt's flat. I am sure the police would be interested. Do you want to see them?" Lech asked sarcastically.

With a tilted head the young man kept his gaze on Lech. Finally he had the lad's attention. A bit of a smirk widened Lech's face.

He waited until the lad finally asked, "What do you want?"

Lech lifted up the other envelope. "I don't know how much Boll has paid you, but I will pay more." He ran his fingers through the envelope, exposing a large amount of money. The lad's pupils dilated.

"What do you want me to do?" the lad asked greedily as he glowed at the banknotes, his thick foreign accent coming more and more to light. The sudden approach of a Beetle, made them move to the verge. A young female driver was shaking her head as she barely managed to roar past them.

Lech retorted with a dirty look and returned his attention to the lad. "I still want you to do the same as what Boll paid you for. But I want you to do it my way."

The lad glared at Lech dubiously. "I don't understand," he taunted.

"Which part you don't understand?" Lech groaned and jerked his head. "I guess you've got half of Boll's money already. I will pay you for the exact same job. Boll doesn't have to know and you can keep his cash too. What's so difficult to understand?"

The lad scratched behind his ear, clearly mystified by Lech's suggestion. "Why would a person want to pay for the same job I would have done anyway. I can't kill Hunt twice. And it's supposed to look like suicide." The young lad shook his head, bewildered.

Lech on the other hand suppressed an impish smile. He thanked God silently. Now he knew why Boll had hired him. He had guessed so, but was not sure. It was his intention right from the beginning to find out what the lad was up to. He only needed to get him on his side now.

"Because I don't want Hunt only dead, I want to torture him. Obviously not physically, after all it's supposed to look like suicide. I want him to pay for what he has done," Lech explained with a chilling expression.

The lad raised his eyebrows. First he'd thought Lech was a cop. When he discovered that he was followed the other day, he did vice versa and followed him. He knew now that his pursuer was a comrade of Hunt. Wondering what Hunt had done wrong to be abhorred so much, the lad reminded himself that only the money counted. He never asked for details. He just carried out what he was paid to do. He would do as he was told and take the cash. The thought of all the money made his mouth watery. He moved his tongue around his lips to clear up the spit that had built up. Getting double paid for the same job, who on earth would say no?

He proffered his hand towards Lech for a handshake. "Deal! I am Pablo. What do you want me do?"

CHAPTER 67

Lucy's mum was poking along her daughter. The sound of pebble stones underneath her loafers grated in her ears. They walked past David's vehicle, which sat in his usual spot. She was slightly fretting about her daughter's frame of mind. When Lucy first told her she was moving in with a married man who had two children, she had been outraged. But when she met David, she changed her mind. David wasn't just handsome. He was also a very charming person. She had finally understood her daughter and gave her blessing. Yet she should have known better. He became coltish and because of his good looks and the pilot licence women were slobbering at his feet. He began cheating on her daughter, the same as he had done to his wife. It was still early in the day. They were on their way to collect the rest of her daughter's belongings from the flat. In her opinion her daughter deserved better and hoped this was the end of their relationship.

Lucy on the other hand had still very strong

feelings for David. She wished, that after some time elapsed, they would end up back together. She was also afflicted by some strange sensation. Perhaps it was down to the fact that she couldn't get hold of David? Unsure if he purposely didn't pick up the phone or if indeed something was wrong, she entered the flat with mixed feelings. With her mum in tow, she stood in the dark hallway, the door to the bedroom closed. The shutters in the whole flat were down. Only the small glow through the window gap in the lounge allowed them to negotiate their way. Lucy assumed that David was still asleep. She proceeded towards the lounge and pulled on the string to open the shutters. The room was in a mess. Dirty laundry dangled from the sofa, dirty dishes stuck to the table and papers were tossed across the carpet. It wasn't like David. He was usually a neat person and detested jumble.

Lucy headed for the bedroom. Her mum, in an attempt to shed some light on the kitchen, was occupied moving some beer bottles out of her way. Precariously Lucy called out for David. To a certain extent she feared catching him with a girl in bed. She rather preferred to warn him beforehand. She didn't need to see any live action and just the thought of it set her tears in motion. The rattle of the beer bottles attenuated her shouts. When she didn't get a reply from the bedroom, she slowly pulled the handle and widened the door. She silently prayed for emptiness. The room was pitch-black and Lucy's fingers slid to the switch on her left side. She was assuaged when she found it empty, but also surprised. Where was he? His car sat outside and David rarely went out by foot. The bed was unmade and the room was in a similar state to the lounge.

"Lucy, are you alright?" Her mum's breath was crawling down her spine. Lucy turned on her heel.

"Yes, I am fine, don't worry. Not sure what's going on here. David's car is here but no sign of him."

"He might have gone for a walk?"

Lucy threw back her head. She glanced at her mum, sceptical. David, gone for a walk, no way!

"So much the better, I honestly don't need to see this person right now. I am not sure if I could keep my temper." Her mum furiously went on.

Lucy looked at her mum, beseeching. "Please, Mum. Don't be so contemptuous. You used to like David. It hurts when you talk like this."

A scornful sound emerged from her lips. "Yes, I used to. But that's gone now." She regretted her words immediately when she spotted her daughter's watery eyes. "Sorry Lucy, sometimes I can't help myself. Please don't get upset." Lucy's mum couldn't stand to see her daughter unhappy. She averted her eyes and fixated on the bedside table.

Lucy followed her mum's gaze and her attention was promptly drawn to the surface. Lucy advanced to it and her glance adhered to a piece of paper. "Oh my god. It's a suicide note," she screamed as she snatched it from the surface. Lucy wobbled towards the window and grabbed hold of the ledge. She felt faint and her head was washed over in utter pain. "He killed himself. He did it this time for real. Oh Mum, it's my fault!" She crouched down, covered her mouth with both of her hands and began weeping like a child.

Her mum, still in the doorframe vaulted next to her daughter. Slowly she took the piece of paper from her daughter's hand and studied it. "But where is he?" Lucy's mum furrowed her eyebrows as she scanned around the room. She suddenly felt sick. She was not prepared for something like that. She had always considered herself as a strong person. And yet for the first time in her life she didn't know what to do. "Maybe we just should call the police."

Lucy slowly lifted her head. Her mascara was smudged all over her face. She arose and tumbled towards the hallway. She snuffled whilst tears spilled down her cheeks. So far they had been in all the rooms except the bathroom.

Her mum in tow, pleaded, "Please Lucy. Don't go in there. You don't know what's behind that door. Let's just call the police. Let them do their job." Her mum was all of a sudden terrified of what her daughter was about to find. But Lucy waved her aside.

"I don't think he is in there mum. He's done it probably somewhere else." But was she fooling herself? The corners of her mouth turned down and her face ash pale, she approached the bathroom door. The night when he ran out with a shotgun in his hand came to her mind. Maybe this time he really did it. Close to a mental breakdown, she glanced once again at the note in her hand. Wiping off her nose with the sleeve of her jumper, she raised her hand and pushed open the bathroom door.

CHAPTER 68

Lucy was a nervous wreck. She was trying to control her trembling as she approached the sink and splashed water on her face. In principle she should feel relieved, the bathroom was empty. But the anxiety stayed with her. And it would be as long as she didn't know where David was. A noise at the door startled Lucy from her crouched stance. Her mum, resting against the door-jamb, flinched. The jiggle of a bunch of keys in the door lock had caused the noise. Lucy stepped out of the bathroom, her mum already long on her side. Both of them stared apprehensively at the door. The door moved inwards and David entered the flat. He was casually dressed in a tracksuit bottom and T-shirt. Circles of perspiration on the front of his shirt and underneath his arms suggested he had been for a jog.

Signs of surprise showed on his face when he saw his unexpected visitors. A glimmer of hope developed in his eyes. Had Lucy decided to come back? But one look at Lucy's mum, and hope faded away. "What's going on here?" David asked. He lifted up his T-shirt and used it to rub off the sweat from his face. His upper body was exposed to them. Lucy's mum, suddenly abashed, averted her eyes.

"How can you do this to me?" Lucy squalled with swollen eyes. She beckoned with the suicide note in her hand. David tapped his forehead, annoyed with himself. He had completely forgotten about the letter.

"I am sorry," David tried to explain. "I felt a bit suicidal the other day. I am OK now. Just forget about it." Lucy shook her head in disbelief. With a jutting chin and her hands pressed into fists she stepped forward and lurched at him.

"'I felt a bit suicidal.' That's all you have to say about it? I was worried sick and just about to call the police. And you are telling me you felt just a bit suicidal?" Lucy mimicked.

David bowed his head in shame and muttered an apology. But Lucy was still not conciliated. She threw the suicide note into his face.

"How dare you? You drop me some lines to say goodbye. And at the same time you mention your lover. Wanting me to go to her house to collect your belongings? Are you out of your mind?"

David was at a loss for words. He had forgotten about that. He was tempted to make excuses. But with Lucy's mum on her side, he ditched the idea and said nothing. Lucy, with her hands on her hips, held back and lifted her head up. She was waiting for another apology.

Instead of satisfying Lucy's wish, David snatched the note from her hand and ripped it to pieces. The pieces plunged to the floor. Lucy wasn't about to give up. She waited for another minute. But when no sound came out of David's mouth, she tiptoed to reach David's height and spat in his face. She then rushed past David and stormed out.

Lucy's mum shrugged her shoulders and followed. On her way out she paused and hissed, "Please, do me a favour. Leave my daughter alone once and for all. You have hurt her enough."

The slam of the door echoed in David's ear. His first instinct was to run after Lucy. He discarded the thought. It would just be a waste of time. He headed for the lounge and stretched out on his couch. Within seconds he zonked out.

CHAPTER 69

David was woken from a dream by the sound of his phone. "Blimey!" he burst out. He had been dreaming of flying again. The phone stopped ringing. He rubbed his eyes and sprawled. The quietness of his flat brought him back to reality. Astounded by the glance on his wristwatch, he swung his legs across the arm rest and stood up. He had slept for more than ten hours. It was still daylight, but the twilight was around the corner. David was supposed to be at work right now to commence his night duty. However, he had no intention of doing so. He couldn't even be bothered to inform his captain. Instead he grabbed a bottle of whiskey from the kitchen cupboard and poured some into a tumbler. He wasn't a drinker. Yet today was a different matter. He took a big sip and contorted his face in distaste. The bitterness of the beverage dwelled on the tip of his tongue. David was not used to spirits.

Returning to the living room, he lowered himself onto the couch and switched on the TV. He flipped through the channels and his blank expression crimped to the screen. David was struck by depression. How had he managed to lose so much control of his life? How did he get into the situation he was in right now?

One thing was for sure, he had stepped into a trap. He had no prospect of winning. If they wanted him out they would be able to succeed. Life was so unfair. Sixteen months grounded for no real reason, he still didn't get it. He was avoided by all his comrades and to be honest he even didn't care. David felt let down by the whole team. Today he had received a reply in regards to his complaint to the commissioner. It only said to wait for the outcome of the appeal. His gut told him the captain had his fingers in the pie.

Unfortunately all the correspondences within the armed forces had to go first through their hands. Stupid policy! Overwhelmed with black despair, he sank with his forehead on the glass table and shed tears. That wasn't like him, he wasn't a weeping person. He was the opinion that only women cried. Today, however, was different. The pain was too deep. Not just because of his job, it was also the loss of Lucy and his financial problems. After no tears were left, David hauled out his shotgun from the cabinet and loaded it with ammunition.

He stopped in his tracks. *Shit, what are you doing?* he asked himself. But there was no way out of it. Not anymore. He had to do it. Everyone would be better off without him. He was just a pain to the world.

David sprang to his feet and stooped down in front of his hi-fi system. He grasped a record from The Beatles off the bottom shelf and began to play it. He moved the stylus forward to reach his favourite song 'Yesterday'. He grabbed his tumbler, filled it up again and once more sealed his lips with the top of the glass. He fetched some plain pages and a pen from his desk and this time chose the carpet as a settee. With trembling fingers David removed the lid from the pen and began to write. The last remaining bits of daylight shone through the half-open shutters. Once again he paused and wagged with his head. What was he about to do? Could he really do this to his children? Yet whatever sense he tried to talk into his head, turned out to be a waste. He reclined onto his side and actuated the pen. *Dear Lucy…* he began afresh.

The slam of the car door ceased David's movements. He assumed it was his landlady. He glimpsed at the alarm clock, the cursor on nine. He had lost track of the time. He ought to be on duty an hour ago. The whiskey served its purpose and David's tipsiness became apparent. The fizzling of his buzzer made David jerk. Unless it was his captain to censure David for failing to turn up on duty, he didn't expect any guests. He teetered to the door. The Beatles song 'Let It Be' was blaring now through the walls.

As anticipated his captain, Max Boll in full lengths was showing his face. With a huffish expression, his captain gestured to his watch. David burst out in laughter. "Speak of the devil," he said ironically and hiccupped. Boll was hit with a boozy breath. He covered his nose with his palm and glared at David.

"Are you not supposed to be on duty?"

David leaned against the doorframe to keep his balance and grimaced. "Do you think I give a shit?" David giggled and wiggled his eyebrows disrespectfully.

"For God's sake, you are pissed. What's wrong with you?" Boll turned his face away in disgust as he was struck by another boozy breath. David chuckled, followed by another hiccup.

"I thought you wanted to get rid of me. You should be pleased, I didn't turn up. It's another reason for you to suspend me from duty once and for all!" A further hiccup interrupted him. When it stopped, David raised his voice. "Because by now you should have realised I won't resign voluntarily. Only over my dead body will I leave the army." David straightened up and banged the door in his captain's face.

CHAPTER 70

With the door slammed in his face, Boll needed several seconds to recover. When he heard that Hunt failed to turn up on duty, he decided to pay him a visit. He had also come to give Hunt a last chance before he would get the ball rolling. Boll shook his head, annoyed, and turned on his heels. Because Hunt wasn't interested in listening, Boll had no other choice. Hunt had it coming. With his hands in his pockets he strolled along the footpath leading to the street. A woman in her late thirties dressed in a blue skirt and white blouse stood on the pavement. He recognised her immediately. He had met her in the past, when visiting Hunt. She was Hunt's landlady, Carla Sturm.

"Oh hello. How are you?" he sweet-talked.

"I am fine. Oh, I remember you. Are you a colleague of David Hunt?"

Boll caught sight of a small travel bag beside her. "I am his captain. Max Boll is my name," he said with some authority in his voice, his big belly puffing out.

Carla noticed his side glance. "I am on my way to visit my sister. I got a call, she isn't well. I am just waiting for the taxi."

"Are you staying overnight?" Boll asked innocently.

"Yes. Unfortunately for only one night, I have to be back tomorrow morning." She sighed. "I have no other choice. I have some people coming around to view the ground-floor flat. They are moving out. His girlfriend left him. Poor guy!" Streaks of brown hair cascaded on her cheek as she shook her head in compassion. "They were so much in love and now it's over. I think he is heartbroken. Well, it's not easy these days, being still married with kids and starting a new relationship. And such lovely kids he has."

Boll nodded and clothed his face in smiles. "Yes they are."

He peeked over her shoulder and pointed with his chin towards the flat. "That's why I am here. He was supposed to show up for duty tonight. He didn't. So I came by to see if he was alright. Unfortunately he is in a bad state. He has taken it to heart badly. He just consumed half a bottle of whiskey. I had to take the other half off him," Boll blagged. He dug into his pocket and fished his car keys out. "Well, not much I can do for him now. I advised him to get his head down."

Outraged by the news, Carla clapped her hand on her mouth. "Oh my god! I hope he will be OK. I will check on him tomorrow when I get back. Do you want me to give you a call after I have seen him?" she queried.

"No, don't worry. I will get in touch with him

myself. Have a nice evening and hope your sister will get better soon."

"Thank you. It's just a bit of flu. And there is no one else to take care of her." She elevated her hand and waved to the taxi that stopped right in front of them.

Boll scudded off. His mind was racing. That was enough information fed to Hunt's landlady. He didn't want to say too much. He roared off in his vehicle and two blocks down the road, he came to a halt and entered a phone box. Pulling out his address book from the inside pocket of his coat, he swiftly looked up the number for Pablo, the man he had hired to kill Hunt. He thrust some coins into the slot and while pressing the receiver between his head and his shoulder, he used the other hand to dial the number. After the third ring, Pablo answered. "Change of plan," Boll panted. "We have to improvise. It's going to happen tonight. It can't wait until tomorrow."

Everything had been planned for the next day. However, Boll changed his mind the moment he espied Hunt in a drunken state. It just would make things easier, especially with Hunt's landlady out of town.

"Can you be ready within an hour?" Boll ordered and this time it was him who smirked.

"No probs, whatever you want. But what about my money?"

Boll rolled his eyes. "Don't worry. I will get it for you now. I will meet you in an hour at our usual place." Boll placed the receiver back to its place. He rubbed his hands in elation, confident that tomorrow he would be free of his worries. Pablo was meant to vanish directly after it was done. Just in case something went wrong. Therefore Boll would pay him beforehand. He wasn't worried that Pablo would run off before accomplishing the job. Pablo was aware he would be found. Boll was cognizant of the whereabouts of Pablo's family. He could absolutely count on him. Boll squeezed his palm against the glass door and gave it a firm jolt. In a trice he was on his way home to collect Pablo's money.

CHAPTER 71

"He wants me to do it tonight," Pablo divulged. "In about an hour!"

Lech, on the other line, furrowed his brow. Why so suddenly? According to Pablo it was supposed to take place tomorrow. Perhaps something didn't go as concocted. He froze. "Wait!" Lech croaked. "Where does he want you to do it?"

He knew David was on duty tonight. No way Boll would risk executing his plan at the barracks. It wouldn't make sense if Boll wanted to keep a low profile. The army would be all over it and the truth about the incident and the flight prohibition could be revealed. So why did Boll change his mind?

"I guess at the flat. The way it was arranged. I will call you after I've met Boll," Pablo replied.

Well, one day more or less wouldn't make any difference. Lech reckoned that David was at home. Perhaps his shift had changed or he was off sick.

"No problem. But don't call me. I will meet you

around the corner of Hunt's flat for about eleven-ish. We will take it from there. This should give you plenty of time." Before Pablo had a chance to butt in, Lech reassured, "No worries, I will have the money ready. In the meantime I will try to find out where he is. In case he isn't at home." The handset lapsed from his hand.

Lech glanced at his image in the mirror. He stood in the hallway of his own house. It was an antique exemplar from the 1900s, once owned by his great grandmother. It was one of those mirrors that could freak you out if you believed in ghosts. After the death of his mum, he did not have the heart to get rid of it. He tugged on his ear as he picked up the phone once more and rang Hunt.

After ringing umpteen times Lech was about to let go, when he heard a whizzing sound eluding from the other line. The drunken voice belonging to David surprised him. He didn't know David much as a drinker. In fact he only vaguely remembered ever seeing him drinking at all. At least he now grasped why Boll had altered his arrangements with Pablo. David was in no fit state to parade on duty tonight, the perfect opportunity for Boll to fulfil his intentions. A man off his head was easier to take out than somebody with a clear one. Something must have occurred to David. Yet there was no time to go into details. He kept his chat as brief as possible and hung up. Still, everything would go ahead as envisaged, just a bit earlier than hypothesised.

Fortunately his girlfriend was at her mum's. It saved him from an explanation as to why he was staying out all night. One more phone call and Lech would be ready for action. This time he didn't have to wait long. "Can you get ready now?" Lech scratched his moustache, hoping that he wouldn't be left in the lurch. "It's going to happen tonight. I will pick you up in twenty minutes."

Ten minutes later Lech glanced in the mirror one more time. He moistened his fingers with his spit and smoothed his spiky hair to its side. Satisfied with his looks, he grabbed his coat from the wardrobe and stormed out of the house. He was relieved that his friend was free tonight. He knew he could rely on him. On his way to David's house, Lech stopped at his friend's house, who lived in the city centre of Mitzen. With his back against the house wall, his friend lingered outside his place.

A cigarette dangled from his mouth. Dressed all in black, he resembled a thief. Like Lech he was in his late twenties. With his receding hair on top of his head, he looked slightly older. He was of a beefy build and therefore came across as a bully. Lech brought the van he had chosen for tonight to a halt and his friend swung open the passenger door. He took one last drag of his half-smoked cigarette, threw it on the floor and hopped inside. As they drove off, Lech gave him a brief insight as to why things had changed.

When he finished, his friend replied with a sadness that couldn't be missed. "No worries. I didn't have any plans anyway. You know me." Lech just nodded. His friend was going through a nasty divorce and without doubt he was hurt. "Let the fun begin," he tried to cheer and made himself cosy on the passenger's seat.

"Yes," Lech chuckled.

CHAPTER 72

Down in his basement Max Boll entered the workshop room situated next to his sauna. He proceeded towards his safe. The door was secured with a combination of numbers. Boll loped straight to work and within thirty seconds the money neatly tied up in bundles accompanied him to his vehicle. His wife, who watched him from next door to their dwelling home, shook her head, annoyed. Her husband hadn't even bothered to greet her. She was pondering what he was up to. She winced at the phone, as it came alive.

"Hello?" she answered. First she was unable to place the voice. It sounded groggy. "Pardon me. You want to speak to my husband? Who is calling again?" she inclined. "David Hunt. Oh yes, of course. Hold on." She felt a smidge of awkwardness for not distinguishing David right away. He just sounded so different today.

Of course she remembered him and always would. He had fitted the sauna. Both of them had been flirting very heavily with each other. Her husband still resented her for this. At the time he had been very jealous, although nothing happened. Their marriage was over for different reasons. It was just a matter of time until they got divorced. She was working hard on her husband to agree to sign the papers. She had had enough of him and couldn't imagine spending the rest of her life with such a selfish, dodgy person. She detested him. Sad when you thought that once they'd been in love with each other. Or maybe it was just because their child had been on its way. "Hold on, David," she said in a sweet voice. Her husband didn't like it when she called Hunt by his first name.

She smiled, as she opened the window and shouted at her husband who was rushing to his car. "Max, David is on the phone."

"Who is David?" Boll grunted, infuriated, with one foot already on the floor of the driver's side. He knew exactly who it was. His wife called David by his first name deliberately, just to piss him off. He still sometimes mused over whether his wife and Hunt had slept together. If yes, surely his wife would have told him by now. Just to get him to sign the papers. His wife wanted a divorce. Yet he was not willing to let go.

"David Hunt, darling!" The ironic in her voice unmistakably.

"For fuck's sake, he is Mr Hunt for you and not David." He ambled inside and snatched the phone from his wife.

David, not able to control himself, clamoured from the other end, "It's your entire fault. You took everything from me. I make sure you will be blamed for it."

Boll threw back his head and burst out in laughter. "You could have told me so thirty minutes ago when you slammed the door in my face," Boll simpered, plunged the phone back to its holder and scooted off.

A short time later he pulled his car into the same car park at the keep fit trail than the other day. Pablo was already waiting. The interior light beamed at his head which was concealed behind a newspaper. Boll sprinted towards the driver's window and rapped. Pablo, immersed in the headlines, was startled. He opened the door. "Are you ready?" Boll whooshed. He was still riled because of his wife.

"I am, you have the money?" He lowered the newspaper to his lap and gleamed at Boll full of expectation.

"Yes." Boll thrust the money into Pablo's hand.

"OK, I assume it's still as discussed? With the shotgun?" Pablo looked up at Boll. Boll nodded.

First he had thought of the hanging method. He changed his mind when he remembered Hunt's shotgun. He wanted to be sure it was done properly.

"Yes. Don't forget to vanish immediately. Obviously if there are any problems, let me know. Otherwise, good luck for the future!" Boll gave him an encouraging pat on his shoulder.

"Understood!" Pablo nodded. He gave Boll a wink by placing his left fingers on his temple and set his vehicle in motion. Boll, with a big smirk plastered around his face, watched him leaving. Soon it would be all over. He returned to his own vehicle and set out in the direction of home.

Boll was conscious of the questions he would have to answer, once it was done. He was well prepared for this. That Hunt was having huge problems at home, not just financially but also in his love life, was beneficial. He was sanguine that his superiors would rather focus on this and not suspect that it had anything to do with the incident back in February. After all, it had been more than five months ago. And thankfully the complaint to the commissioner and the appeal to the lieutenant colonel never left Boll's desk. The acknowledgement Hunt had received, had been Boll's draft, just another forged document. He also had in mind to pay Carla Sturm, the landlady a further visit in the morning. To tie up any loose ends!

CHAPTER 73

Pablo came to a halt in a lay by outside Bueckenau. He put the gear into neutral. With the engine running he began counting the money in the envelope. Satisfied with his findings, he wiped off his sweaty palms on his jeans and roared off. In ten minutes he would meet Lech and more cash would fly his way. So far everything went far beyond his expectations. Not long to go and he would sit in an airplane finally turning his back towards Germany. A red traffic light at a T-junction not far from Hunt's flat forced him to stop. He stretched himself and leaned forward to reach out for his glove compartment. He tugged at the lock. It released and between a pile of papers, receipt and other junk, the barrel of a gun was visible.

He carried it with him at all times. It was just a precaution, in case something went wrong. There was also this uncertainty about Lech. Why did he want to do the dirty work himself? Wasn't it a bit odd? Something about this man didn't add up. But research showed that there was nothing unusual about him. At the end of the day it was the money that mattered for Pablo. And if he had to use the gun to protect himself, he would. The lights turned green and he was back on the move. He swung the steering wheel into the estate. As arranged Pablo parked at the rear of Hunt's flat. It was the street one turn beforehand. He jumped out of his vehicle with the gun under his waist belt. Speeding up the footpath leading to the flat, he spotted Lech from the corner of his eye.

Lech stood on top of the track against the neighbouring house wall with his arms crossed in front of his chest. Pablo once more brushed for his gun. He felt more relaxed by the touch of it. He converged with Lech, who gestured with his chin towards Hunt's flat. "He is in the house. Are you ready?"

Pablo nodded. "Can I see the money first? After all, I take a double risk here." He slid his fingers in his pockets and paused in anticipation.

Lech with clenched teeth uncovered an envelope from his jeans pocket and pressed it against Pablo's chest. Pablo allowed himself a quick glance at the contents and nodded his head in contentedness. "So how we gonna do this? Are we just knocking at the door?"

"Yes," Lech murmured and shoved himself off the wall. "He will let us in. He trusts me."

*

By now David had consumed more than half a bottle of whiskey. Perhaps for somebody else it would have meant nothing. For David it meant quite bluntly he was utterly pissed. Still chafed about the phone call to his captain, he picked up the letter from the floor and drew up the last sentence to his beloved Lucy. He then put it away into the drawer of his bedside table. Whilst sat on the edge of his bed, he cupped his face with his palms and rocked back and forth with the shotgun in his lap. He was gravely considering setting an end to his misery.

The thud at his front door made David pause. He struggled to his feet and dressed only in boxer shorts staggered to the door. Along his way he had to latch onto walls and furniture, whatever came first to keep his balance. With one eye closed and the other peering through the peephole, he yanked at the door and pulled it open.

With his left arm reclined on the handle, he glanced at Lech equivocally. "What are you doing here?" David's words were very clearly slurred.

"I need to speak to you. Can we come in?"

"We?" David's eyes widened and his gaze wandered off to the person beside Lech. He blinked several times to adjust to the darkness slinking its way into the lobby. "Who is this?" David beckoned to Pablo.

"It's a friend. We are here to help you. Are you alone?" Lech glared cynically at David's bathrobe.

"Of course I am alone. What do you mean here to help me? It's too late. Everything is too late!" David shouted and attempted to shift into an upright position. His left hand was still pegging on the door handle.

"Come on. Let's talk inside," Lech reasoned. David reluctantly budged sideward and beckoned them to enter.

Lech went ahead with Pablo in tow. "You know the way." David pointed to the lounge whilst studying Pablo's face in puzzlement. David had no idea who this stranger was. He stepped forward to shut the door, when suddenly a shadow seemed to appear from nowhere and loomed toward David.

The shadow turned out to be a man, dressed all in black and his face was shrouded by a balaclava. David gawked at him, slack-jawed. The man in black slowly raised a gun from underneath his black jumper and pointed it directly at David's forehead. David widened his mouth to unfurl a scream. However, the only words he managed to form were, "What the fuck?"

Yet it was too late. The man dressed all in black stared at David through the slashes of his balaclava and pulled the trigger.

CHAPTER 74

David opened his eyes slowly. Was he dreaming or was he so drunk that he began to hallucinate. Or perhaps he was dead and this was heaven? Had he not just heard a shot? With his eyelids squeezed, he pinched himself to test if he was able to feel the pain. "Ouch," he mumbled as the pang pierced through his skin. He was crumpled on the floor in the hallway.

"Are you alright?" Lech asked, hovering above him.

"What happened?"

"You went down when the shot was fired and passed out. Only for a few seconds though."

David sat up and peered disconcerted at Lech before his sight roamed to the dead man sprawled across the carpet. Blood was dripping from his head. He had expected to see the man with the gun he had secretly begun to call Balaclava Man, yet he had erred. It was the man who had entered his flat with Lech.

"What the hell…?" David indicated the pool of blood, struck by horror. "What have you done?"

David's gaze bored at Lech accusingly.

The balaclava man, emerging from Hunt's bedroom, loomed large beside Lech. He jerked down his balaclava, displaying his face in full view. The beard stubble surrounding his mouth and cheeks somehow gave him a scruffy appearance.

"Who is that?" David pointed to him precariously. He recalled he was the one who had fired the deadly shot. The balaclava man now without his gun, but holding David's shotgun, outstared him. What was David's shotgun doing in his hands? He recollected that he had last left it in his bedroom. And why was he not wearing his balaclava anymore? That could imply only one thing, couldn't it?

Feeling menaced by the balaclava man's demeanour, David jumped up and took a step back. Whilst swallowing nervously, he swiftly scanned the room for any useful object to utilise for protection.

Balaclava Man was the first who broke the silence and grumbled, "We don't have time to mess around, Lech. Let's get moving."

David had no idea what he was on about. He squared his shoulders, and formed his right hand into a fist ready to strike if inevitable. His eyes flitted to the now closed front door. When the balaclava man lifted up David's shotgun, David leapt frenziedly towards it. Unfortunately the amount of alcohol flowing in his body thwarted him. He tripped over a pair of trainers and landed head first against the front door.

He propped himself up with his palms, pushing against the floor and opted for another go. His head felt heavy and the thudding of his heart blared in his ears. He peered down at himself, eventually awakened to the fact that he was still in his boxer shorts. He didn't care. He was fighting for his life here. Something terrible was going on in the privacy of his home and he had to get away from it. He again charged for the door, but the balaclava man was quicker.

He grabbed hold of David from behind, tugging on his bathrobe and shoved him towards Lech. "Move him away. There is no time. Come on, quick."

Lech placed his arm around David and shifted him roughly to the kitchen. Pushing him down on a stool by pressing his palms against David's shoulders, he gripped another chair and lowered himself. Lech, facing the back of his chair, leaned forward. He bored into David's eyes and with an ominous undertone, he growled, "David, listen to me. You need to calm down." Lech swiftly leapt up, snatched an empty glass from the cupboard and filled it with some tap water. "Drink, you need to get a clear head. I am doing this for you. Give me a minute and I will explain it to you."

He patted David on the shoulder and returned to the hallway. When he glanced down at Pablo's lifeless torso, for an instant, remorse sidled through his mind. Pablo had been far too young to die. Yet it was his fault. He certainly would be still alive if he hadn't met Boll.

Lech bent down and encircled his fingers around Pablo's wrist. His friend did the same to the ankles. In one go, they lifted him up and hauled him to the bedroom. They swung him onto the bed, undressed him and covered his genitals with the duvet.

In the kitchen David gulped the glass of water down his dry throat. Submerged in nausea and a bad headache, he elevated from his stool and drew closer to the door that was left ajar. His unwanted visitors had moved to the bedroom. David listened to the muttering of them, unable to make out their words. He weaselled through the door and attempted to catch a glimpse. Disconcerted that the corpse had gone from his lobby, David wondered what was taking place in his bedroom.

Were they trying to hide the body in his flat to blame him for the murder?

Cold sweat ran down his spine. He tiptoed towards the open gap to sneak a peek. The dead man was resting now on his bed, half covered with the duvet. Whatever was going on in here, David didn't like it. He snatched his car keys in a swift motion from the key hooks adjacent to the coat rack and sprinted towards the exit. His head felt much clearer now thanks to the glass of water.

The sudden noise behind him caused him to crouch. Without revolving, he understood he had been caught. Once more he bestirred himself to leg it and lunged out. Unfortunately it was too late. A sharp pain whooshed through his head, followed by a dark cloud and darkness.

CHAPTER 75

Lech's mouth hung wide open. He needed a few seconds to regain his composure. Eventually he gasped. "What have you done?" His friend surprised him every day, but this time he went too far. Glaring down at David's lifeless body on the carpet, he rubbed his left eye raw.

His friend shrugged with an innocent gesture. "I had no other choice, man. He just wasn't calming down. Or do you want to get done for murder?"

Lech scratched his head. "Of course not," he exhaled. "I know where you coming from. But that makes it even harder for us. How do I get him to come around? We won't have much time. He is hammered. No chance will he wake up anytime soon." Pacing up and down with his hands behind his head, Lech cogitated over what to do. "He was supposed to write his own suicide notes. What am I gonna do now?" he grumbled.

"Did not this lad," he pointed his chin towards the bedroom, "bring some along? Surely your captain must have thought of them."

"No, he told me Boll had forgotten and he noticed it too late."

His friend tilted his head. "Can we not do it? Copy his handwriting? It can't be that difficult."

Lech glanced at him, puzzled. "What, the suicide notes? I am not good at this. Anyway, how am I supposed to know his handwriting?" Lech's veins bulged out from his neck as he rammed his fist against his other palm. "Son of a bitch."

His friend, mumbling more to himself, loafed to the lounge. "There must be something with his writing." He began scouting around in the cabinet, the only furniture beside the couch and David's hi-fi system, left in the room. With no luck, he proceeded to the bedroom rummaging through the bedside tables.

Drawers opening and closing could be heard followed by a deep drawn sigh. "Look at this," his friend called out.

Lech, who hadn't budged until now, joined his friend in the bedroom. "He's done the work for us." His friend gesticulated with some loose pages between his fingers. His cheeks were beaming with joy.

"What do you mean he's done the work for us?" Lech drew closer. "Listen, we have two bodies here, one dead, one alive. There is no time for messing around," he censured exasperatedly. His friend pressed his bony finger on the first page.

"Just look and stop moaning. Like I said, he has done it already. It looks like he was about to top himself. It's a suicide note, two pages, addressed to…" he looked closer. "Lucy."

Lech furrowed his brow. He was slightly confounded by the news.

"That's his girlfriend. She used to live here. She left him the other day." Lech rubbed his forehead. He was trying to gather his thoughts. His sweaty shirt adhered to his skin. "Is there anything else?" He pulled on his shirt to get some air onto his flesh.

"What do you mean by anything else?"

Lech approached one of the bedside tables. "I mean any more of them. Where did you find it?"

His friend pointed to one of the open drawers. Lech kneeled down. His gaze averted to the exanimated body of Pablo. The blood had oozed down to the pillow and sheet. Lech began to retch but managed in time to keep it down. Blood always aroused his nausea. He spun his head back, focusing on the drawer in front of him. One suicide note already done? Hunt must have been serious! Surely he couldn't have been writing only to Lucy. There must be one to his parents or children. Full of eagerness, he began scrabbling around the entire flat.

Ten minutes later he gave up. "Nothing." Slouchy, he joined his friend in the lobby. Wary like a watchdog, he monitored Hunt, who lay still unconscious on the floor. Lech wondered why Boll hadn't thought of this one. Possibly because of the precipitance, after all it was meant to happen tomorrow.

"Isn't one enough?" his friend grizzled. "It's time to clean up, come on." He lightly shook Lech's arm.

"That's not enough. Just think. If you are about to

say goodbye forever, would you not at least write to your parents too? Perhaps not to your estranged wife, and the kids are too small. But at least to your parents?" Lech sounded angrier than he intended to. He had pictured it to be easier.

"So what do you want to do then?"

Lech shrugged his shoulders. He tilted his head and studied the two pages. "My writing is similar," he discovered. "I'll give it a go. I'll write one to his parents. Best to mention the children too, so it sounds more realistic. Let's find some paper and a pen!"

CHAPTER 76

Boll patted his friend on the shoulder, escorting him out. Benjamin Kraft had nipped in to talk things through again. "Don't worry. Everything will soon turn out to be OK." He understood why Kraft was quite perturbed about the whole situation. If the truth ever came out, then their whole career, they'd worked so hard for, would be down the drain. And it wasn't even his friend's fault. He had started it and Kraft had just supported him. That was one of the reasons he now preferred to keep his friend out of it. The less he knew, so much the better, just in case anything came back to them. He would have to take the blame then. What had happened tonight had nothing to do with him. Boll watched Kraft driving off as he stood on the porch of his house. He bit his lower lip in uncertainty. Something plagued him. He was deluged with worries he couldn't explain.

David Hunt was supposed to be dead now. But what if something went wrong? Running his hands through his hair, he attempted to shake off the bad thought that slowly crept to his mind. Maybe he had been wrong all along and couldn't trust Pablo. Maybe he ran off with the money without completing the job? He abandoned the idea. Boll knew where his family lived. Pablo would not jeopardise his family. Still, he felt uneasy. Perhaps he should check for himself. Just to make sure the job had been done properly. Or was it too risky? What if a neighbour saw him? After all, it was supposed to look like suicide and not murder. That had been the plan from the outset.

And then it dawned on him. Because he had to rush things, it was meant to happen tomorrow, he'd forgotten about the suicide note. Without a letter left behind for your loved ones, it might not look like suicide.

Enraged about himself, he banged his clenched fist against the house wall. With no other alternative left than to return to Hunt's flat, Boll sprinted back to his house to get the key. The other day Hunt stupidly abandoned his house keys in the canteen. Boll took the opportunity and stealthily made two copies, one for Pablo and one for himself. With his wife lingering in the house, Boll decided to write the suicide letter in Hunt's flat. He swiftly grabbed his coat and headed for the door. His wife dogged on him. "Do you have the decency to tell me where you are going at this hour?" She began nagging.

He rolled his eyes and stole a quick glance at his watch. It was almost midnight. "Just getting some cigs." Perhaps it wasn't a good idea to leave now. His wife was supposed to be his alibi, just in case. Still, he had no other choice and hastened away.

A short time later he pulled up around the corner of Hunt's flat. He didn't want his car to be seen in Hunt's street. Too risky! He scampered along the kerb, concurrently inspecting the windows in the area for any noise neighbours. No light was shining through any of them. Indeed most of the windows were hidden behind closed shutters. The whole community seemed to be asleep. By the time he approached the flat he was out of breath. Boll dipped in his jeans pocket for the key to the flat. The full moon, with his emanated intensity, glowing above him made him an easier target to be spotted. Not only this unsettled him. Boll in general became twitchier during full moon. He was a strong believer that it somehow swayed a human's frame of mind. With one last skim through the neighbourhood, he was satisfied that no other person was loitering around.

As he inserted the key into the lock, Boll wet his mouth in anticipation. His head lifted, he pulled the door towards him and rotated the knob. His heart was throbbing madly. On one hand with pleasure to finally see light at the end of the tunnel, but then on the other hand with discomfiture over whether everything had truly happened as hypothesised.

He squeezed his upper arm against the opening and reeled inside. He blinked his eyes when the murkiness of the dwelling met him. With his fingers patting along the wall, he scouted for the light switch. Unable to locate it in a jiffy, he shut the door and fished his lighter from his pocket. The flame enabled him to locate the switch and in a swift move he pushed the button. As the hallway lit up and Boll's eyes adjusted to the abrupt brightness in the room, he was all at once petrified with horror.

"Oh my god," he whispered and covered his mouth with his palm.

CHAPTER 77

Stunned but also annoyed about his own stupidity, Boll lowered his hand and moved closer to the object that had frightened him to death. His own scarf! He had left it on the wardrobe in the lobby. His name was embroidered on one side. He briskly clutched the end of it and threw it around his neck. He jammed the door shut and went hot-foot to the bedroom.

The door was ajar. He slowly pushed it inwards and peeked at the bed. The air reeked of blood and mugginess. Although over the last few days it had cooled down, a sign of the late summer, the temperature in here was high. A quick satisfied look on the surface, verified that Hunt was dead. He was reclined on the sheet, covered up to the waist with a blanket and, due to all the blood and brain parts hanging off his thick hair, his head was beyond recognition. The shotgun rested on top of his chest, still with the index finger wrapped around it. Boll had seen enough. His mouth enlarged to a bright smile.

The only thing still missing was a suicide note. Boll jiggled closer, scanning his surroundings in a quest for a pen and paper. He purposely averted his gaze from the body. Despite the fact that he was a soldier, he wasn't able to bear the sight of death. His eyes came to a halt, at the top of the bedside table. The layer was smothered in half-empty packs of sleeping pills and anti-depressants, part of the plan to make it look more real. An empty bottle of whiskey and a half-filled tumbler stood next to its side. He paused when his eyes caught sight of some loose pages. A big gasp of relief escaped from Boll's mouth and his eyes began to sparkle, as he took the contents in. Two suicide notes addressed to Hunt's parents and partner and identical with his handwriting! Pablo must have somehow taken care of it. *Good lad.* Boll nodded contently.

He whirled around, darting for the doorway. The dee to turn his back from here was suddenly overwhelming. Everything was going as planned, no reason to be in here any longer. He leaped to the front. When he caught the slam of a car door, his legs went heavy as lead.

He abruptly paused and pressed one ear against the front door. The crunch of gravel from the other side caused by footsteps sounded very close. No doubt it was heading his way. Beads of sweat protruded on his forehead. Fidgeting with his hands on his waistband, he considered his options. If he got caught in here with a dead body, regardless of whether it looked like suicide, he certainly would arouse suspicion. With no other exit than the front, he contemplated the window. But as quickly this thought came into his mind, he discarded it.

Most likely the police would grow sceptical. Perhaps it would prompt the police to treat it as murder. No, the windows had to be shut. Whoever was entering the flat would possibly run straight out and call for help. His moment to sneak out!

On the hunt for a hiding place, he retreated from the front door and bounced to the kitchen. The jiggle of a bunch of keys became perceptible. Boll now in the kitchen, adapted to the darkness of the room. A small reflection from the hallway light facilitated him to seek a spot to lie quiet. It was the first time he set foot into the kitchen. The cooker, along with a sink and a fridge to his immediate right, didn't provide him with a hide-out. A small table with two matching chairs wasn't adjuvant either. The only place to take cover was behind the door. Musing about the owner of the key bunch, he presumed it to be Hunt's ex-girlfriend. Boll hastily vanished behind the door. Too late to pull it behind him, he ducked down as best he could.

The doorknob on the exterior was turned around. Stamping of heavy footwear reverberated in the hallway. It sounded rather more like the footsteps of a man than a woman.

Boll's breath quickened and with clammy palms he supported himself against the wall. Slightly turning his head, he peered through the gap between the door hinges and the frame. A shadow restricted his view and the door was suddenly torn open. It slightly bounced back off Boll's torso. He swallowed and stopped breathing. Any time now and he would be discovered. With millions of thoughts going through his head, Boll persevered behind the door like a statue. In an instant the beating of his heart accelerated. He was confident it was audible in the room.

Slap-bang and the light was switched on. The sharp brightness in the kitchen bedazzled Boll for several seconds. Automatically he closed his eyes and wished the ground to open up to swallow him.

CHAPTER 78

Lech, with David Hunt's keys juddering between his fingers, made a move straight to the kitchen. He was still annoyed about his carelessness. He had left his spectacles behind. He'd realised it as soon as he sat behind the steering wheel. The whole situation was getting slowly out of hand. And to make things worse he had to go back to the scene to collect his glasses. But it was the fact that his friend was slowly losing his mind that bothered him. Since going through the divorce, he sometimes acted like a maniac. One reason Lech had chosen him, but it was about time to repress him.

The first thing Lech noticed was the illumination in the hallway. He was pretty sure they had switched off the light when departing. Lech, still puzzling about it, stepped into the kitchen.

He turned on the light, and whilst the room was filled with luminosity, Lech caught sight of a shadow behind the kitchen door. A deep growl almost escaped from his mouth. He spotted a shoe jutted out from behind the door, and deftly grabbed a dirty knife from the sink.

Abruptly, he stopped dead. Hadn't he seen this one before? It was a quite distinctive one, a brown leather brogue with a red line across the front. Lech instantly placed it to Boll and stopped breathing. To avoid any confrontation with his captain, Lech swiftly snatched his glasses from the kitchen worktop. On his way out he dragged the hood of his jumper deeper into his forehead. After a quick exit and once outside the building, he finally began to breathe again. With the knife still embraced in his palm, Lech disappeared out of sight.

The minute he was back in the van, Lech let his mind wander. He was certain that his captain had not recognised him. Without question he would have challenged him. Lech had been astounded to find the captain in the flat. Perhaps he wanted to make sure the job was done correctly? Or he remembered the suicide notes? Hopefully Boll wouldn't scrutinise the corpse and discover that it wasn't Hunt who was resting on the bed. He doubted it. The face was beyond recognition and the body frame, the hair and the tan was almost identical to Hunt's, one of the reasons why Pablo had to die. Lech decided to keep his discovery quiet. Within seconds the vehicle pulled onto the road and headed out of town.

*

After the intruder's departure Boll slowly opened his eyes. His shaking hand wiped off the wetness foaming up around his lips. He still couldn't believe his luck. He got away without being detected. He'd never had a chance to even look at the person. He had kept his eyes closed, like a child who had done something wrong and wished to disappear in a hole, before being caught by their parents.

Now he regretted it. He waved it aside. Most likely it was Pablo, who had forgotten something. Anyone else would have certainly seen the body through the wide gap of the doorway and called out for help. Most likely Boll would never come to know if it was indeed Pablo. It didn't matter. And there was no time to muse about it. Boll had to get out as quickly as possible. He took one last gander around the room before finally turning his back to it.

CHAPTER 79

David's head was hurting like hell. When he recovered consciousness he was surrounded by murkiness. Where was he?

The sound of an engine and the constant jouncing back and forth indicated he was in the back of a moving van. He attempted to budge his hands as the sound of cars rumbled past his ears. Why could he not move his hands? It took him several minutes to realise that his hands were tied to his back. He wiggled with his feet and with relief discovered they were free from shackles.

Recollecting the last events of the evening, he chuckled at the thought of Boll when he came by to give him a lecture for not turning up on duty. What a joke. He remembered that he'd also been writing a letter to his beloved Lucy with the thought of ending his life. The bitterness in his mouth reminded him of the amount of alcohol he had gulped. He'd never consumed so much in his life before, one of the reasons he struggled with his memory.

And there was something else nagging in the back of his mind. He summoned up the last moments in the flat. The sight of a dead man and Lech's face flashed in his head.

Struck by sudden fear, he writhed with his whole torso on the cold, greasy floor. Shaking his head in disbelief, he tried to convince himself that it had been only a dream. But why was he now in the back of a van? And why was he tied up?

He distinguished male voices in the front of the van. One of them belonged to Lech. A cold shiver ran down his spine. So it was true, Lech had been in his house today, implying the dead man must be for real. Overwhelmed by fear and despair, David began struggling at his bonds. Crawling alongside the chilliness of the ground, he began fumbling with his legs and torso for anything he could use to free himself.

Albeit still suffering with nausea and headache, David felt sober. The reality had cleared his head. It dawned on him that he was only dressed in boxer shorts. He could sense his nudeness. Heat surged through his veins, a sign of his embarrassment. They must have carried him to the van. Nothing made sense to him right now.

"Where are you going with me?" he shouted at the top of his lungs with his voice unusually high-pitched. "Who are you? Let me speak to Lech!" David banged up to gaze through the window that separated them. He was sure it had been Lech's voice before. But who was the other person? The back of the vehicle began to reel and David collapsed on his bottom. Due to the van going too fast, he was unable to keep his balance and began dragging himself along the floor by arching his bottom and tummy towards the door.

He crouched in front of it and tried with his elbow to catch the latch. Once more the van began to totter and David was hurled down to the floor. He started yelling afresh. His wail was tuned out. Due to the speediness and hubbub from the outside, David concluded that they were travelling on a fast road. His physical tenseness , but also emotional condition was distinct and visible as he craned his neck.

Approximately ten minutes later, for him it seemed forever, the van came to a sudden halt. Dreading the incertitude, David leapt up and floundered with his bonds behind his back. Teeth clenched and with his right knee ready to strike out, he waited. The back doors suddenly squeaked while pulled open. The blood drained from David's face.

Balaclava Man, again without balaclava, stood with his burly frame full length in the doorway. Behind his back David doubled his fists, not that they would be of any use in bonds. Still, it gave David some reassurance. The darkness foretold it was still night. Raindrops flitted to the inside of the van. David assumed it was a car park of a service station. Though the only view he had was a field adjoined to a forest. "Who are you?" David snarled with his chest out.

"You don't have to know!" Balaclava Man retorted. David was somehow eased for once not to have a gun pointed at him.

"Where is Lech?" David demanded one more time. Instead of a reply, he was faced with a blank stare.

David's head was rattling. Many thoughts went through his head. Yet the main one stuck with him. Why wasn't Balaclava Man wearing a mask to cover his face? He had killed somebody in front of him. David would be able to identify him. He didn't like that and his pulse began to quicken. There was only one reason why a killer was showing his face. He wouldn't get a chance to identify him. He would never be a witness in court to say who the murderer was. The sudden titter from a passing couple raised David's hopes. Balaclava Man's gaze followed the sound and swayed his head.

In a swift move David lunged forward and attempted to head-butt his assailant. But he never had a chance. Balaclava Ban shook his head, reached into his waistband and drew the gun, pointing it once more at David.

CHAPTER 80

Bewildered, David stared at the gun. His eyes darted to the outside in a quest to spot the giggling couple. There was no sign of them. Some light from a nearby building shone into the interior of the van. The sound of fast cars was humming in David's ears. He reckoned it was coming from a nearby motorway. David took a step back and raised his eyebrows. His bare toes tottered up and down on the floor. Caused by the constant chafing against the bonds, the skin around his wrists felt sore. His attention was drawn to a noise at the front of the vehicle. Out of nowhere Lech cropped up with a water bottle in his hand. With flushed cheeks, Lech gazed at them furiously. David, uncertain if it was towards him or Balaclava Man, wrinkled his forehead.

"Come on. What's the matter with you? Put the gun down!" Lech demanded and grasped the barrel, pushing it downwards away from David. Balaclava Man let the gun slip back to his waistband.

David glanced at Lech, sceptical. "What's this all

about? What have I done to you?"

With raised eyebrows Lech looked offended. "Why? What do you mean? I am here to help you, you know that." Lech held on to the handle and vaulted up to the inside of the van.

"So why did you kidnap me? And for God's sake why is this guy constantly pointing a gun at me?" David motioned his chin towards Balaclava Man, who stood back.

Lech rolled his eyes. "Listen, I know there are lots of things to take in. First of all, we never intended to kidnap you. We just had to get you out of the flat. And obviously you were not very cooperative."

David turned around, gesturing to Lech to unleash him. Lech pressed the water bottle between his thighs, fished out a pocket knife from his jeans, slit open the bonds and dropped them to the floor. David revolved and rubbed his chapped wrists in achiness.

Lech pressed the water bottle against David's chest, who gratefully took it from him. "Listen, if it hadn't been for us, you would be dead by now. You know that."

David slowly comprehended. He rubbed his eyes, instantly feeling very drowsy. "So the dead guy in my flat is the one who was supposed to kill me?" David grimaced and took a big sip from the water bottle.

"Yes." Lech nodded.

"So what now?"

Lech signalled to balaclava man. "Could you get the bag from the front please?"

Balaclava Man did as he was told and vanished out

of vision.

"Is this the man you call your friend?" David asked, rubbing his chin. Lech had no chance to answer. Balaclava Man returned with a black travel bag in his arms. He threw it at David's feet and marched off without a sound.

As David ducked down to check the contents of the bag he let out a deep sigh and grinned. He removed a T-shirt from the bag and threw it on. Finally, it was over. He gazed at Lech, who patted him on the shoulder. "Everything as discussed, a new passport, enough money and obviously some clothes." Lech smiled.

"Thanks for everything. I owe you big time. Still, tell me, why all this show?"

Lech sighed. He jumped out of the van and shifted his head back and forth to establish that his friend was out of earshot. He then leaned towards David who slipped on some trainers he had found in the bag.

"Well, first of all I am truly sorry. It wasn't planned to knock you unconscious, let alone bind you up. But everything had to go fast. As you know, the whole thing was planned for tomorrow. And you being pissed didn't help either. I rang you to get you out of the house, but you were too slow on the uptake."

Lech bolstered his right foot on the loading bay of the van and tapped his forehead as he whispered, "Well, and my friend, he lost it a bit. He wasn't expecting you in the flat and panicked. He is fine now, don't worry. He won't do you any harm. Just likes to show off, you know."

Lech was right. The whole show was supposed to

take place tomorrow. And David was meant to be out. He hadn't expected it to happen tonight, one of the reasons he had lost it and indeed looked too deep into the bottle. At some point he'd really considered pulling the trigger instead of disappearing off the face of the earth. He couldn't even remember Lech calling him. So when he saw Lech in front of his door step with his friend pointing the trigger at him, and then later being knocked unconscious and transported in shackles in the back of the van, he'd really thought everything had been a set-up and Lech was actually working for Boll.

Just a few days ago, Lech stopped by at his flat and told David about his discovery. David was at first in shock. He couldn't believe that he'd received forged documents to make him believe that he'd lost his licence forever. He was very much enraged and tempted to confront his captain. Lech stopped him just in time. He revealed to David that Boll had hired a contract killer to get rid of him once and for all by making it look like suicide. David saw sense and finally comprehended that he had no chance in winning the battle.

When Lech suggested to vanish off the earth to start a new life somewhere else, David eventually agreed. What other choice did he have? First David wondered why Lech was so keen to help him. When he asked, Lech had reminded him that once when he had been in trouble, David jumped in and helped him out of his misery. It was when Lech went AWOL during duty and David gave him an alibi. Not a big thing but still…!

Lech also loathed the captain and didn't want him

to succeed. David's only concerns were the future of his children. That is why they both came up with the concept to still make it look like suicide. Then his wife and children would be financially sorted. She would be entitled to a lump sum, a widow and an orphan pension for both children. Also it would keep Boll off his back. And luck was on their side. The person who was supposed to kill David, resembled him. Pablo didn't deserve any different. After all, he was about to end David's life. He had probably killed many other innocent people in his role as a contract killer. But who would actually pull the trigger? And then Lech came up with this brilliant idea. He knew this lad, kind of a friend to him, who was unscrupulous and did anything for a bit of cash. The money was no problem. Boll had paid enough to Pablo. There was something in it for everyone.

And fortunately Pablo had kept the money in his vehicle. He was supposed to vanish immediately after the murder. He had planned to go back to his home country, the Balkans. Lech would get rid of his vehicle, and with no family in Germany, Pablo wouldn't be missed. Perhaps his family back home would. But people go missing all the time and occasionally don't come back.

The only condition Lech's friend had asked for, was to pull the trigger without Hunt's presence. He wanted to stay anonymous. So David wasn't supposed to be in the flat. And Lech had no chance to explain to David the exact plan, another reason David feared for his life more than once. Yet Lech had no other choice than to go ahead with it. So everything went a bit out of control. However, everything had turned out to be fine and Lech managed to calm his mate down.

"I guess I don't have much time." David looked up.

"No, you don't, best to get moving."

"By the way, thanks for writing the letter to my parents. In all the rush, I had forgotten about this one."

Lech had told David that he had written one, when David was out on the floor.

"No worries. I noticed that. Well, it was supposed to happen tomorrow and not today." Lech chuckled with his chin cupped in his open palm and the elbow supported by his knee.

"Well, when I didn't turn up for duty, Boll popped in to tell me off. I presume I proper pissed him off. I also looked a bit too deep into the bottle, but frustration took over. It's not easy for me to leave everything behind, you know?" David glanced at Lech with blushing cheeks. He felt slightly ashamed.

"No worries. I know where you coming from." Lech straightened up and gave David another companionable pat, this time on his back.

"What about your friend? Will he keep quiet?" David motioned with his chin towards the dark.

Lech nodded. "Don't worry. He is 100% trustworthy. And don't forget he killed someone. We always could hold this against him."

David sprang to his feet and clapped his hands. "I am ready then." Yet David didn't stir from the spot.

He was suddenly overwhelmed with different emotions. It was hard to say goodbye to his old life. It felt like dying. With mixed feelings he remained in his position, contemplating whether there was another way out of it.

As if Lech could read his mind, he pressed. "I think it's time for you to go!" Lech's eyes became watery as he gently conveyed David out of the van by placing his arm around his shoulders. "The car is around the corner. Good luck." Lech slid some car keys into David's open palm. He didn't mention one word about Boll being in David's flat. He didn't want to disconcert David. He was certain that Boll hadn't recognised him.

He wished David to finally find his peace. They arranged to get in contact with each other only if David's new life was in jeopardy. So wherever David ended up, Lech would eventually come to know of David's whereabouts. David embraced Lech with tears in his eyes. He thanked him for everything.

"Don't ever forget the code. The code is the only connection we have. And I will only use it if your existence is compromised."

"Don't worry! It will stick with me for the rest of my life." David had it scribbled on the back of a photograph he would always carry with him. It was a picture showing him and his two young children on their last holiday together.

Again, his eyes welled up with tears, but not only the thought of his children hurt him. He would miss Lucy too, no doubt about that. David bent over and picked up his travel bag. With a swift wave to Lech, he skittered away. By now the tears were spilling down his cheeks. He pulled himself together and disappeared into thin air.

FINAL PART

NOW

CHAPTER 81

Twenty-Five Years Later

Lucy emerged from the plane; the strong heat struck to her face. She was not used to it. Still dressed in jeans and a T-shirt, she yearned for a light summer dress. She followed the crowd, consisting of many different ethnicities, entering the terminal. It had been a very long flight during which she was sat next to a grumpy man, none of her choice. With butterflies in her tummy just at the thought of a reunion with her first love, she ambled to Passport Control. She still questioned whether she was doing the right thing here. After all these years of not knowing, Lucy all of a sudden doubted whether she wanted to confront the truth. With clammy hands she removed her passport and holiday visa from her handbag and waited for her turn. Since the contact with Zoe, the past had been haunting her. It had even affected her marriage. After all these years, all of a sudden being sought out by the daughter of her first love, Lucy realised that she had never stopped loving David.

Lucy's life had changed since then. She became obsessed with the idea that David was potentially still alive. Lots of things, leading up to his death, hadn't made sense. At the time she didn't notice. She had been very young and hurt. She only saw daylight when Zoe showed her the folder. Now, Lucy puzzled, if she had known would she have started looking for him earlier? At the end of the day she still wasn't sure if the man who she was supposed to meet tomorrow, was indeed David, or if he was in fact buried in a grave in Bueckenau. During her frequent online research, she almost couldn't trust her eyes when she found a man, with a similar name and who looked identical to David, just an older version, residing on the Bahamas. He worked as an architect.

She even found a private address for him. Rather than using the email address of his office, she chose to write to his private one, using the old fashioned way of pen and paper. She included her email address and the newspaper report of Zoe, before sending it off by express delivery. She kept it quiet from Zoe, wanting to be sure that it was indeed David, before raising false hopes.

First there was no response. Then after Lucy had already booked the flight, he replied by email. In his email he denied being David, stating he was from

Austria and had never lived in Germany. Lucy wasn't the kind of person to give up easily. Something had bothered her in his text. It had just sounded so much like David. She decided to still go ahead with her trip to the Bahamas and to look for herself.

She wrote back to him, this time by email. She politely asked if he would still agree to meet her, despite the fact that he wasn't David, so she could see with her own eyes. He agreed. And here she was facing the truth on this beautiful island.

The queue seemed to be endless. To blame were the tourists, who hadn't filled in their visas on the plane. Lucy's mouth felt very dry. She was desperate for a bottle of water and ravenous for a large plate of seafood. In front of her was a family with two young children from France. The parents struggled to keep them under control. Lucy empathised with them. The flight must have been a long time for such young children. Finally it was Lucy's turn. She tugged some strands of hair behind her ear and approached the window. Without any problems she was done in no time. Whilst heading for the luggage area, she stuffed her passport back into her handbag.

Less than ten minutes later, she sat on the rear seat of a local taxi. The journey to the hotel lasted less than thirty minutes. It was just outside Nassau. After being checked in, Lucy retreated to her hotel room. With her luggage in tow, she trod into her room. It had a decent size and was well-appointed with modern furniture. She dumped her luggage in the corner and made hot-footed to the window. Suddenly overwhelmed by the stunning view, she watched tidal waves impinging against the cliffs. With a bright blue sky and the rays of the sun, the ocean had a turquoise colour. No wonder they said the Bahamas was a paradise. Further down to the right was a long stretched beach with beautiful white sand and tourists sunbathing. A promising promenade with restaurants and shops surrounded by massive palm trees completed the picture. Lucy loved it. She slowly began to enjoy her holiday, almost forgetting the reason she had come.

CHAPTER 82

David glanced at the picture of the newspaper article resting on the passenger seat. He had read it on numerous occasions. The photograph of his daughter stared back at him, somehow accusingly. Or perhaps it was just in his head? He shrugged his shoulders.

After his wife had opened his mail and found the letter from Lucy along with the newspaper article – thank God she hadn't been able to read it as she didn't speak any German – he had managed to convince her of mistaken identity. And when he read the article, David realised he had no other choice than to make contact with Zoe. It was clear she wouldn't stop until she knew the truth. If she continued with her enquiries into his death, everything would eventually spill out. Too many lives were at stake, but the main thing that bothered him was Boll, his former captain. He feared that he was able to hurt his daughter. After all Max Boll, had hired a contract killer all those years ago to kill him.

And Boll was clearly of the opinion that he had

indeed succeeded. So now with Zoe rummaging in the past, Boll most likely panicked that he would be found out and was probably doing his best to stop it. So David had to warn his daughter. He had no other choice.

But first of all David had to confront the problem that was right in front of him. It was Lucy, who had come to the Bahamas to meet him. David once more stared at his iPad and read the email from Lucy. Sat in his black Mercedes, he began shifting anxiously in his seat. Every now and then he glanced at the patio of Café Rosella. He was meant to meet Lucy in about fifteen minutes. After he had received the email, he replied denying his existence. Unfortunately Lucy didn't believe him. She had booked a flight to the Bahamas, insisting on meeting him so she could see for herself.

It was so much like Lucy, she was very determined. Eventually he agreed. It was just before ten in the morning, but the city was already fully awake with lots of tourists lingering in the streets. Ten minutes later, a taxi pulled up outside Café Rosella. A middle-aged woman emerged from the vehicle. David recognised Lucy instantly. Apart from getting older, she had not changed much. She was still attractive, wearing a beautiful light brown summer dress covered with flowers, and a pair of beige sandals. Her curly hair was slightly tousled by the strong breeze emanating from the ocean. David remained in his vehicle. He was parked on the other side of the road. He put on his sunglasses and watched Lucy from behind tinted windows taking a seat on the patio. Minutes went past, but David didn't stir.

He was tempted to leap out of his Mercedes to embosom Lucy one more time in his life. Yet he knew it was too risky. He perceived Lucy's disappointment in her posture. Every time a car went by her cheeks flushed and the pupils of her eyes bubbled with hope, followed by slouching her shoulders.

Deluged by desolation, he averted his gaze. When it came to women resilience was one of David's worst weaknesses. He coerced himself to stay away. He couldn't afford to put his current life at stake. Not after he was given a second chance. He observed Lucy for nearly an hour consuming three cups of coffee in a row and chain smoking ten cigarettes. Ultimately he brought the engine back to life and pulled into traffic. As he roared past, he allowed himself to sneak a peek. Lucy stared right back, locking eyes with him. David didn't stop. He continued his journey with tears stinging his eyes.

David came to a halt not far from Café La Rosa. He took a deep breath and clenched his mobile phone. Fully aware that this would not stop, unless he made the final call he had withheld too long already, he touched the icon with his daughter's phone number displaying. The one Lech had given him. The familiar ring tone of his home country reminded him, with every inch of his body, what he had left behind all these years ago.

The other line was picked up with a hello. David's heart began to race. His palms sticky with sweat tightened around his handset. It had been more than twenty-five years since he last listened to his daughter's voice. Unsure how to begin, he first started with a warning. He still attempted to evade the disclosure of his real identity. However, his sixth sense told him his daughter wouldn't stop until she knew the truth.

Hoping for the best, that she would keep quiet as too many lives were at stake, he finally plucked up his courage and spluttered, "It's me. It's your dad."

FINISHED

ABOUT THE AUTHOR

Conny Ge is originally from Germany. After leaving Germany in her early twenties and travelling all over the UK and backpacking in America and Mexico, she settled in the North of England. In 2011 she graduated with a Foundation Degree from John Moores University in Liverpool. A few years ago, besides working full-time and being a mum, she began writing her debut novel, a thriller/mystery – *The Folder*. Since her early adulthood, she has been passionate about writing and reading books, mainly in English, her second language. She is intrigued to write further novels in the thriller genre and gave thought to the idea of writing a sequel to *The Folder*.

28982881R00221

Printed in Great Britain
by Amazon